Justice & Mercy

A Post-Civil War Mystery

Lea Wait

Sheepscot River Press
Post Office Box 225
Edgecomb, Maine 04556

Chapter 1
April 14, 1865 Hestia, New York

"Captain Stone?"

I forced the mists that often marked my hours in those days to part. Owen Hindley stood at the dining room door, leaning on the grayed wooden staff he'd depended on for support since his rheumatism had become crippling. He'd been a hired man here for forty years, more or less. Certainly since before I was born. Since the war took most able-bodied younger men he was the only one left attempting to keep Aunt Cornelia's grounds and animals in order.

"Before she left this morning Mrs. Livingston asked me to walk the borders of the property and report back."

"Yes?" That walk would account for the mud covering Owen's boots and darkening the bottom eight inches or so of his staff. Katie would have to mop the hall again after he'd left.

"I've been out to the north field." He stood, clearly waiting for a response.

"The north field's the one planted with corn, correct?" I said, dredging up a blurred memory of playing hide and seek with another child in a cornfield near the towpath.

"Used to be," Owen said. "Some years ago Mr. Livingston decided corn was too much trouble. For a few years he leased it to

1

William Burns, who lives just beyond, for hops. But in '61 most men went to soldiering. Land's been sitting fallow, like most of us, waiting for the war to end."

I focused on his boots. Their brown leather was cracked. His feet must be sodden from the mud, like those of soldiers who'd been marching for days. What did he want from me?

"Waters took good topsoil, and left rubbish on the land," he expanded. He took off the wide-brimmed felt hat he would've already removed if I'd been Aunt Cornelia, and scratched his head. "You should come with me, Captain. Look for yourself."

"I can't see what need there is for me to look at a field that's lost some soil because of flooding. I believe you, Owen."

"It's not the field you need to look at. It's what the waters left behind." The old man straightened up and raised his voice slightly to be sure I understood. "There's a body, Captain. Where the canal waters pulled back, there's a body. Or what's left of one, anyways."

That was how it began.

Mud is what I remember most about the early spring of 1865. Wagon wheels sunk deep into impassable dirt roads. Farmers stranded far from town. Horses, mules and oxen hobbled with hoof disease. Fields impossible to plow, and even more impossible to plant. "The Devil's pulling seeds right down to Hell with him," said old men to young. "It's this war as has been goin' on too long. There's no good left in the world."

The upstate New York winter had been a harsh one. Frequent ice storms froze heavy drifted snow, leaving those living in the small towns and cities lining the Erie Canal isolated from commerce or war news. The canal had been drained in the fall, as usual, and filled again in March. Then, as if nature was laughing at men already tested by war and weather, melting snows were followed by drenching rains, and the canal overflowed on the long level between Utica and Syracuse.

Scows were stranded in open country. Determined men slept short hours for weeks rebuilding the sides of the canal and the washed out towpath. Flooding like this came once in a lifetime, folks said, and then only if you were unlucky.

I hadn't noticed our country being blessed with a lot of luck in the past few years.

Since 1861, when it all erupted down at Fort Sumter, I remembered cold and hunger, sore feet, and filthy soldiers picking lice off one another, waiting for the next battle. Hoping to survive a few more days or weeks.

My back and legs carried scars reminding me how close shells and bayonets had come to ending my soldiering days. I'd been laid out by problems a gentleman – and I'd thought of myself as a gentleman back before the world changed – would never mention, especially in polite company.

But the war wasn't polite. We soldiers all suffered the same indignities, shared the same whores, and dreamed of home, wherever that might be. Those days, those images and sensations, are now never far from my mind.

And then there was the Wilderness.

Long hungry days marching through torrential rain and deep mud on roads close to impassable. We tore up railroad tracks, destroyed telegraph lines, and burned bridges as we advanced. Confederates ambushed our detachments as we tried to dig trenches in the wild tangled Virginia landscape. Days merged in my memory, until the moment Lee's forces came toward us out of the fog in numbers far greater than we'd anticipated. My ears echoed with gunfire and screams as Private O'Brien of Albany fell next to me, his guts mixing with mud and decaying leaves.

Nothing else was clear until I woke out of deep darkness and felt my arm afire with pain. A saw grated on bone and, from a distance, I knew it was my bone. Pain arced through my body. I fell into darkness again.

When next I opened my eyes I was in one of the low tents that passed as field hospitals, lined with cots and pallets and heavy with smells of blood and vomit and shit and men who hadn't bathed since the last rain washed caked filth away. The man to the right of me was still. The man to the left was wailing, a high-pitched cry. My left arm throbbed incessantly, although nothing was there but blood soaked bandages. I remember thinking I was certainly feverish. This must be a nightmare. Someone dripped water between my lips and injected me with what I now know was the blessing of morphine. After that I was able to observe the nightmare from a distance. The world was easier to accept when I was removed from it.

Most people would say my war ended in the Wilderness.

But I'd been out of that tent a year now, and knew it would never end. I'd never again pass a dooryard fence without seeing bloated body parts hanging there. See a wheat field without remembering where we'd dug trenches for mass graves. Hear the privy door slamming in the night and not feel my heart race as though I were running through a sea of cannon fire and bayonets. Assume a man's appearance defined his worth.

Doctors in the hospital in Washington, and then in New York City, and even here, in the isolation of upstate New York, agreed the throbbing in my missing left arm would be quieted by morphine and by the little white opium tablets I carry with me at all times. Sometimes the injections and pills also help me drift above the day, so I see the world through a soft, comforting, mist. But the mists are not guaranteed. They can part at any time, and a tree branch be transformed into the flayed body of a suspected spy, or a woodpile become a pile of severed limbs.

Months ago I learned not to share these visions. They merely increased the distance people put between my mangled body and themselves. Fighting in the war might make one a hero at a distance. Close up, people stared, and then looked away. Did they think I was also blind; that I wouldn't notice?

When I finally could go home to New York City last October I was anxious to resume my life as it had been before the war. But Father looked away when I struggled to cut a slice of pork on my dinner plate using one hand. Mother cringed if she saw me before the boy she'd hired to help me dress and wash had ensured I was properly covered.

Everyone ignored the reality that using one arm rather than two lengthened the time it will always take me to accomplish even simple tasks such as pulling up and buttoning my trousers or adjusting the paper I'm writing on to avoid ink splotches and smears.

They waited for the boy they knew to return. For life to be as it was before the war. I waited for them to accept me as I am today. The world had changed, and I had changed with it. We both longed for the comfort of the days before the war.

I was no longer the boy to whom my family had waved good-bye and sent letters and packages of extra socks.

My beloved Margaret was one who looked away from what wasn't there, despite my desperate need to have her look and touch and accept. It became clear her promise had been to marry a man who was whole, not to accept the changes the war had brought. The normalcy of future marriage and family I had held close throughout the horrors of the war was not to be. Not with Margaret; perhaps not ever.

My arm was gone. My mind, if sometimes shrouded by the haze

of the white pills, was still intact. I was despondent and angry; ready to begin a new life, but with decreasing hope of any new life opening to me.

After the Christmas holidays, when the letter came from Aunt Cornelia in Hestia, I felt relief flooding our home on Gramercy Square. Uncle Henry had died, at a proper age and in his own bed, and Aunt Cornelia was alone, and could use my assistance in running her estate. Just for a while, until her grief subsided.

Someone had found a use for me.

Despite Mother's polite protestations, I think we knew it would be best for all of us if I left.

But once I was here in Hestia it was clear that, in actuality, Aunt Cornelia needed no one. Perhaps she'd sensed that I needed her? I'd felt close to Aunt Cornelia and Uncle Henry since the summer of 1849 when my parents sent me to stay with them to escape the cholera epidemic in New York City that killed Ben. We all understood: they couldn't stand losing their younger son, too.

After that I'd visited Hestia when I could, and spent many carefree summer days exploring the fields and woods and leaning on the fence at the edge of their property watching the exotic men and women who trafficked on the Erie Canal.

Now I took advantage of Aunt Cornelia's acceptance and the pretense that my presence in Hestia was necessary. I planned to stay an appropriate number of months to get perspective on my situation; to dispel the demons haunting me.

That morning in April I was in her spacious dining room. Its walls were stenciled with pale red flowers on a beige base, and it faced east, so was usually bright in the morning. It had become my habit to spend the early part of each day sipping coffee Katie, the hired girl, kept hot for me, and reading the *Utica Register* I'd spread out on the large cherry table so I could turn the pages with one hand. The newspaper was several days old by the time we obtained a copy, but reading it made me feel as though I was still part of the world.

On April 3 we'd received word of the fall of Richmond, and on April 9 the *Register* announced General Lee's surrender at Appomattox Courthouse. Bells were rung; canons in Hestia were fired so even those of us far in the countryside could hear them. Bonfires were lit throughout the city wherever enough dry timber could be found to keep them ablaze. A public holiday in celebration had been announced to take place April 20, and I was looking forward to the official end of the suffering for our country and for my brothers still in arms.

The union had been preserved. Our fight had not been in vain.

Despite the country's excitement, my own life had not changed. The stump that had been my arm still throbbed severely. Doctors shook their heads and said it was my nerves that pained me, not my missing limb.

That April morning I hadn't slept well for several nights, and had already taken my third pill of the day. Focusing on life outside my pain was difficult. It was the kind of day when reading the *Register* could take a morning.

Aunt Cornelia knew to leave me to myself at such times. Her schedule was inviolate. She'd driven her lightest carriage into Hestia herself that morning. Several days each week she visited the orphan asylum. When I thought about her days, which wasn't often, I wondered what she did there. What could anyone do with forty or fifty children?

Occasionally I thought of asking her; even of asking if I could be of some assistance. I'd always liked children, although my experiences with them had been limited. Ben had been four years older than I, so we hadn't been playmates, and after his death I spent most of my time with nannies or tutors, except for those summer months in

7

Hestia. And when I was older the children of our family's friends had been small, sometimes amusing, creatures who were quickly relegated to the care of others when their behavior became inappropriate.

Someday I hoped to be a father, but I assumed the care of my children would be Margaret's responsibility. Or that of whoever might be my wife.

In the meantime I was shy with children; afraid of the questions they'd ask.

Certainly on that April morning children were far from my mind.

There was a body in the north field.

Chapter 2

I struggled to pull on the heavy frockcoat I'd worn throughout the winter. Temperatures were still cooler than normal for April, and I wasn't ready to give up the comfort of wool. Owen watched my efforts to adjust the heavy garment with my right hand, but didn't offer to help. Like a stubborn four-year-old, I was determined to do it myself, even if that meant my coat would hang askew. There was no one here to care, in any case. No one aside from myself, and my own pride. I left the buttons undone. At least my hat provided no challenges.

Outside, despite blue skies, the dank smell of mud was everywhere, as it had sometimes been on the battlefield. Although those fields had absorbed other smells as well.

"You've seen lots of bodies, I expect, Captain. But here in Hestia we don't come across many," Owen pointed out conversationally.

Indeed, the prospect of viewing another body had aroused curiosity rather than horror. I'd seen enough of death in the past several years to feel more numb than nauseated at the thought. I couldn't imagine this body would move me in any way, other than to stir my interest. Why would a body be in the quiet north field?

Owen led the way carefully through the muddy barnyard that in past springs had been full of clucking chickens and young men hammering high trellises for the hops fields. Now it was silent, awaiting the return of those hired to keep the estate productive and in order. Aunt Cornelia and Uncle Henry never had children of their own, but over the years they'd hired many young people to help run their lands and care for their home.

"They need training up in what's expected by an employer," I remembered Uncle Henry saying. "When they've got that figured out, they're ready to work in town and earn a better salary than I can pay. In the meantime, they're better off in the countryside learning skills they'll use for a lifetime than working their lives away over in the Globe Mill, or in one of the garment factories."

Many of those young men who'd learned farming skills now wore blue uniforms. I wondered how many would be back after their units were disbanded. In a month or two they should start returning, eager to begin their lives again.

Would any ask for their old jobs? I should discuss the matter with Aunt Cornelia. I wasn't sure what operations she would wish to start up again. Growing hops for beer? Corn? Renting out fields to others? If fields weren't prepared within the next few weeks we'd miss the planting season this year.

I followed Owen past the drying and storage buildings and around the weathered barn, now empty except for the old bay horse, a wagon for supplies, and a sleigh.

Before the Army'd confiscated them there'd been half a dozen or more horses here. Only two remained: the bay, and the mare Owen'd harnessed for the carriage earlier today. Somehow Aunt Cornelia had managed to talk the local Union provisioning officer into understanding the need for a lady so far from town to have one decent horse, and the old bay hadn't been sound enough to serve the Union.

Our winding path, deep with decaying leaves and small branches broken off by heavy winter ice and snow, led through perhaps a quarter mile of woods, the stark black and brown bark of the trees not yet softened by budding leaves. Owen must have lifted or pushed aside larger branches when he'd been here earlier.

Droplets of blood among the decaying wood and leaves stopped me. Then I shook my head and re-focused my eyes. What I'd thought droplets of blood were only remnants of red berries that had frozen and survived the winter.

"All right?" Owen called back, seeing my hesitation.

"Fine, Owen." There was no sense admitting that once again my mind had tricked me.

He nodded and continued on. This rough walk was not easy for him.

If there were strong young men available later this spring I would advise Aunt Cornelia to hire two or three. Owen knew the lands and buildings, and he could advise and perhaps supervise in Uncle Henry's place. It was clear he could not be counted on to perform any tasks that required speed or lifting. I wondered how he'd managed the kitchen garden for the past few years, even with help from Katie.

The wooded area opened onto the twenty-acre north field marked off by snake rail fencing. I remembered the field as an endless expanse of pale yellow grain, fragrant and clean; an open space between the quiet woods and the bustling canal just north of it. On summer evenings the moving lights of the barges and packet boats reflected in the canal waters had seemed magical and exciting.

Now the field was barren, oozing with mud, scared by rocks the waters couldn't move and debris left behind by flooding. Canal sewage, rotting vegetation, human waste, gutted perch, and the occasional decomposing chipmunk or woodchuck whose burrow had filled with water were strewn as far as I could see.

The sucking sound of wet soil on our boots almost drowned out the only immediate sign of spring: mating songs of the barn swallows swooping overhead and cardinals in pine trees on the other side of the fence. Cold water soaked through the seam of my left boot and chilled my toes.

Owen stopped about twenty-four feet from the canal, and pointed.

Ebbing waters had revealed a skeleton half covered by sodden muck.

"Thought you should be the one to tell Mrs. Livingston," said Owen. "You being her nephew, and a captain, and all. A body's a body, for all it's just bones." He hesitated. "Of course, if Mr. Livingston were still alive, he'd have known what to do."

He was right, of course, on both counts. The situation was my responsibility to resolve. And Henry Livingston had always known what to do. If he hadn't, his wife had reminded him.

I suspected Owen Hindley had lived his life in the wake of Livingston decisions. Now I was here to help make them, although so far Aunt Cornelia had not seemed to need my assistance with anything of consequence.

My arm ached. I resisted the temptation to take another small white pill.

"Body's been here a while," Owen said, patiently.

I walked carefully around the bones. The skull and most of the upper torso were visible, but mired in mud. The lower torso and legs were still beneath the soggy earth. "Are any family burying grounds nearby? Maybe the flooding opened a grave."

Owen shrugged. "Not that I've heard of. None on Livingston land, for sure. Your folks always buried their own in the church ground in Hestia. And a family would surely bury kin deeper than this body was covered."

"Then you have no idea who it might be."

"All sorts come and go on the canal. Will you be wanting me to bury it, then?"

For a moment the haze descended again.

I looked down at the muddy bones and saw Richard's startling blue eyes; his light brown hair, and his body, long and lean. I almost heard the low laugh always just below the surface, whether in a tavern near Columbia College, where we'd met, or at Gettysburg, just before the battle. "See you on the next hill," he'd called as he'd headed out to join his unit.

Richard. His gray jacket mended where he'd ripped its sleeve after that young rebel caught the cloth on his bayonet, just before Richard turned and bashed the boy's skull in with his rifle stock, the killing imperative but horrible, as were so many acts during war. Over mugs of rum or cider Richard and I often questioned the necessity of brutality, but on the battlefield we did what had to be done to stay alive and keep our comrades safe.

Richard, his pipe sticking out of one pocket, and the letters from his mother in another. Richard, who joined his unit that day at Gettysburg and disappeared. My closest friend. The only one who'd known how much I missed Margaret, and how I'd wished the war to end so I could join Father in his law firm and establish a place for myself where there was peace and justice.

I knew how much he admired his widowed mother and wished to be at home caring for her and his younger sister, and that he was writing to two young ladies, one in New York and one in Washington City, and had pledged his future to neither.

After the battle I'd seen to my men, and then sought out his unit to see how he'd fared. He wasn't there. I searched the battleground, body by body, with others who were still able to stand. I walked miles to see if he'd been taken to one of the hospital units. No one had seen him.

Even now, two years later, his family was still waiting for him to come home. Perhaps he was in a southern prison, as they hoped, or lying in a hospital no one had checked, or he'd lost his memory and been found and cared for by some Pennsylvania family. I'd visited his mother before I'd left for Hestia last January. She was refusing to wear black. She'd kept his room as he'd left it.

She was not the only mother who waited and refused to mourn.

All over the north and south, families were waiting for word of loved ones who were among the thousands of young men whose bodies couldn't be identified, or whose families were unknown, or who'd broken from their units and skedaddled to the west, leaving old lives behind. The end of the war without the return of those sons and husbands and brothers would be heavy blows to those waiting with hope.

"Don't bury it, Owen. Leave him. Or her. Someone in Hestia will know what to do. Someone connected to the police, I should think."

"Policemen try to prevent crimes. There's nothing here to prevent. Best to let the fellow rest," asserted Owen quietly.

"There must be a way of finding out who it is. We can't just pretend the body isn't here."

Somewhere there might be a mother, or sweetheart, or brother or sister, waiting. On the battlefield there had been hundreds, and no time. This was one person; one soul, as the Reverend Ames, our unit chaplain, would have said. And I had time; there was no call on my hours now.

I shrugged off my coat and laid it carefully over the exposed bones. "I'll find someone to take a look. Until then, don't tell anyone about this. I don't want it touched."

Owen looked at me doubtfully, but nodded. "If that's what you want, Captain."

"It is." As I stood up I thought for a moment I saw a young boy standing among the trees on the far west of the property line. But when I looked again the boy had disappeared. "Owen, does a small boy live near here?"

"Robbie Burns lives to the west, beyond the woods."

"The son of the man who used to rent this field?"

"That's the one. Haven't seen him recently, but in the winter even the young'uns stay to home. Why're you asking?"

"I thought I saw a boy in the trees over there," I said, pointing.

"It's possible." Owen shrugged. "Boys wander."

I looked, but didn't see him again. I headed back to the house, my long strides leaving Owen behind.

A pair of red-winged blackbirds, patches of scarlet brilliant in a glare of bright sunlight, spiraled after each other in a wild mating dance near a birch tree ahead of me. It was spring; life was renewing itself.

Chapter 3

For the first time in months my mind was filled with swirling images not caused by injections or pills. In truth, I considered the possibility of another injection when I got back to the house, but then, contemplating the walk to town which seemed my next logical step, I decided to risk the pain in favor of keeping my feet firmly on the muddy road and not becoming distracted or weary with memories or visions.

"Katie," I called. The girl came running from the kitchen, strands of long brown hair slipping out of her braid, and her apron askew. Both her hands and apron were white with flour, and a splotch of white on her cheek showed where she must have brushed a strand of hair behind her ear.

"Captain Stone? Sir? You called?" Katie was clearly perplexed by my summons. I rarely saw her except when I wanted some item of food or drink at an inappropriate hour or requested my chamber pot be emptied or my room cleaned. After I arrived in January I'd made it clear she was not to enter my room without specific permission. Years of living with hundreds of men had taught me to value privacy. And, perhaps vainly, after Margaret's rebuff, I was not yet ready to display my mutilated body to a young woman. Even a maid.

Katie had followed my dictum and stayed in the shadows, doing whatever it is that maids do, although I'll admit to summoning her occasionally out of boredom.

But Mrs. Langdon, Aunt Cornelia's long-time cook, had left in early March, and my aunt had declared this the perfect opportunity for Katie to learn a new skill.

Putting Katie in charge of the kitchen meant the cleanliness of the house was reduced considerably, and we were immediately treated to an assortment of culinary errors which might have been found amusing by a young and loving new husband. After a few days, however, I lost my patience with bread which refused to rise, potatoes salted beyond credibility, and beef burned on the outside and raw in the center. My appetite now was considerably less than it had been in the past; despite the starvation rations we'd been forced to live on during the war, I'd lost even more weight in the past year. One doctor said the loss was a result of boredom; another, it was related to my medications. In any case, Katie's unpalatable cooking did nothing to tempt me to eat more.

When I mentioned to Aunt Cornelia that something must be done about the kitchen, she was less than sympathetic.

"Young women not fortunate enough to have been raised in homes with money must learn ways to help support themselves and their families."

"Yes, of course." It was unfortunate, but women of that class seemed to manage, so far as I knew.

"I was one of the founders of a ladies' group in Hestia concerned with social reform which, I'm proud to say, recognized that problem some years ago. If young women do not have appropriate employment opportunities they can easily fall into deplorable behavior."

"And you and your friends decided to rescue such young women?" Clearly this was another of Aunt Cornelia's causes. I knew she'd often employed young men and women. I hadn't realized hiring them was part of an organized crusade.

"We did try that for some time, but our efforts were not altogether successful. We found we were more productive finding girls before they were led astray. Local clergy help us identify girls in situations which might lead to their sinking to unfortunate occupations. We seek them out and offer them opportunities to earn fair wages, live in proper homes where they can observe and emulate womanly deportment, and learn a skill or trade."

"Katie is one of these girls?"

"Katie's mother died years ago. She was living alone with her father and older brother, both of whom are known to be intemperate. A girl should have a woman's care and direction in her life. Katie was no longer in school, although her teachers and priest said she was bright. She was given a choice of either working in the mill, or working here. She's mastered the basic arts of housekeeping, and I'm sure will learn cooking as well. When she's ready to leave us she will be prepared to get an excellent job in another household."

"Perhaps some day she'll have her own home," I put in. "She's an attractive young woman."

"She's still very young," said Aunt Cornelia, giving me a glance whose purpose was not hidden. "She's learned a lot in the past two years, and those skills could certainly be put to use should she be lucky enough to find a good, sober, God-fearing man who will appreciate her. I'm pleased with her progress, and have told her so."

I said no more about the cooking, but was secretly delighted when, a week later, Aunt Cornelia loaned Katie out to Mrs. Sampson's cook for ten days of training. The girl had now been back two weeks, and there was an appreciable improvement in her efforts in the kitchen. Bread now rose and stews were not usually burned. Beyond that, my comments on her culinary efforts are best kept to myself.

"Katie, I'm going to walk to town. Are any of Mr. Livingston's old cloaks or coats still in the house somewhere? I'd like to borrow one, if any are available."

"Have you lost your blue frockcoat?" she asked.

If one of our maids in New York City had been impertinent enough to ask a question of that nature my mother would have fired her instantly. But it didn't seem to concern Aunt Cornelia that Katie occasionally spoke her mind, and generally the girl was amusing, so I wasn't bothered by her comments. Many people in the country appeared to believe their thoughts worth sharing. Aunt Cornelia and my mother, despite being sisters, had different standards for their help.

"My coat is not available just now."

"Some of Mr. Livingston's clothing is still in the upstairs hall wardrobe. Mrs. Livingston gave most of his things to the poor, but I remember her saying she'd keep some outer garments should guests be in need."

"Then please get me a cloak or coat. It makes no difference."

Katie shook her head slightly and looked at me as though I were slightly mad. Perhaps I was. "Yes, sir. I'll see what is there." She ran up the stairs as though a hound were at her heels, and returned carrying a dark cloak with a circular cape top and two long openings for arms. "This might do, sir. Mr. Livingston didn't wear it much."

I put my right arm into the garment, and, without being asked, Katie pulled it up on my left shoulder. She gave it one good tug and we could both see it might fall off the shoulder without being held by another arm. Before I could say anything she reached out and fastened three of the brass buttons. "That should hold well enough, sir. Until you find your own coat."

Hestia was almost five miles away. On the right day it might have been a pleasant walk. But although the sun had been out only minutes earlier, clouds were now thickening. The freshness of spring was just below the surface of breezes that threatened a late freeze. I set out with determination. Perhaps I could meet Aunt Cornelia at the orphan's home and ride back with her in the carriage.

During the late 1840s, in an attempt at modernization, the road had been covered with planks designed to cover ruts and ease the difficulties of spring traveling in mud. But the plan had failed. The wood had rotted, and planked roads were no longer used. Now the street was back to what it had been – a crude road pitted with holes made by wagon wheels, hooves and boots that had sunk into the mud.

In the past four years I'd probably marched the difference between my aunt's home and Paris and back. In worse weather, for sure. And on worse roads. But most of the last year I'd spent inside, in a hospital or at home, reading, or resting by the fire. Today the miles in front of me stretched further than I'd anticipated.

The distance gave me time to think. I'd never minded being alone. Growing up I'd learned to amuse myself, especially after Ben died. Father was usually at his office, or having dinner with business associates, and Mother was easily bored by such fascinating subjects as railroad cars and those new additions to the New York streets, policeman detectives.

I must have played with other boys on occasion, most likely when my governess took me to Gramercy Square Park. Several boys about my age had also lived near the house in Hestia and I learned to seek them out when I visited Aunt Cornelia and Uncle Henry.

Where were those boys I'd played hide and seek with now? Aunt Cornelia hadn't mentioned them, and I hadn't thought to ask. Most likely they were in the Army of the Potomac. Or had been.

The bones Owen had found might belong to one of my childhood playmates.

That possibility increased the length and speed of my steps.

I was glad when finally the road was less pitted, and I passed houses more frequently. At first they were wooden one-story structures boasting only small muddy yards, kitchen gardens in the rear, and perhaps an attic where the children slept. Closer to the center of Hestia houses were of brown or gray brick, two or more stories high. Many of those boasted flower as well as kitchen gardens, and the sound of hammers and axes came from stables in back of several.

I moved aside for an oxcart carrying barrels of cider, and was relieved when a brick path emerged on the side of the road so I could walk without sharing the street with an increasing number of animals and carriages. The center of town was marked by several dry goods establishments, a blacksmith, druggist, and the Hestia post office. The Oak Tavern was on a side street, near the school, and a public stable. My destination was a three-story home on the east side of town. A hedge of hawthorn surrounded the grounds, and one brick walkway led from the sidewalk to the front door, and another to a red painted door on the side of the house. I knocked at the red door.

The man who answered was massive, his stomach barely breached by a set of braces. His shirt collar was open, and he pulled on his waistcoat as he opened the door. From the rumpled appearance of both his shoulder length hair and the pillows on the sofa I could see in the background, I suspected my knocking had woken him, despite the hour being closer to two in the afternoon than dusk.

"Doctor Litchfield. I've come to seek your counsel."

"Good to see you, my boy." He opened the door wider as I moved sideways past his girth into the study that served as his consultation room. Prior visits had established that the door to the left of his desk opened into a small examination room where cabinets held the various instruments of his trade. The room we were in was by far the more comfortable of the two. A bookcase filled with medical texts propped up by an actual human skull was behind his desk. Half a dozen tarnished candlesticks of varying heights and a whale oil lamp whose glass had not been cleaned after its last use stood on the top shelf.

He motioned to one of the heavy upholstered chairs, and then sat in another. "I've been meaning to check on you, Aaron. I saw your aunt at church last Sunday. She said you're still staying at home most days."

I ignored the unstated question as to why I hadn't been with Aunt Cornelia at church. "I'm mending."

Doctor Litchfield nodded and leaned toward me. "What about pain? Are you sleeping well?"

"Some pain. The pills help with sleeping."

"Are you still using morphine?"

"When necessary."

He sat back somewhat. "Use what you need, Aaron. Potions are God's gift to us. They'll do you no harm, and will make life easier to endure."

"They do help me sleep," I agreed. "But they bring nightmares." And sometimes visions during the day, I added to myself. Despite the assurances of many doctors, I didn't feel myself with the medications, and yet was finding it harder and harder to live without them. I hadn't determined whether I was more at ease with pain or with the confusion that sometimes followed my taking the drugs.

"Sleep's what's important. Rest is what you need to heal your body and spirit." He got up and rummaged in one of the deep drawers of his large desk. "Take these. When you need additional morphine, you can get it at the pharmacy."

"Thank you." I pocketed the vials of opium pills he'd handed me. "But I didn't come to see you about my health. I've come to ask a favor."

"Yes?" Dr. Litchfield eased himself back into his wide chair.

"Owen Hindley found a body in our north field."

The doctor sat up, so far as his stomach would allow. "A body?"

"Actually, more of a skeleton," I amended. "It appears to have been buried long enough for all but the bones to be gone. Recent flooding washed the ground away from the skull and some of the ribs."

"What do you want of me?"

"I want to know how long the bones have been there, and how the person died, if possible. I want to identify the body."

"Why should you mind about it, Aaron?" He sat back and waved his hand dismissively. "No doubt it's a tramp or gypsy or someone who headed west years ago. Perhaps someone who died on the canal. There'd be no way of knowing. You're here to help your Aunt Cornelia and heal yourself. Why be concerned with the body of a vagrant? Tell Owen to cover the bones, or bury them outside the field, and be finished with them."

"Aunt Cornelia doesn't need my help, and I'm healing well enough. Someone died and was buried. With your help I'd like to find out who it is, and why. A family may be waiting for word from someone. Perhaps we could answer their questions. I remember Aunt Cornelia's saying you're the coroner for Hestia."

"I am."

"You were the one who confirmed Uncle Henry died of natural causes."

"Most deaths are natural, Aaron. I'd known your Uncle Henry for over thirty years. His heart was weak, and it gave out. I didn't have to see his body to know that. Of course, many times I do examine bodies closely. But a coroner's work is usually with the more recently deceased than your man or woman appears to be."

"But you could look at the bones."

"I'm not sure how much I'd be able to determine." He looked at me closely. "But of course, I'll give it a try, if it's that important to you."

"Thank you. It is."

"You left the bones in the ground?"

"I covered them with my coat, to protect them a bit."

"We'll have to get them out of the ground to examine them. It's been years since I did an autopsy on bones, and not a body. Not since Jeremy Phelan plowed up that old Indian skeleton near his apple orchard. I'll need to remove them to my office. Do you have a board or canvas at your place we could put them on?"

"I'm sure Owen could find one."

"I have appointments this afternoon, and then it'll be too dark to do anything. I'll bring my wagon 'round in the morning, and we'll see what we can make of your bones."

Chapter 4

The orphanage wasn't difficult to find. Only a few blocks from Dr. Litchfield's home, it was an imposing three story Federal style building like so many elegant homes built early in the century, but more recently updated by the addition of four Greek-style columns and a pediment. A high ornate wrought iron fence surrounded both the building and yard. Near the entrance a brass plaque read "Bradford Asylum For Orphans". Whoever built that imposing fence could not have been worried about orphans breaking in.

The gate was unlocked.

"Yes, sir?" The woman who answered my knock on the heavily carved oak door wore a pinafore similar to uniforms worn by New York City maids to identify their rank and function. I suspected this particular pinafore served a purely practical purpose, since its front was stained with a number of substances I had no desire to identify. "May I help you?"

"I'm looking for Mrs. Cornelia Livingston. I'm her nephew. I believe she was coming here today." I glanced past her, into a wide, dark paneled hallway interrupted by a carved staircase leading to the second and third floors. I could imagine ladies descending it in flounced and crinolined gowns, pausing on the landing just long enough to make dramatic entrances.

"Would you wait here a few minutes?" She walked quickly toward the back of the hallway.

This had once been a wealthy family's home. The large doors on each side of the first floor hall would then have opened into parlors and perhaps a library or music or smoking room, as well as dining and reception rooms. The rooms above would have served as bedchambers for the family and, perhaps on the third floor, the staff. Although somewhere in the distance I could hear a young child crying, the building was surprisingly quiet for one now housing many children.

The woman returned. "I see you're looking at the building. We're lucky to have had such a place donated. This is the children's naptime. Another half hour and you'd have no doubt where they were. Come with me. Mrs. Livingston is available."

I followed her to the back of the hall, its parquet floor still damp from scrubbing, to where another, smaller, hallway joined it at an angle. From the sounds of rattling brass and iron and the surprisingly appetizing smell of spiced potatoes, I surmised the second hallway led to the kitchen. I couldn't think my aunt contributed much to that area of the orphanage, unless she had hidden talents that had not been obvious during the week Katie had been away from our home to learn basic cooking techniques. Aunt Cornelia's efforts in that direction had been worse than Katie's.

My companion opened a door almost hidden within the paneling below the shadow of the wide staircase.

"Mrs. Livingston, your nephew is here," she said softly. After a moment she opened the door further and gestured that I should enter the room.

My aunt was sitting at a table in one corner of a small bookcase-lined room lit by several oil sconces. It might once have served as an intimate study or retreat for the gentleman of the house. Now the bookcases were filled with an assortment of what at quick glance appeared to be threads and needles, yarn, and piles of fabrics and clothing. One section contained medicinal supplies – laundered bandages, bottles of antiseptics, and so forth. A worn leather ledger lay on the desk.

Two other women were with Aunt Cornelia. It was clear I'd interrupted some sort of female gathering.

But Aunt Cornelia didn't seem upset to see me. "Aaron! You've surprised me." She smiled, and then indicated the two women sitting with her. "But of course you're welcome. I don't believe you've met Mrs. Neilson and Miss Burns."

I bowed slightly in greeting. "I haven't had the pleasure."

"Lidia, Nora, this is my nephew, Captain Aaron Stone, who I've spoken about. He's been with me since January, helping me run the estate."

"I'm so glad to meet you," said Mrs. Neilson. She was a plump woman, with graying brown hair, wearing a dark blue morning dress covered with a sort of sprigged pattern and finished off with a modest white lace collar and cuffs. Despite her welcoming smile and the gaiety of her attire, the deep lines in Mrs. Neilson's weather-beaten skin said she must be approaching forty, and those years had not been easy ones. Perhaps she was one of the many women, in both the north and south, who'd been forced to do men's work in fields and barns to keep food on their tables. She glanced at my empty sleeve and then raised her eyes to my face. "Cornelia has mentioned you often, of course. How kind it is for you to help her out in these difficult days."

I nodded slightly. "I'm pleased to have been of some use." Of but little use, I thought to myself. "Now that the war's over we can hope for the return of our soldiers. Work in the fields and farms can resume as it should, and I can be of more help."

Mrs. Neilson nodded, but did not smile. "Of course we're all blessed that the conflict appears to have finally ended."

Had she lost a husband, or perhaps a son? The thought disappeared quickly as I looked at the other woman in the room. "And you are Miss Burns?"

Miss Burns was unlike any other woman I'd seen in Hestia or in New York City. Her face was also slightly sun-darkened, but she was much younger than Mrs. Neilson, and her skin, instead of being lined, glowed with the health of youth. Perhaps she was as young as twenty; surely not older than twenty-two or twenty-three. But most astonishing, Miss Burns had cut her hair short. It fell just to her ears. I'd heard of women who did such things; the nearby Oneida Community, which had a reputation for a number of behaviors unacceptable to civilized people, was said to encourage their women to wear their hair short. But I myself had never met a female who would choose to eliminate what, for most women, was the most visibly feminine part of their appearance. Miss Burns' hair was a memorable dark auburn. Perhaps she had been ill? Occasionally doctors recommended cutting heavy long hair to help cure a fever. As I stared at her, Miss Burns lowered her eyes slightly, as was appropriate for any attractive young woman.

Aunt Cornelia clearly had seen my amazed and admiring look at her friend. "Miss Burns is our neighbor, Aaron."

Burns. I'd heard that name only this morning. "It must have been your father, then, Miss Burns, to whom my Uncle Henry rented out the north field in years past." And perhaps her brother I had seen in the woods this morning?

"My father did rent out the Livingstons' back field, to grow hops," she agreed, looking almost questioningly at me for a moment. Her brown eyes were sparked with green, and she wore a plain brown dress, of a somewhat old-fashioned cut, mended in several places. The dress was modest, but suited her well, although the knit shawl around her shoulders hid most of her shape. I'll admit that even at that first meeting my eyes lingered on her longer than was necessary.

I turned to my aunt. "I'm sorry to interrupt your meeting, Aunt Cornelia, but I walked into town, and hoped that perhaps, when you were ready to return home, I might join you in the carriage."

"Of course you may." Aunt Cornelia hesitated a moment. "I think, ladies, that we have accomplished what we can today. Our plans are made, and we've prepared what we can. Lidia, I will see you at church Sunday. And, Nora, we will be in touch as soon as we know more details about the situation."

"Certainly, Cornelia," said Mrs. Neilson. Miss Burns nodded agreement. Both of them rose.

"Nora," Aunt Cornelia said, "Why don't you and Robbie join Aaron and I on our ride home? There's room in the carriage."

Robbie? Then the young boy I'd seen *had* been her brother. How had he managed to get here so quickly? I glanced at my pocket watch. Almost three o'clock. I'd forgotten how long I'd been with Dr. Litchfield.

If this young woman and her brother were to ride with us, perhaps I could learn more about her. But that circumstance was not to be.

"No, thank you, Cornelia," said Miss Burns. "I have several errands to do before I start for home, as you understand. Perhaps I will see you Monday."

"Whenever the time is right," answered Aunt Cornelia quickly. She turned to me as the door closed on the two women. "Now then, Aaron, we'll be on our way, and you can tell me what has brought you to town."

Aunt Cornelia's horse and carriage were in back of the orphanage, where a surprisingly large stable held several wagons, carriages and horses, "for taking the children on outings, or use in securing supplies." The Bradford family had funded the asylum well.

"How many children live here?" I asked as we started toward home. "It's a much larger establishment than I'd imagined."

"Before the war there were about two dozen children, of various ages. They stay here until they're fourteen, when most leave to go into service at a local home or work at the factory," said Aunt Cornelia. "But the war has taken a major toll. We now have over forty orphans, plus twenty-three half orphans. Most lost their fathers in the war, and their mothers must work to support themselves, so cannot care for their children. Most dream of the day when their situation will improve, and they can bring their sons and daughters home. We also provide some training for the mothers, so they are better prepared to find employment, and to care for their children without a husband's help."

Neither of us spoke for a few moments. My experiences of the war had been, of course, with men on the battlefields; soldiers who cherished letters from home and longed to be with their wives and children. The children and their mothers who benefited from the services of the Bradford Asylum for Children were victims on the home front.

The past years had not been easy for anyone.

As soon as the carriage was outside of Hestia I told Aunt Cornelia about the body Owen had found in her field, and about my meeting with Dr. Litchfield. Thank goodness, she was not the sort of female to faint or be flustered.

The mare picked her way down the pitted surface of the road. "Then Dr. Litchfield is coming tomorrow, to examine the bones and take them away," said Aunt Cornelia, holding on to the side of the carriage with one hand as it pitched over the ruts.

She'd handed me the reins as we left town, and I held them with difficulty, and tried to keep us steady. I hadn't attempted to drive a carriage since I'd been home, and driving with one hand was difficult.

The horse seemed nervous, clearly noting the hesitancies in my directions. "Yes. I'll talk with Owen tonight and see if he has a plank to put them on. It may be a bit difficult for us to carry it to Dr. Litchfield's wagon, but I don't think the bones will be heavy. It's just the matter of getting through the muddy field."

With my having only one arm and Owen's having a bad leg, I thought to myself,

I should have asked Dr. Litchfield to bring someone with him to help tomorrow. Although that would have added to the list of those who knew about the bones.

I was concentrating on my driving, and at first didn't notice Aunt Cornelia's silence.

"Aaron, have you thought this through? Sometimes circumstances are best left as they are."

"Surely you don't mean we shouldn't try to identify the body, Aunt Cornelia. Everyone should be given a decent burial, and every family deserves to know what happened to a relative."

"In most cases I believe you're correct, Aaron. But from your description of the bones, this person has clearly been gone for some time. Perhaps his family has already laid him to rest, in their minds. To literally dig him up now could be uncovering old wounds. Emotional sores. Sometimes it's better that we not know exactly what has happened in the past."

"Knowing the truth is always important."

"'Always' is a strong word, Aaron. And truth does not mean the same thing to every person. There are times when digging up the past can have unforeseen influences on the future."

"You mean we shouldn't know who those bones are, or why they're in your field? That doesn't make sense to me. Knowing ends questions, and possibilities. It allows healing."

Aunt Cornelia nodded, almost reluctantly. "Only the future will tell whether those bones should have lain quietly where they are, or whether you should have brought them to light."

I glanced at her. Clearly she did not feel as I did. "The bones are on your land. Perhaps I acted impetuously. I never imagined you wouldn't agree with me. If you wish, I will tell Dr. Litchfield I've changed my mind. We can bury the bones quietly."

Aunt Cornelia smiled, almost sadly, and shook her head. "It's too late for that, Aaron. Dr. Litchfield knows you've found that body, and all the town will know by tomorrow night, if they haven't heard already." She looked over at me. "Perhaps there's a reason those bones appeared now. Today is the first in many days when you've found something you cared enough about that it took you five miles into town. Perhaps identifying those bones is something you need to do before you can leave the past behind and start living your future."

In Hestia that Friday evening of April 14 was a quiet one. Aunt Cornelia retired early, and I stayed up, sipping Uncle Henry's best cognac in his study, and wondering about Aunt Cornelia's strange reluctance to identify the bones.

At one point I took down the daguerreotype my parents had sent my aunt and uncle after I'd enlisted. The picture had stood on their mantel throughout the war. I stared at myself as I'd been four years ago. My uniform was new and immaculate. My expression was serious, and I'd posed, as directed, holding my saber in my now missing left hand. I looked very young. That daguerreotype was the only visual record of my life before the war. Just looking at it made my arm ache.

I poured another half snifter of cognac, and I wouldn't be truthful if I didn't admit I thought about the lovely and enigmatic Miss Burns, and what excuse I might find to meet her again.

Chapter 5

I shall never forget the events of that Saturday.

It started simply enough. Owen and I searched the barn and other outbuildings for a plank appropriate in length and width to be used as a temporary ossuary. Katie found an old patched sheet that would do as a cover for the bones.

We all assumed Dr. Litchfield would be joining us early in the day, but no wagons appeared in our drive. I paced the length of the piazza, uneasy about the next steps we were to take. Owen had thought of possible logistical challenges and placed old work gloves, a tin bucket, a shovel, and even a large pair of iron ice tongs near the plank and the neatly folded sheet on the side of the piazza. All was in readiness.

I remember in detail where everyone was, as they say happens when something occurs that changes your world.

Aunt Cornelia was settled in the parlor, embroidering blue and yellow wildflowers on a dark green velvet quilt square. Owen was sweeping the brick walkway that led around the house. Katie was supposed to be in the kitchen, although I saw her face at the library window at least twice, looking out toward the front of the house. We were all waiting.

It was a quarter to eleven when Dr. Litchfield's horses finally pulled his wagon into the front drive. He got down from the wagon remarkably nimbly for someone of his size and age. I met him at the bottom of the porch stairs.

"Have you heard?" he asked in a low tone. His eyes were slightly swollen, as though he'd been crying.

"Heard what?" I asked. "We've gathered what we thought necessary for the removal." I gestured at the pile on the piazza, but Dr. Litchfield ignored me.

"Then I must tell your aunt first," he said, pushing by me and opening the front door of the house without knocking. "Come."

I motioned to Owen, who was listening by the side of the house, and we followed the doctor in. I sensed clearly that whatever had happened was something that needed saying to all of us, no matter position or rank.

As soon as we entered the parlor, Katie edged to its door, holding a white dust cloth in her hand.

Dr. Litchfield stood by the mantel, looking at all of us. "Word came by telegraph at eight this morning to the *Register* offices. Last night our dear President Lincoln was assassinated while attending the theater in Washington."

Aunt Cornelia dropped her sewing. I heard Katie gasp.

"An attempt was also made on the life of Secretary of State Seward. He lies gravely injured in his home."

The room was silent. Owen took off his hat, and tears fell down Aunt Cornelia's cheeks; the first I had ever seen her shed.

"In Hestia there's talk of nothing else. The major issued this notice." Dr. Litchfield pulled a much-folded piece of paper out of his waistcoat pocket and read,

'A great calamity has befallen the nation in the murder of its chief and the attempted murder of the chief officer of his cabinet. Citizens of Hestia are requested to close their places of

business and suspend their usual avocations from noon 'till 2
p.m. today, during which hours all the bells of the city will be
tolled.'

Flags have already been lowered to half-mast, and most people in town have put on mourning bands and placed black wreaths on their doors. The streets are silent, but for their tears."

Katie blew her nose loudly into her dust cloth.

"He led us through so much," Aunt Cornelia said quietly. "Now, at last, when finally there is promise that our union is preserved and the suffering over, he has been taken from us." She looked up at the doctor. "Who is responsible?"

"It is assumed to be a group with southern loyalties, but there is no word yet on who committed the murder. Certainly more than one individual is involved, since Lincoln and Seward were attacked close to the same time. I cannot believe those remaining in the government and the army will allow such individuals to escape."

Aunt Cornelia, despite her tears, recovered first. "Katie! Go to the front bedroom and unpack our mourning wreaths and crepe from the trunk. Wreaths must be hung on our doors and windows, and the piazza hung with crepe. Owen, raise our flag, and arrange it so it hangs at half-mast." Aunt Cornelia looked pale. "It was good of you to come, doctor, to let us know. Living in the country we miss hearing news as soon as we would like."

"I would have been here earlier if it hadn't been for the excitement. The town is alternately in despair and anger."

"I can imagine." Aunt Cornelia said. "May I offer you a cognac? I think on this occasion I would like one."

"I wouldn't refuse, Mrs. Livingston," said the doctor.

"Aaron, would you get the cognac and three snifters from the library? I assume you will join us."

I'd never seen Aunt Cornelia sip even a drop of sherry. As a child

I remembered her attending temperance meetings at the church and chastising Uncle Henry for his occasional lapses. Yet I knew where the liquor was kept – for medicinal purposes only, I had been told as a child – and for the first time I realized that my occasional glasses of whiskey in the late night hours had never diminished the supply there. The bottles must be replenished regularly. I said a silent thanks to Aunt Cornelia as I poured three snifters full of the potent oak-colored liquid and passed them around.

"To our President! And our country," said Aunt Cornelia, raising her glass.

"Our late President," said Dr. Litchfield. I echoed his words. Somehow it didn't feel strange to be sipping cognac on a Saturday morning. The day which had started full of tension and excitement now felt empty, and strangely ominous. What would become of our tenuous nation now, without the leader we'd focused on for the past four difficult years? I supposed we had a new president now. President Andrew Johnson. The phrase sounded somehow odd.

Katie was already outside the parlor door, her arms filled with black mourning cloths. "Katie?" said Aunt Cornelia. "Hang the largest mourning wreath on our front door, and before you hang the crepe take one of the other wreaths over to the Burns house and tell them what has happened. Nora will hear bells tolling at noon and be anxious."

"Yes, Ma'am," said Katie, disappearing toward the front door.

I knew better than to volunteer to take over Katie's mission; a gentleman did not leave an honored guest to pass information on to a family he does not know, even in so unusual situation as the assassination of the president. But I glanced at my pocket watch, and vowed to note how long Katie was absent. That would at least indicate somewhat how far away the Burns residence was.

There was some conversation for the next moments; I do not

remember what it was. I do remember watching out the window as Owen carefully raised the American flag on the pole in front of the house, and then lowered it slowly to half-mast. For a blurred moment I saw the many flags raised in battle and lowered by shelling, and the flag that hung at perpetual half-mast near the hospital for the Army of the Potomac in Washington.

"Aaron?" I realized Dr. Litchfield must have been speaking to me. "I brought my wagon. We might as well go about the somber task that brought me here this morning. It seems fitting under the circumstances."

I nodded and drained my snifter. "Aunt Cornelia, this shouldn't take us long."

"Take whatever time is necessary. This is a day for sadness, and Dr. Litchfield is right. Your plans seem more appropriate now then they did earlier."

Outside, Owen and the doctor and I loaded the plank and tools onto the wagon. "If we take the back drive," suggested Owen, "we'll be able to get the wagon within a few hundred feet of the bones. That road hasn't been used this spring, but I walked it yesterday afternoon and moved aside the largest of the branches that fell during the winter."

As the horses pulled us around and down the back drive clouds blew across the sun, and the day darkened. Our slow progress was accompanied by the distant tolling of bells in Hestia.

It was now after noon. The country was mourning. And I had not yet seen Katie return. I would not be able to see her from the north field.

Despite the now chilly air, Dr. Litchfield knelt on the damp ground and leaned over the bones. "We must remove the body carefully, retaining as much as possible the relation the bones have to each other in the earth. The mud and hardened dirt may be concealing some clue as to who this was, or how he or she got here. Some of the bones look as though they're in place; others have been separated by mud. Or animals."

Owen stood next to him, leaning against the shovel. "A lot of mud will come with the bones, Doc."

"It will. I'll wash the dirt off carefully in my office later when I'm examining the body. There's no way to do that adequately here, and we might miss some of the smaller bone fragments." He looked at me. "They're beginning to decay. Do you still want me to do this? I don't know how much information I'll be able to find, given their condition."

There was no sense turning back now. "Those who loved this person need to know what happened." For a moment I listened to my own words and wondered if there were anyone, anywhere, who had not been loved by someone. Then I dismissed the idea as maudlin. Even the orphans in Hestia had women like Aunt Cornelia to care about them.

"Bones alone won't tell who it is," cautioned Dr. Litchfield.

"But you will be able to tell if this is a man, or a woman. And we'll have an idea of how old the person was. And perhaps how long the body's been here."

Dr. Litchfield nodded as he reached out to gently rub some of the mud off a shoulder bone. "I can already tell you the body's been buried at least three years; most likely four or five. Owen, this field hasn't been planted in some time, has it?"

"Not since before the war. Maybe '60 or '61. Mr. Livingston's records would say for sure. William Burns leased the field to grow hops before that. After the war started there was no one to work it."

"Burns enlisted?" I asked idly.

"Most men here abouts did," said Owen. "Would have gone myself if I'd been a few years younger."

We were all conscious of the continuous tolling in the distance.

"That would confirm the body's not been here longer than the field's been idle."

Dr. Litchfield ran his fingers carefully down the bones, separating them slightly from the mud encasing them. "Hops roots can be ten or fifteen feet long. It would've been difficult to dig a deep grave in a field where they'd been grown. This body wasn't buried more than two or three feet beneath the surface. A plow would likely have hit it. No wonder the flooding uncovered parts."

"It isn't usual to bury a body less then six feet under," Owen pointed out. "Two or three feet's too close to the surface. Animals are likely to dig it up." He paused. "There's no coffin, or trace of clothing."

Dr. Litchfield rubbed his hands together to remove some of the mud clinging to them. "Fabrics could well have disintegrated after four or five years in the ground. This wasn't a formal burial. It was done quickly. Perhaps there wasn't time to dig deeper."

"Doesn't look as though a lot of prayers were said over this soul," I agreed.

I'd helped bury too many men under difficult circumstances, with time constraints keeping us from being either as respectful as we'd like, or as careful. But those were battlefield conditions. How would those situations apply to an isolated field in northern New York State?

"You're right," said Dr. Litchfield. "We're less than twenty-four feet from the canal path. Could have been one of those ruffians who work the barges. Or someone heading west who didn't complete the journey. Maybe became ill and died and those traveling with him didn't want to waste the time it would take to give him a decent burial."

"He might have died of something contagious, and they wanted to get the body off the barge," I suggested.

Owen moved back. "Could we sicken from whatever it was he died of?"

"I doubt we have to worry about that." The doctor's mud-encrusted fingers were moving along the skull. He looked up. "I'll need to look at this carefully, in good light. But it feels as though there's a hole in the back of the skull. If I'm not mistaken, this fellow was helped along his journey to eternity by someone wielding a heavy object."

Chapter 6

Many nights sleep escaped me in those days, and the night of April 15 was no exception. My dreams returned me to the battlefield; to gathering up fragments of what had been friends; to running through fields exploding with shell fire on legs that would not move; to sweaty sessions with women making a few cents from soldiers trying to fill their needs for home and peace and comfort with a woman. Any woman.

I woke, drenched with sweat, dreaming of a one of those women I almost remembered from the trek through Maryland. A woman who now had Nora's face.

Several times I reached for my morphine, but stopped. Tonight our president was dead. Tonight I was a soldier who needed to feel. To mourn. Dulling my pain would be denying the fates of so many.

By dawn I could no longer remain in bed. Owen had left the flag flying at half-mast through the night. It seemed the right thing to have done.

I walked through the yard and garden, and found myself on the path to the north field. I needed to make sense of what the world had become.

After Dr. Litchfield examined the body I'd talk with the sheriff. His name was Newell; John Newell. I suspected he'd have no interest in the bones, or why they were in this field – past was past — but my legal training told me I needed to report their existence.

The quiet crack of a breaking branch startled me. Ahead, near where we'd removed the bones, stood the boy I'd seen two days before.

I walked closer. He looked at me, but didn't run.

"Robbie Burns?" I called out.

"Yes," he answered, standing with bare feet planted solidly apart on the cold ground. "Are you going to tell Nora?"

"Tell Nora what?" I asked as I approached him. He was small; perhaps four or five years old, although I was no expert in determining age. His fists were tight, as though he was prepared to take me on.

"That I'm on your land without anyone's say so."

"It's my Aunt Cornelia's property," I answered. A technicality that would mean nothing to either this boy or his sister, I suspected.

"Did you lose your arm in the war?"

"Yes."

"Did Rebs cut it off?" The boy starred at my sleeve as though trying to memorize it.

"They shot it up, and then a doctor amputated it. Cut it off."

"Did it hurt?"

"Yes."

The boy moved closer to me, his eyes focused on my arm. "Does it still hurt?"

"Sometimes. But not like at first."

The boy nodded seriously, as though the answer made sense to him. He pointed at the now-empty grave. "Did you take the bones? I saw you looking at them the other day."

"Dr. Litchfield and I took the bones, yes."

"Why'd you dig 'em up?"

"I want to find out whose bones they are. How did you know about them?"

"I saw 'em. I was exploring. Lots of things got caught in the flood."

"Did you find anything else interesting?"

"I didn't take nothin' you'd want."

Clearly Robbie wasn't going to share whatever he'd found. "That's all right. I'm sure you can keep whatever you found."

"It's only some boards and a broken chair. I'm goin' to fix the chair for my sister."

"That's a fine idea. Maybe I could help you?"

"I don't think so. You only have one arm. How could you hold something and hammer at the same time?"

The boy was right. "Maybe I could hold and you could hammer."

"Maybe." He looked at me consideringly.

"What are you doing out here so early in the morning? Won't your family be worried?"

"It's just Nora. Ma's dead and Pa's in the army."

Then Nora had the total responsibility for her brother. And no mother to advise her in the ways young women acted and dressed. Although surely she knew few women of any age wore their hair the way she did. "Perhaps your Pa will be home soon, then."

The boy shrugged. "He don't write."

"Well, Nora will worry about you, then."

"She's gone. She won't know."

"'Gone?'"

"Sometimes she goes walkin' at night. I wake up and she's not there. She's always back in the morning."

Where would a young woman be going by herself in the middle of the night? There could only be one answer. I felt a twinge of jealousy.

"Well, the sun is up now. She'll be coming home, and she'll be worried if you're not there, won't she?"

"I suppose. I wanted to see the bones again. But you took 'em."

"Why'd you want to see the bones?"

"I hadn't seen people bones before." Robbie looked over at where the bones had been, and then at me. "I wasn't scared. I wanted to see what the insides of us look like."

"I didn't think you were scared."

"Some might be. Some talk of ghosts."

"Have you ever seen a ghost?"

"Nah. But there might be some near here. 'Cause of the bones. Nora says ghosts are only in people's minds."

"I think Nora's right."

"It's Easter Sunday, ain't it?"

"It is."

"Then Nora'll be after me to clean up and go to church."

I nodded. "It's a good Sunday to say a prayer."

"President Lincoln got killed."

"Yes."

Robbie backed up a bit. "When I get growed up I'm goin' to kill the people that did that." He turned toward the woods.

"Can you find your way home?"

"I got here, didn't I?" He took off across the field, clumps of mud flying behind him, and entered the woods near where I'd seen him two days before.

I turned and headed back for the house. I'd go to church too, I decided. This Easter there was a lot to pray for.

Chapter 7

I hadn't made a regular habit of attending services with Aunt Cornelia, but this Sunday I dressed without hesitation, putting on the dark gray frock coat, trousers and embroidered waistcoat my parents had given me for Christmas. Father's tailor had eliminated the left sleeve on both the shirt and coat, which was not my preference, but it did make the clothing fit well. Aunt Cornelia was, of course, dressed in black, from her crimped bonnet to her buttoned shoes. She was still in mourning for Uncle Henry. But Katie was also wearing black, and asked permission for us to drop her at St. Patrick's, as it was Easter, after all, and it would be right and proper to say a prayer for Mr. Lincoln and our country. Even Owen, who I'd never noticed attending services, suggested he drive us all, and perhaps join some acquaintances at church.

I hoped Owen was not being overly dramatic when I saw he'd decorated our carriage with crepe, but as soon as we neared town I realized my reticence at public mourning was highly misplaced.

Never, before or since, have I seen any demonstration that approached the public sorrow expressed in Hestia that day. Every house displayed a mourning wreath or banner or crepe. Every carriage was swathed in black; even horses wore black crepe decorations. Every household which owned a United States flag displayed it proudly, and at half mast; black borders had been stitched around some flags to form somber frames. Both St. Patrick's, where Katie was helped down from the carriage by a worn and bent bearded man who Aunt Cornelia quietly informed me was Katie's father, and the First Presbyterian, were draped in black, inside and out. Parishioners of every denomination were dressed in grays and blacks and violets, in formal mourning for "Father Abraham."

Reverend Pinkston, a tall, stately, man of God whose only apparent vanity was the wide white mustache he had clearly waxed with care before ascending the dais, wore the pulpit gown and bands usually reserved for funerals, and devoted his Easter sermon to the greatness of our fallen leader, the devastation of our country's loss, and our national responsibility to work together as individual citizens and as states to bring our country together. On Thursday he might have planned his words to be those of joy and beginning; the long war was at an end, and it was Easter. The Lord had risen, and the world would soon rejoice in spring and rebirth. Now he described those new beginnings as growing out of the pain of national grief.

Every pew was filled, and a dozen somber men stood in the rear of the sanctuary. Periodically the sound of sobbing was a counterpoint to Reverend Pinkston's words. All the sadness and discouragement and broken hopes of the past four years were on display that morning as men and women remembered the husbands, fathers, brothers, and sons who'd filled family pews now occupied by women alone. Farms had been neglected; families bankrupted. Middle class women had entered fields and factories in numbers impossible to imagine four years before. Neighbors had banded together to keep food on the table. Soldiers, especially those not officers, often waited months for the paychecks they'd hoped would buy shoes and grain for their families at home.

Our world had changed because of this war, and President

Lincoln had led us through the victories and defeats; the devastation and the ultimate celebration. He'd given us a beacon to follow: a hope that all we were sacrificing was for the good of the nation, and, ultimately, for the good of mankind.

Now he was gone.

After the service people gathered outside the church and talked quietly. Their grief was communal.

Aunt Cornelia's friend Mrs. Neilson was in purple mourning, and, I noted, driving her own carriage, despite its being larger and more elegant than most, and designed for a driver and passengers. She was one of the first to leave the gathering. I saw no sign of Nora or Robbie Burns, but they were likely at St. Patrick's. I hoped Nora had returned home safely from wherever she had been early this morning. The thought of her meeting a man in the silence of the night was still strangely upsetting to me.

Dr. Litchfield tapped me on the shoulder, breaking into my reveries as I stood at the side of the crowd waiting for Aunt Cornelia to complete her socializing.

"Aaron, I've unloaded your skeleton, and, if there are no other calls on my time, will examine it tomorrow afternoon."

"May I come then, and watch when you do? I'll admit to a curiosity about the process."

"If you wish. You were trained as a lawyer before the war, were you not?" asked the doctor.

"I was."

"Then the examination of a body, even if the body be nothing but bones, is something you should be familiar with. In the practice of criminal law it is not uncommon for a lawyer to observe an autopsy."

My study of law had been academic; classrooms, and the leather-bound books in my father's office, in which every transaction between men in the State of New York was measured and considered. Right or wrong. I knew, of course, of the volumes that covered our legal system's attempts to convict felons and murderers, and to free those who were innocent, but those were not the clients I'd anticipated serving, so I'd paid little attention to criminal law. It was not the sort of law gentlemen like my father practiced.

But in the moment Dr. Litchfield suggested it would be appropriate for me to be present at his autopsy, I realized that should the unknown soul whose bones we were to examine have been murdered, as the doctor assumed, then a lawyer would be required to ensure that whoever committed the crime would be prosecuted.

And that I wanted to be that lawyer.

That Easter Sunday when our nation mourned the man who was perhaps its greatest leader, I also mourned the unknown individual whose life was ended at the hand of a cruel and heartless murderer. I made a silent vow not only to identify the victim, but to bring his or her assailant to justice.

Chapter 8

As I lay in bed that night my mind churned with seemingly unrelated scenes: assassinations and autopsies; lawyers and courtrooms; and the lone women I'd seen in church that day. Many were awaiting the return of loved ones, but some, I also knew, would be disappointed in their wait. Mother had written that Margaret had already found someone to replace me in her heart. For the first time I allowed myself to wonder if perhaps someday there might be another woman who could love me, despite my damaged body. I dared hope it could be so.

When I could no longer take the long empty hours of whirling thoughts I hastened their end by a dose of morphine. I'd grown used to the peace and numbness it brought.

After that I dreamt of trying to decipher the sounds of voices and carriage wheels and hoof-beats. They could have been battlefield noises, or sounds I'd heard in Hestia. My mind refused to translate them into anything approaching logical sequences, and I floated with them, willing my body to relax, and my mind to ignore them.

I rose in the morning rested, but not refreshed. I was glad I hadn't promised to meet Dr. Litchfield until afternoon. By then I would have regained my focus.

I was still not fully awake when I dressed and descended the stairs.

Katie was in the kitchen, kneading bread for the day, or perhaps for the week; whatever it was women did. "A cup of coffee, with cream if you have it, and three boiled eggs with ham and some toasted bread. I'll be in the dining room."

"I'll get them for you, sir. You have an appetite this morning."

Perhaps filling my stomach would help the mists in my mind recede. "Is Mrs. Livingston dressed yet?"

"Mrs. Livingston left before dawn, so far as I can tell," said Katie. "Owen says her carriage is gone, so she must have harnessed the mare herself. We thought perhaps you would know where she went, sir."

"I have no idea." I ran my hand through my hair. I must cut it soon; it was almost down to my shoulders and more shaggy than was acceptable even in the country. "She didn't mention any plans."

"I'll be getting your breakfast for you, then." Katie turned to a bubbling pot on the massive wood-burning Franklin stove she was learning to master. The glow from the logs inside was barely visible through the soot-covered mica windows on the stove's door. I would have liked a newspaper to read this morning, and would have given up several days' breakfasts for a *Harper's Weekly*, but it was published on Saturday, and rarely did a copy make its way to Hestia until Tuesday or Wednesday of the following week. Perhaps Aunt Cornelia had gone to Utica in search of one? I suspected not. Like the rest of the nation, I would have to wait for the answers to my questions.

Had Lincoln's assassin been found? Did we indeed have a new president? No doubt men were sitting at breakfast tables in dining rooms throughout the country wondering those same things. The president's death had brought the country together. Or at least brought the grieving north to one point of view. I had spent too much time in southern states to imagine there were many tears there.

By late morning there was still no sign of Aunt Cornelia. I was beginning to be concerned. In the months I'd lived with her I'd never known her to be absent, however briefly, without telling anyone where she was to be.

But worrying about someone who'd left at her own discretion was of no value to anyone. Aunt Cornelia had lived her life as she chose, even when Uncle Henry was alive. They'd seemed a happy couple, but had never been blessed with children, and Uncle Henry had tolerated, and, in truth, seemed to support, the many causes that had always filled Aunt Cornelia's life. Temperance. Rights for women. Abolition of slavery. Now the plight of orphans.

I could only think she'd been delayed for some reason, and would not want us distressed. Assuring Katie that Aunt Cornelia would be home at any moment, I left for Hestia, and Dr. Litchield's office.

Hestia's streets were filled with small groups of men and women talking in low voices, and the buildings hung with curtains of black crepe gave the impression that the whole city was a stage set. Flags were flying at half-mast, and I suspected would do so for days to come.

"Dr. Litchfield?" I knocked on his door, opening it slightly.

"Come in; come in, Aaron. I'm glad you're here. The world is a mournful place today, is it not?"

"It is. Have you heard when the funeral in Washington will be held?"

"The news came in on the telegraph this morning. Services in the capitol will be Wednesday, and many churches throughout the country will hold memorial services at the same time. Churches here in Hestia have already announced they will do so, and the veterans' organizations and fire department are planning a parade to take place afterward. As a veteran, Aaron, you will, of course, be expected to participate."

"I will see. I'm not a member of any local company. I assume

Lincoln's burial will be in his home state?"

"It will. But the outrage and sorrow of the nation's citizens is so deep that his body will travel to Illinois in a slow train, stopping in many cities along the way, so all may pay respects to our fallen leader. One of the stops will be in Utica. A number of local people are already planning to be there, to honor him in person."

"He was a great man," I agreed. "No doubt of that. I had the privilege of seeing him once in Washington, when I was in the hospital there. I shall never forget his genuine caring for those of us who'd been injured, nor his sadness for those families who'd lost loved ones."

"And now he is our great martyr," added Dr. Litchfield.

We stood silent for a few moments.

"Would you like to see what I've found so far?" asked the doctor, breaking our silence.

"Please."

He led the way to his examination room. The bones, most of them now clean of dirt, lay on the table.

I looked down at the skeleton. Today I saw only bones; not a person. Perhaps I was becoming callous? "What have you found? Is it a man or woman?"

"Definitely a man. The narrowness of the pelvic area makes that clear. In addition, the skull is larger and thicker than a female's would be. Men's brains are, of course, physiologically larger and therefore stronger than those of a woman."

"And his age?"

"An adult. He had all of his teeth. I'd guess he was between the ages of thirty and forty, but he might have been a bit older. The large bones still appear strong, which is one reason so many of them survived being in the ground for years. They would have deteriorated more quickly if he'd been sickly, or older."

I nodded. I knew nothing of the study of bones, but what the doctor was saying made sense.

"It's difficult to determine with absolute certainty how many years the gentleman had been in the ground. I've never examined bones as unprotected as these, buried in damp earth most of the year. If he'd been in a coffin decomposition would be quite different. There might even have been some skin or hair left to help us in our identification. Or some pieces of fabric." The doctor paused. "But I'm still guessing he was buried between three and four years ago."

"There's nothing else to help identify him?" I thought for a moment. "How tall was he?"

"About five feet seven inches. An average man, Aaron, perhaps slightly shorter than you are." He reached over to his desk and picked up two envelopes. "I did find a few hairs, though. Most look dark brown, or perhaps very dark auburn, mixed with strands of gray. And there were two bone buttons in the mud near his neck." He handed the envelopes to me.

I looked in the envelopes, but didn't touch the hair or buttons. "Knowing the color of his hair might help identify him. But the buttons might have belonged to anyone."

"At least we know the man was most likely clothed when he was buried. And the buttons are somewhat distinctive. They weren't made of metal, shell or wood. A small piece of information, true. but it might help in narrowing down who the man was. For example, if he'd been in uniform, the buttons would most likely have been brass. Although in the early years of the war not all soldiers wore uniforms."

I shook my head. "Few did, even later. We have so few clues. I'd hoped you'd find something on which to base an identification."

Dr. Litchfield picked up a small piece of hardened leather on his desk. "I did find this. It could have been part of a boot, or a brace, to hold the poor man's pants up. Or even a section of a purse. But I've found nothing that might have been in a man's pocket."

"Such as coins, you mean."

"No coins; no watch; no chain. That could mean he was the victim of a robbery."

I walked around the table, trying to imagine what this man had been like. "Last night I asked Aunt Cornelia to look through my uncle's records of the field where we found the bones. Owen remembered correctly. William Burns planted that field in hops from 1856 through 1860. He didn't renew the lease in 1861. That agrees with your conclusion that the body was buried then, or slightly thereafter."

"The body could have been buried in 1862, but I think we can rule out 1863 or '64. Bodies decay and molder and blend with the soil. Ashes to ashes, dust to dust, as preachers say. It's the way of nature."

Suddenly I had a vision of piles of severed limbs covered with flies and maggots stacked outside a surgeon's tent in Virginia. I knew too well what insects would do to a body. And vultures. And then there were animals. I shook my head slightly to chase the visions from my mind.

"Do you remember whether any men in Hestia disappeared in 1861 or '62?"

Dr. Litchfield gestured toward the door, and we both returned to the reception area and sat down. "Aaron, you're asking a question that's impossible to answer. In 1861 and '62 many men joined up and headed south. Most families in Hestia lost a man or two. And unless they were badly wounded, few of those men were able to come home quickly. Many were recruited again from the ranks, enticed by a signing bonus at the end of their terms, and re-enlisted. Some are still gone."

I nodded, beginning to understand the vastness of the task I was undertaking. "Which would also be true of this man. Or, if he did come home, he didn't leave again. I could check census records and make a list of all men between the ages of 30 and 45 from this area. And check Army records for those who enlisted."

"That would be a start," agreed the doctor. "But only a start. Before the war most men were born here, married here, and died here. A few went west, or to the city, or married someone in another county and moved there. But their families generally knew where they were. Or at least where they'd headed. Some men who enlisted haven't been heard from in months, or even years."

I remembered the letters to wives and mothers I'd written for men who were illiterate. And the soldiers who never waited for the mail. They seldom received letters or packages because their loved ones couldn't read or write. "Families of those who died in the war should have received letters of notification." I'd written too many of those.

"Most, yes. But Caleb Parker, who hadn't been heard from in over a year, walked into his mother's kitchen last week. She'd thought for sure he was dead. I'm sure there are others who haven't been heard from who will be home still. Or at least accounted for." Dr. Litchfield got up. "A drop of brandy?"

"Thank you." I accepted the glass and took a decent swallow. The warmth filled me for a moment, and then vanished. "I'm assuming an immense task, aren't I?"

"And you haven't taken into account the possibility of your man being from some other part of the country entirely. Thousands travel east and west each year on the canal. Few stop in Hestia. Or," here Dr. Litchfield shook his head, "there's always the possibility that the man enlisted – but in the Confederate Army."

I looked at him. "From Hestia?"

"At least a few, to be sure. Some people here have family in the south, and others are anti-abolitionists. Some broke with their families locally to go. There's been no word from most of those.

Communication lines to the south were officially closed, and families with men fighting for the south wouldn't have shared information if they'd heard from loved ones. Having a son or brother fight for the Confederacy is not popular here."

I nodded, cradling the snifter in my hand. "I hadn't thought of that. But on several occasions I posted letters to northern parts from Confederates I met between the lines, or in the hospital tents. I'm sure Rebs did the same when asked. Fighting each other didn't mean we didn't show each other simple courtesies when the occasion arose."

"Aaron, last night I thought a lot about what you want to do. Newspapers are saying at least four hundred thousand men, north and south, died in the war. Many of their families will never know what happened to them. Their men were most likely killed in battle and buried by soldiers who didn't know their identities; or died of sickness away from their regiments, their families clinging to the idea that their man is alive somewhere. They'll hope that perhaps he skedaddled, as they say in these parts. A nice way of saying he deserted, or went west. Or decided to make a home somewhere other than Hestia. Or was injured and somewhere someone is caring for him. Mothers and wives won't want to think about a skeleton. The war's been over less than a month. Most units haven't yet been disbanded."

"If it were my father or brother, I'd rather know he'd been murdered than think he chose not to return home."

But as I sat in Dr. Litchfield's comfortable study, sipping his brandy, I knew men in battle didn't just fear death. They feared being labeled cowards. They feared making judgment calls that would endanger themselves, or the men with them. Feared being called deserters for running from certain death. For some, returning from war crippled or labeled a coward would be worse than disappearing and starting life again where no one knew them, or what they'd done. Or not done. No one who hadn't been in battle could imagine.

Dr. Litchfield seemed to sense what I was thinking. He shook his head and spoke softly. "The war is over. Let the past rest in peace."

I was about to reply when the door to his office burst open. "Doctor," cried out the heavy-set man who rushed in. "Jake Neilson's been shot. We found him just down the road from Proctor's Tavern."

"Jake Neilson?" Dr. Litchfield threw bandages and surgical tools into his bag as he spoke. "I didn't know his regiment was back."

"Don't know nothin' about that, Doc. But Jake's here, for sure."

Neilson. That was Aunt Cornelia's friend Lidia's last name.

Chapter 9

"You've seen more than your share of gunshot wounds, Aaron," said Dr. Litchfield as I helped him harness his horse to his wagon. He threw in a pile of blankets to cushion the victim, if necessary, and added, "You're welcome to come with me. I could use another hand. Others from Proctor's Tavern may volunteer to help, but anyone coming from there at this time of day is not apt to be in complete control of his faculties."

"I'll come," I agreed, not pointing out that he and I had each just finished a brandy, and that within the past 14 hours I'd also injected morphine and taken several opium tablets. I felt fine, but that could well be the result of the drugs.

"Neilson's home is only a mile or so beyond the tavern," Dr. Litchfield said, as he slapped the reins. "If he can be moved we'll most likely take him there. The question is how badly he's wounded. The tavern's an old stage stop on the road to Syracuse. I'd guess it's ten miles away."

I held on as we jounced down the road leading southwest out of town. Chickens and dogs scattered as we approached, and several people stopped to watch. The sight of the doctor heading somewhere in a hurry was clearly a sign something serious was happening. In a week when the town was already in black, no one wished for more tragedy or pain.

I suspected Proctor's Tavern hadn't changed much since stages were the primary mode of transportation for people and mail and supplies. In this area of the world the canal had filled that function for almost fifty years, and now even the waterway had been superseded by the faster railroad, which could operate all year and not be concerned with freezing waters and flooding. Stages still existed, but their importance was minimal.

The tavern door opened into a large low-ceilinged room filled with heavy oak trestle tables and chairs. The smell of beer was stronger than that of the venison stew simmering on the stove. A short grizzled man, too old for military service, stood in back of the bar. Jake Neilson was lying on top of one of the long oak tables, surrounded by four men, three of whom held tankards of beer. No one appeared to be doing anything to help him.

Dr. Litchfield strode to the table, checked Neilson's pulse, and then stepped back.

"He's gone." The front of his coat was soaked in blood. I was no doctor, but it was obvious Jake Neilson had been shot in the chest.

"That's what we figured. We thought at first there might be some life in him so we brought him here, and poured whiskey down his throat to see if that would revive him. But it didn't help."

Dr. Litchfield made no comment on the failed treatment. "Any of you have an idea how Jake got himself shot?"

"Harvey and me found him, 'bout half a mile west of here. We was heading back to my place," said a man whose dark beard had spots of blood or dirt in it. "He was just lying on the road. Harvey took off to get you, Doc, and I came back here to get help. We moved him here. That's all I know."

"Who's the fellow with you, Doc?"

"This is Aaron Stone. Captain Aaron Stone," said Dr. Litchfield, gesturing toward me. "Cornelia Livingston's nephew. Been living at her place a few months now."

"Wounded in the war, were you?" asked the man behind the bar.

"Wilderness Campaign. Virginia," I answered. There were sympathetic nods around the room.

"I'm going to have to take Jake to my office, to do an official autopsy," said Dr. Litchfield. "I'll notify Sheriff Newell and tell him what you've said about finding the body and moving him here, but he may want to ask you again. A man doesn't just end up dead on the road and have nobody notice."

"We didn't have nothing to do with it," said the dark-bearded man again. "We were trying to help. Be Good Samaritans."

"I'll know for sure after I've thoroughly examined the body," said the doctor, "but I don't think you did Jake any harm. A gun shot from close enough to leave powder burns like that would likely have killed him pretty fast. Any of you know his wife well enough to tell her?"

The room was quiet, and the men self-consciously looked away from the body and the doctor.

"She's a long-time patient of mine. I'll tell her. Then I'll report the shooting to Sheriff Newell. He'll probably get the reverend to go out and talk with her. Best she have some people around in any case. Most likely the sheriff'll want to come out this way to see where you found Jake."

"Glad you're taking him, Doc. Good to get him out of my tavern, for sure," said the man near the tap. "Bodies don't make for good business."

"I don't suppose they do," said the doctor. "Now, would a couple of you help put him in my wagon?"

Jake's body safely stored and covered in the back of the open wagon, Dr. Litchfield and I continued down the Syracuse Road, at a slower pace than before.

"It's never easy to tell someone of a death in their family," the doctor commented. "I've done it more times than I'd like to remember. I keep thinking it should get easier, but it never does. Mrs. Neilson's been waiting two or three years for Jake. They never had children, so it's just the two of them. Either he didn't make it home, or he was killed just after. Maybe on his way to the tavern. If he'd been coming from the tavern someone would've said. His wife was alone in church yesterday; if he'd been home then, he would've been with her."

"If he just got home after being away for a long time, I'd think he would have stayed with his wife. Not gone to a tavern."

"You're young, and not married, Aaron. Marriages are strange creations. People in them don't always act the way you might expect."

He pulled the wagon into a wide drive between a row of trees leading up to a house that had clearly been home to at least two generations. On the left was a small wooden one-and-a-half-story structure; no doubt the original house. Attached to it was a dramatic two story Gothic Revival addition built on a foundation of cut fieldstone and proudly displaying tall slender windows shaped like pointed arches and a steep roof topped by an octagon-shaped tower. Despite its elegance, the house was now sadly weathered and in need of paint, and several of its slate roof tiles were missing.

"Interesting house, isn't it?" said the doctor as he saw me looking at it. "Mrs. Neilson's family home. Her father made money on the canal and wanted to build a mansion in town, but her mother insisted on staying where they'd always lived. So they compromised."

By then I was staring at something even more startling than that tower. Aunt Cornelia's carriage and horse were ahead of us in the driveway.

Chapter 10

The doctor checked that Jake's body was still completely covered. I hoped Mrs. Neilson wouldn't look in the wagon. Jake's body wasn't pretty.

The doctor raised the tarnished brass eagle door knocker and then dropped it. There was silence for a few minutes, so he knocked again, and the door finally opened.

"Yes?" said Mrs. Neilson, looking from Dr. Litchfield to me and back again. Clearly she was surprised to see the two of us together, and at her home.

"Mrs. Neilson, we have news. May we come in?"

She opened the door wider, onto a long dark front hallway covered with red and green flowered wallpaper and hung with two precisely spaced horizontal lines of Currier New England scenes. The parlor, to our right, was brighter, the drapes open, and the walls papered in a geometric beige on beige pattern. The room was almost large enough to be a drawing room, and held two carved mahogany sofas and a sideboard, as well as several chairs. Six mahogany-framed Alken hunting prints hung on the far wall, and an embroidered screen stood near the fireplace.

Mrs. Neilson, dressed in a surprisingly stylish morning dress with a scarlet wool Garibaldi shirt trimmed with black braid and buttons and a wide black silk skirt trimmed with red, appeared to be alone, despite the carriage out front.

She was composed, but clearly waiting for us to state the purpose of our visit. "News, Dr. Litchfield? Captain Stone?" She sat on the edge of one of the sofas and indicated we should be seated on matching chairs. She didn't offer us refreshment.

"I wondered if you'd heard from Corporal Neilson recently," asked the doctor.

"I had a letter from him a little over a month ago," she answered. "He's with the 117th New York, in North Carolina. They took part in two expeditions against Fort Fisher, near Wilmington, in January; the second time they captured the fort. Jake wrote how exciting it was; how proud he was to plant his regiment's colors on the parapet. Now the war is over, I'm hoping he'll be home soon. At church yesterday Mrs. Daggett, whose son Rufus is also with the 117th, said she'd heard they'd be mustered out by June, or July at the latest."

So Jake Neilson hadn't made it home before being shot. What was he doing in Hestia if his regiment was in North Carolina?

"I'm afraid I have bad news for you, Mrs. Neilson," said Dr. Litchfield. "Your husband must have been trying to get home, but he didn't make it. Some fellows leaving Proctor's Tavern this afternoon found his body a half mile from here on the Syracuse Road."

Mrs. Neilson's face turned pale, and then pink. She didn't move, or say a word. Then she said, very softly, "Are you sure it was Jake?"

"No doubt. They called me in, on the chance he could be revived, but he was gone. It was Jake."

"I see."

Somewhere in the distance I thought I heard a baby cry, but the sound was brief. Probably just the creaking of a country house, or wind in the trees.

I waited for Mrs. Neilson to faint, or cry, or show some sort of emotional distress, but she sat silently across from us.

"Mrs. Neilson, can I get you something? Some water, perhaps, or some tea?" Dr. Litchfield started to get up.

"No; no!" she answered. "Nothing. I just need a little time to get used to the idea that Jake's …. He's been away so long. Since August of '62. I thought he'd be home soon, now the war is over. I didn't expect this." She pulled a white handkerchief from her skirt pocket and dabbed at her eyes.

"Of course you didn't. You need time to absorb the news."

"I'll be all right. I appreciate your coming. When … I mean, what will happen now?"

"I'll have to do an autopsy, Mrs. Neilson."

At those words Mrs. Neilson visibly paled, and held on to the arm of the sofa as though she needed support. "Is that necessary?"

"I'm afraid so. But I'll confirm that when I talk with Sheriff Newell."

"Sheriff Newell?"

"Jake was shot, Mrs. Neilson. The sheriff will want to find out who did that."

"No. No; not Jake." Mrs. Neilson was clearly beginning to let go of whatever control she had over her reactions. "Shot? Right here in Hestia? On his way home? It wasn't a war injury? Maybe he was wounded and they sent him home early."

Dr. Litchfield shook his head. "It looks as though he was shot here. I know this isn't easy, Mrs. Neilson. Would you like me to get one of your friends? Someone who can be with you for a little while?"

"I'll be all right. I just need a few minutes."

"Mrs. Neilson, where is my Aunt Cornelia?" I could no longer stay silent. If Aunt Cornelia was here, then why hadn't she mentioned that? On the other hand, if my aunt wasn't here, then why was her carriage in the front drive?

Dr. Litchfield looked at me as though I were out of my mind.

"My aunt's carriage is in the driveway," I said. "She left our home before dawn this morning."

Mrs. Neilson stood up. "Of course. Your aunt is here. I'll get her for you."

As she left the room, Dr. Litchfield said quietly. "If you knew she was here, why didn't you mention it earlier?"

"I didn't know what to say. And I didn't know for certain she was here; just that her carriage was. But if she is here, why didn't Mrs. Neilson tell us? She has someone with her."

"Dr. Litchfield; Aaron." Aunt Cornelia stood alone in the doorway. "I've been here since this morning. I promised to help Lidia with some sewing she was doing." She looked at me. "You were going to see Dr. Litchfield this afternoon, I remember."

Sewing? I'd never seen my aunt sew anything other than embroidery. And leave before dawn to do embroidery? As I was trying to make sense of the situation, I realized my aunt was not in her usual mourning attire; she was wearing a dark green dress I didn't remember. It didn't fit her well; perhaps she'd lost weight since she'd last worn it.

"Mrs. Livingston, we've had to deliver the sad news to Mrs. Neilson that her husband was found dead about half a mile from here. He appears to have been shot this afternoon." The doctor saw my aunt looking at me with some question in her face. "Captain Stone was with me when I was told Jake was injured; he came along to assist me. I'm relieved to know you're here. Mrs. Neilson's not reacting to the news yet; she may be in shock. I'm afraid she may fall apart when she's had a bit more time to understand what has happened."

"How awful," said my aunt. "Jake dead! And so close to home.

Why don't I plan to spend the night with Lidia, so she won't be alone?"

"An excellent suggestion," agreed Dr. Litchfield. He rummaged in one of his pockets for a moment and then handed her a vial of liquid. "Here's some laudanum; it will help her sleep. Give her fifteen drops before she goes to bed, and another fifteen if she wakes during the night. She'll need to have control of herself tomorrow; no doubt neighbors will be stopping in, and she'll have arrangements to make."

"Of course," said Aunt Cornelia, accepting the vial. "I'll be sure she gets some rest." She turned to me, "Aaron, will you let Katie and Owen know where I am, so they won't be worried? I seldom spend a night away from home."

"Of course," I said. "Is there anything else I can help with?"

"I don't think so. But thank you both for coming." She started to walk toward the door, politely dismissing us both. "I'll see you at home tomorrow, Aaron, as soon as I know Lidia is all right, or there is someone else to stay with her. And you'll make sure my nephew gets home, Doctor?"

"It isn't far out of my way. I'd be happy to drive him there."

"I would appreciate that. Now I must see to Lidia."

The door closed, and the doctor and I were outside.

"What a coincidence, that your aunt was visiting her friend at such a time," said Dr. Litchfield. "I wouldn't have felt right about leaving Mrs. Neilson there alone. So far as I know she doesn't even have a girl to help her; the one she had went to Utica for higher wages. It will be a hard time for her, I'm afraid, with no family nearby." He turned to me. "I'll take you home, Aaron. This must have been a difficult afternoon for you. One body in your field, and another on the road."

"No; not at all," I replied. To my surprise, I meant it. I felt more alive that day than I had in months.

Chapter 11

Aunt Cornelia returned home at midday Tuesday. She looked weary, and, to my surprise, was back in mourning attire.

"Aaron, would you ask Katie to get me a cup of tea and some toast? I don't think I'm up to having dinner today." She removed her bonnet and shawl and sank heavily into one of the upholstered chairs in the parlor below the portraits she and Uncle Henry had commissioned from a traveling artist shortly after their wedding. "It was a difficult night."

I sat with her until she seemed refreshed from the tea. "Mrs. Neilson must have been very upset."

"Indeed she was. And is. I did what I could for her, but her next few days won't be easy ones." Aunt Cornelia took a small bite of buttered toast.

"We were all worried about you yesterday morning. You left before dawn, and didn't tell anyone where you'd gone."

"I didn't realize I'd be away so long. I thought it would be a short trip."

"To help Mrs. Neilson with her sewing?"

Aunt Cornelia ignored my implied doubt.

"And that, yes. I had a lot of things on my mind. Aaron, are you still resolved to investigate those bones you and Owen found in the back field?"

"I am. Dr. Litchfield determined that the deceased was a man, perhaps thirty to forty years old, about five feet seven inches in height. His skull was broken. Someone needs to find out who that man was, and who killed him."

Aunt Cornelia put down her cup and looked closely at me. "We've talked very little about your future, Aaron. I've felt it was best for you to take your own time to consider all possibilities open to you. But your training as a lawyer was complete before the war, was it not?"

"It was. I studied at Columbia, and then worked in Father's office for a time before passing the necessary legal exams. And then there was Fort Sumter, and nothing seemed as important as the war."

"Are you now determined to return to the law?"

"Before the war I'd planned to join Father in his firm, as he wished. Now I'm not sure. After seeing the war's destruction, I want to do something that builds. Something of value to people, that helps them live better, easier, lives. Handling people's wills and estates is important, of course. Father says it is, and assures me I can make a handsome income from the practice. But I want to be more involved with people than with paper. Does that make sense to you, Aunt Cornelia?"

"It makes sense that your father wishes you to join him in his firm. That firm has been his life, and he wants to see you provided for. He's worried about you, Aaron. That's one reason I asked you to come here. I thought you and your father needed time away from each other."

"And I appreciate that, Aunt Cornelia."

"It would be a shame for you to throw away the years you spent training to be a lawyer."

"That is so. But I haven't reached a decision as to what profession I'd like to follow."

"There are types of law other than the kind your father specializes in. Law that is, as you expressed it, more involved with people than with paper." Aunt Cornelia looked away from me, toward the front windows, and then turned back. "When you found that body in the field and determined to find out who it was, I thought perhaps you'd found what you were looking for. The practice of criminal law is an important one, Aaron. It's not as emotionally simple as making out wills and helping with probate and such. But it's vitally important. Those who need protection under our legal system must be guaranteed it."

"That's what the Constitution says."

"Says, yes. But the reality is often far different. Men who have money and power too often use the law to their advantage."

"Those who have wealth and influence always come out on top in the world."

"It doesn't have to be that way."

"Perhaps. But it was certainly so during the war. The wealthy paid others to take their places in the draft, and those who supplied the armies with weapons and tents and uniforms are richer now than they were before the fighting, while soldiers who risked their lives and are lucky enough to be going home are returning to farms and homes neglected or destroyed. It will be years before this country, north or south, recovers from the damage of these past years."

Aunt Cornelia nodded and leaned toward me. "Aaron, I'm asking if you might want to try your hand at practicing criminal law; at protecting those who need protection."

She was not speaking theoretically. "I've thought of that possibility, Aunt Cornelia. But I have no experience in that field, and barely know the laws pertaining to it. Who is it that needs protection?"

"Lidia Neilson may need a good lawyer soon. I think the sheriff may accuse her of killing her husband."

"Why would he suspect that? Jake Neilson's body was found shot on the road. I was there when Dr. Litchfield was summoned. I saw the body at the tavern. Mrs. Neilson didn't even know her husband was back from the war!"

"Which is why I think she may need someone to help her. Sheriff Newell came to see her late last night. He insisted on checking her bedroom to see if he could find any proof Jake had been home. It was a dreadful and embarrassing imposition for Lidia to have to show her private room to a man in law enforcement."

"But if her husband had not been home, then the sheriff wouldn't have found anything."

Aunt Cornelia sighed. "You see, Aaron, that's where the problem arises. The sheriff found Jake's army knapsack in Lidia's bedroom wardrobe. And fresh blood was on the floor, under one of Lidia's hooked rugs."

I was silent for a moment. "How does Mrs. Neilson explain the blood and her husband's belongings?" I couldn't imagine that stylish and maternal woman committing any sort of crime, much less the murder of her husband.

Aunt Cornelia didn't answer my question. She asked one of her own. "Are you willing to take on her case?"

"I told you I have no experience in such matters."

"No lawyers in Hestia do. And certainly Lidia has no experience in being accused of murder," my aunt answered. "With the help of the right lawyer, I'm sure her situation can be resolved quickly, and her innocence proved."

"Perhaps someone on the road saw Corporal Neilson being assaulted. Or can testify on Mrs. Neilson's behalf." I stood, and started to pace. The idea of being involved, however slightly, in an investigation of this kind was strangely exciting. I stopped. "You, for example, Aunt Cornelia. You were with Mrs. Neilson all day yesterday."

To my surprise, she hesitated. "Most of the day, certainly. I've told Sheriff Newell that."

"Is she under arrest?"

"No. She's at her home. Sheriff Newell's known her for years, and he doesn't believe she will leave Hestia. He said he would wait to take action until after he'd interviewed people who might have seen Jake on the road, and until he had Jake's official autopsy results."

"But why does he imagine Mrs. Neilson would kill her husband?" I couldn't get my mind around the idea of why any woman would kill her husband.

"You should talk to Lidia about that, Aaron. If you're willing to represent her."

I continued pacing. What if the woman was innocent, as Aunt Cornelia clearly believed, and as I strongly suspected, and I failed her? I'd read about criminal cases, of course; in law books, and in the newspapers, as do most people with a curiosity about the darker side of human nature. But defend someone? To have her welfare, and perhaps her life, depend on my actions?

"Aaron, this would be a great favor to me, and an enormous help to a woman who deserves it."

I turned to her. "I'll admit the prospect of involvement in a criminal case is tempting. And exciting. But I reserve the right to call in someone more experienced if I feel I cannot do as well as should be done for your friend. My inexperience in criminal law is a great liability, Aunt Cornelia."

"You're a veteran; you fought for the union just as Jake Neilson did. You would not allow the wrong person to be convicted of a soldier's murder."

"I would certainly do everything in my power to keep that from happening," I agreed.

"Good. Then you'll go to see Lidia, and talk with her?"

"I will," I decided. "This very afternoon."

71

Chapter 12

In my, admittedly limited, experience, women respond to death with the dual comforts of food and companionship. I therefore expected to find the Neilson home full of sympathetic neighbors and friends bearing soup tureens and platters and pies, and was formulating alternative plans for speaking with Mrs. Neilson alone if such was the case. Instead I found only one rather battered wagon and tired horse in front of her home. I tied my own animal to the granite horse block and dropped the eagle knocker.

To my surprise, young Robbie Burns opened the door. "Hello. I know you."

"Yes, you do. We met in the north field."

His auburn hair, very similar to his sister's in length and color, had been parted in the middle and slicked down, but wavy curls were escaping at his temple, drawing attention to his slightly freckled nose.

His glance took in my horse in the yard. "You rode here. You don't have a wagon. Are you going to tell Nora where you saw me?"

"Quite right. I rode here. And I promised not to tell anyone about seeing you. Now, is Mrs. Neilson at home?"

"Did you bring cake?"

"No. I just brought myself."

"A lot of people brought cakes." He grinned at me, as though we were conspirators. "Who shall I say is calling?"

"Captain Aaron Stone," I answered.

He took one more look at me before scampering back along the central hall that I'd last stood in only yesterday. A minute or two later I heard a door shut somewhere in the depths of the house, and a woman appeared at the end of the hall and walked toward me.

"Captain Stone; how kind of you to come to give your condolences." To my delight Nora Burns was standing in front of me, wearing the same plain brown outfit she'd worn when I'd first met her at the orphanage the Friday before. Today she'd discarded her shawl, and her trim figure was evident despite her loose blouse and skirt. "Won't you come in?" She gestured toward the parlor.

"I assume the young man who answered the door was your brother?" I asked.

"Yes. My brother, Robbie. He can be a bit ahead of himself. Normally he shouldn't have been answering the door, but under these circumstances I could use his help. So many well-meaning people have sent their cooks and maids with food and condolences that it's been hard to greet them all."

"He's a fine looking boy. How old is he?"

"Just four, and usually a good boy. But not used to taking a role in someone else's home."

"Of course not." I spied Robbie peaking around the doorway to the hall, a small cake in his left hand.

"May I offer you some tea or coffee?" Miss Burns asked. "Or perhaps a slice of one of the fancy breads or pies that have been brought."

I realized my aunt's refusal of dinner had also eliminated that meal for me and that, actually, I was very hungry. "Thank you. I should like that."

"I hope you'll understand we're being very informal," she added, rising. "Under the circumstances, and with no help, we've just put the food on the dining room table. Won't you come with me?"

I followed her down the hall, past the oak-framed scenes of New England snows and summers I'd noticed the day before. The dining room was past the parlor, between it and the kitchen. The table there was, as I'd imagined, covered with various food stuffs displayed on an assortment of dishes and platters. When dried beans and corn had been all we soldiers had to eat, pies and cakes and puddings like the ones on that table were what we dreamed of, perhaps with even more intensity than we dreamed of our girls at home. A flash of Margaret's face came and went quickly.

"Captain Stone?"

I had the sense that perhaps she'd asked me something.

"Captain Stone, would you like coffee or hot tea? We also have cold tea." Nora Burns stood near a side window and the sun touched her hair.

"Hot tea would be much appreciated."

She poured from a silver tea set Mother would have admired. Clearly the Neilson family was well off. Or had been. The outside of the house needed considerable attention. Of course, with the war many homes had been left unattended to. "Mrs. Hingham was kind enough to bring us some of her sugar; it's been precious during the war. Would you like some?"

"Yes, please." Aunt Cornelia had not mentioned the sugar shortage. It was one of those luxuries she, and I as her guest, had taken for granted.

Miss Burns spooned a teaspoon of sugar into a pale blue porcelain cup and handed it to me. "Please, do serve yourself from any of the plates. Everything I've tasted is excellent. The women of Hestia have outdone themselves."

And come and gone so quickly, I thought, as I cut a slice of lemon cake and added several spoonfuls of raspberry pudding to my plate. I heard light footsteps behind me, and then a familiar voice.

"That pudding is really good. Mrs. Ames made it, with her raspberry cordial and jam."

"Are there any other dishes you recommend, Robbie?" From the uneven cuts and the profusion of crumbs I'd seen on several of the platters, I suspected Robbie had been taking full advantage of the variety of sweets.

"The apple tarts are good. But don't take too many. You might get a stomachache," he informed me seriously, pointing at a half empty tray of pastries. I suspected his advice was based on experience.

"Robbie, why don't you go outside now and play?" directed his sister. "Captain Stone isn't here to discuss pastries."

"Yes, Nora." Robbie took one more glance at the table, grabbed a large sugar cookie, and ran out of the room.

"He's been very good, but the past few days have been confusing for him, you understand, with Easter, and President Lincoln's death, and now this horrible situation. He's used to being at home with me most of the time. Would you like to bring your tea into the parlor?"

She carried a cup of tea she'd poured for herself and we sat again in the bright front room.

"Robbie seems a fine boy."

"I'm proud of him. Next year he'll be attending school. He's excited at being able to see other children often. We live down the road, across from your aunt's home, you know, and there aren't any other children nearby for him to play with."

"Is your mother here, too?" I asked, forgetting for a moment that Robbie had told me his mother was dead.

"My mother?" Miss Burns seemed a bit startled, and her teacup wobbled on its plate. "My mother died shortly after Robbie was born, Mr. Stone. Of course, you wouldn't know that, since you're new to Hestia."

"My sympathies. I spent time here as a child, but not in the past ten years, until this spring." I sipped my tea carefully while balancing my plate on my lap. "And so you and Robbie are on your own, or are there other Burns family members in your home?"

"My father left in the spring of 1861. He was one of the first to enlist." Her eyes flashed, and her cheeks blushed slightly.

I was questioning her too closely about personal matters.

"Robbie and I do well on our own, thank you, Mr. Stone. As you would know, as you yourself pointed out, if you had been here more frequently. There are few secrets in small towns."

"My apologies." There was silence for a few moments as Miss Burns sipped her tea. I appreciated Robbie's suggestion of the apple tart. It was, indeed, excellent. "Is Mrs. Neilson well enough to receive my condolences directly today?"

"She is keeping to her room. She will be surprised at your coming."

I hesitated a moment, not wanting to broach an indelicate subject, but also knowing that if she were here, she must be a close friend, and perhaps confidant, of Mrs. Neilson. "My aunt suggested that, due to the circumstances of the death of Mrs. Neilson's husband, she might benefit from my services."

Miss Burns looked at me directly. I wondered if my aunt had already discussed this with her friends.

"I am a lawyer," I added.

"Yes. I believe your aunt mentioned that." Miss Burns put down her cup and spoke more directly than most young women of my acquaintance would. "Lidia Neilson is a kind and generous woman. When you first met her, last Friday, would you ever have imagined she could be guilty of such an unspeakable crime as murder?"

"Certainly not!" I answered. "That is precisely why my aunt would like me to speak with her, and, if necessary, represent her, should anyone make that accusation."

"Cornelia told you what occurred here last night?"

"She told me the sheriff had found what he felt might be evidence that Corporal Neilson had been at home, and perhaps was at least injured here."

Miss Burns nodded. "I will check to see if Mrs. Neilson will speak with you."

I stood as she left the room. Robbie was outside, patting the nose of the old mare I'd ridden on, and trying to feed her some dried grasses. I wondered again why more women who'd come to pay their condolences were not in the house, and why, of all the people in town, young Miss Burns and her brother were the ones to take on the roles of host and hostess under such circumstances. Surely there were older, married, women, who would have had more experiences with death.

Although Hestia was a small town. Perhaps the word had already passed that Mrs. Neilson might have killed her husband. If so, I imagined there were women who would not wish to be affiliated with her. Miss Burns was right. There were few secrets in small towns.

In a few minutes Miss Burns led me to a study, its walls covered by dark wood bookcases. Mrs. Neilson sat behind a massive desk that would have looked more at home in a man's office. Yet the books and papers piled on the desk appeared to be in use. Perhaps Mrs. Neilson had occupied her husband's study while he was away.

"Mrs. Neilson, again, I'm sorry for your loss. Aunt Cornelia suggested I might be of use to you."

"Thank you for coming." Mrs. Neilson seemed the same, controlled, woman I had seen the day before, but now her eyes were red and swollen. "I assume Cornelia told you of the difficult situation I've found myself in?"

"She told me little except that Sheriff Newell had been here last night, and had found some of your husband's belongings, and blood under a rug in your bedchamber."

"He did." Mrs. Neilson hardly blinked. I suspected she might be under the calming influence of the laudanum Dr. Litchfield had left for her the night before. "You do understand that I did not kill my husband."

"I believe you. I do not believe any woman would kill her husband, especially a returning veteran. But what the sheriff found is troubling."

"Then let me explain, as much as I can. Yesterday late morning and afternoon I was occupied in the older section of the house." She gestured toward the small wing I had noted when I'd first seen the home the day before. "I was not aware of anything occurring in the main house, or, certainly, in my bedroom, during that time."

I noted that she called the room "my bedroom," and wondered how long a husband would have to be gone for it to evolve from "our bedroom."

"So you did not see your husband during the day."

"If he, or any other person, was here, I was not aware of it."

"You have no explanation for the knapsack, or the blood, then."

"None for the knapsack. The blood, yes. I can account for that very simply."

"Yes?"

"You have met Robbie Burns?"

"He opened the door for me when I arrived this afternoon."

"He has been here, with his sister, for two days now. Perhaps you know that young boys are often subject to unexpected nose bleeds?"

"I am not familiar with many children, but I think I have heard that."

"Robbie was exploring the house while Nora and I were heating barley and bean soup for our noontime dinner when we heard him screaming for her. We both ran, and found him in my bedroom. His nose was bleeding quite dramatically, which scared him. I found a cloth to staunch the blood, and he rested on my bed for a time. We did not have the time to clean up the blood which had dripped onto the floor, and the sight of it upset the boy." Mrs. Neilson sipped a bit of tea. "I'm sure you can understand why I moved a small rug beside the bed to cover the blood, to calm the boy. I expected to go back later, of course, to scrub the spot. Your arrival with Dr. Litchfield put the thought of cleaning out of my mind. And so the blood remained there until the evening, when Sheriff Newell found it."

I hesitated. "That is certainly a reasonable explanation. I assume Miss Burns and Robbie will tell me the same story?"

"They will, I am sure."

"But you have no explanation for how your husband's knapsack came to be, not only in your house, but in your bedroom."

"Clearly, of course, someone put it there. I am saying I do not know who that person was."

"You saw no one in the house."

"So far as I know there was no one in that area of the house at all after Robbie's nosebleed. Even he stayed close to us."

"Mrs. Neilson, there's something else that concerns me. Why would your husband be here in Hestia when, so far as you knew, his unit is in North Carolina?"

"That I can't explain. Perhaps his regiment was dismissed early and he thought to surprise me. Perhaps he suffered a slight wound, and was sent home to recover. I certainly was not expecting him yesterday, or at any time in the immediate future."

"I'm sure the sheriff will check with the Army, and so will I. There are many reasons soldiers choose to leave their units without leave."

"Are you suggesting Jake deserted?"

"I'm merely asking whether that was a possibility."

"Mr. Stone, I married Jake Neilson when I was twenty-one and he twenty-three. That was sixteen years ago. During that time I have learned a lot about men, and husbands, and Jake in particular. One thing I learned for certain, and that was not to guess what a man might do, or what a man might tell his wife. I had not heard from Jake in over a month. I would not begin to speculate what happened during that time."

I nodded. It was certainly true that a woman far from the battlefield could have no idea what was going through a soldier's mind. Few soldiers wrote home about their fears and anger and discouragement. I was only surprised Mrs. Neilson was as aware as she seemed to be of what she might not know about her husband. I'd always assumed women believed what they were told by their men. Certainly, I'd always thought Mother and Margaret believed the optimistic and positive news I wrote to them.

"I realize you have a lot on your mind just now. One more question, Mrs. Neilson, and then I'll leave you. Are there any men in Hestia who wished Jake harm? Anyone with whom he had long-standing problems?"

"He was a man. Men have disagreements with other men, and Jake was not a peacemaker. But I don't know who would have had an argument with him now. He's been away – he had been away," she corrected herself, "for almost three years. Many of the men he knew before the war were in his regiment, or in others." She looked at me directly. "Considering the situation I'm in, I would like to give you a long list of names of men who might be responsible for his murder. But I'm unaware of anyone who knew he was going to be home before his unit, and who would have done him harm. Captain Stone, it would be a great help to me if you would represent me, and find such a person."

I stood up. "I will tell the sheriff I am your lawyer. I am certain he's doing his best to investigate possibilities other than that you killed your husband. Dr. Litchfield will be performing an autopsy, and it's possible he will uncover some information of help in identifying Corporal Neilson's killer."

"Thank you. And, Captain Stone, since it appears we will be working together for the immediate future, until this situation is resolved, I would feel comfortable if you were to call me Lidia."

"Then you, of course, will call me Aaron. I will see Sheriff Newell and Dr. Litchfield as soon as I can. If you think of any information which might be helpful, please let me know. In the meantime, speak about this affair as little as possible."

Robbie gulped something quickly when I saw him near the dining room door. I smiled to myself; no doubt he was investigating the contents of yet another tempting platter. "Robbie! Mrs. Neilson tells me you had a nosebleed yesterday."

He nodded, still struggling to swallow.

"Do you have a lot of nosebleeds?"

He shook his head. "No. But sometimes."

"And you and your sister were here all of yesterday?"

"Must you question a child? If you don't believe what Lidia told you, then I assure you I would be only too glad to answer your questions." Nora Burns stepped toward me out of the room I assumed was the kitchen.

"I need to check everything. That's what a lawyer does," I said, stumbling a bit. "I was going to ask you, too."

"Robbie, go back outside. You're going to be up half the night with a stomach ache." She turned to me as the boy left. "Whatever Lidia told you was the truth. Yes; Robbie and I were here all of yesterday, and last night. As you see, we are still here."

"My aunt was here yesterday," I said, lamely, trying to remember whether Aunt Cornelia had mentioned the presence of anyone else at the Neilson home.

"Yes, she was."

"She didn't mention that you were here."

"Did you ask her?"

"No; actually, I didn't." I thought of the horse and wagon outside. "But your horse and wagon are here now; they weren't yesterday."

"Not during the afternoon. Your aunt drove Robbie and me here. After she left she asked Owen Hindley to bring our horse and wagon this morning, thinking we might choose to leave then. Owen rode home on Cornelia's horse, which he'd tied to the back of the wagon. Which reminds me that I must go and attend to our poor Maud. She's been standing there all day, and Lidia would like Robbie and I to stay another night."

"I see."

"You don't see! You're supposed to be Lidia's lawyer; ensuring she's not found to be the murderer of her own husband. Lidia is a good woman; a kind woman; a woman who's helped many people in her life. All you have to do is ensure she isn't punished for doing something no one with any sense will believe she did."

"I am going to try to do just that, Miss Burns," I said. "I was about to leave. Would you like me to unharness your horse for you?"

She looked pointedly at my empty sleeve. "I can manage fine on my own, Captain Stone. I always have. Cornelia said you could help us. Please, go and do that. Don't bother about things we can handle without you."

I took my leave.

I would need to speak with Aunt Cornelia again, and with the sheriff. But first I needed to see Dr. Litchfield. He now had two bodies in which I had an interest.

Any personal interest I had in Miss Burns would clearly have to be postponed until a calmer moment.

Chapter 13

Dr. Litchfield was not alone that afternoon. When I knocked on his red door, the short man who answered carried himself with a bearing that promised he would countenance no nonsense.

"Aaron!" Dr. Litchfield called from inside the building when he heard my voice, "Today is not a good time to talk about your skeleton. I'm discussing Jake Neilson with Sheriff Newell."

"It's Jake Neilson I've come about," I called back to him, as the sheriff opened the door wider so I could walk past him and inside. "I've been retained by Lidia Neilson."

Dr. Litchfield shook his head. "The woman's no fool." He looked from me to the sheriff. "I don't believe you two have met. John Newell, this is Cornelia Livingston's nephew, Captain Aaron Stone." He looked at me and smiled slightly. "Captain Aaron Stone, Esquire. Lidia Neilson's lawyer."

"Pleased to meet you, Captain Stone," said Newell, staring at my empty sleeve, as people who've just met me tend to do.

"And you," I agreed, offering my right hand to the sheriff. He ignored it. I turned to Dr. Litchfield.

"Doctor, I've come to see if you have the results of Jake Neilson's autopsy."

"He was shot, Aaron, as you could see when we got to the inn

Monday. Two bullets. Both were to the chest, and from a fairly short distance. Certainly under eight feet."

"Were there any other injuries?"

"Scratches, on his back and arms. They could have been made by fingernails; weren't deep enough for thorns. Nothing lethal, certainly. And they were under his shirt. No reason to think they were made by the same person that shot him." The doctor paused a moment and grinned, glancing at the sheriff. "'Course, they could have been, but not at the same time he was shot. He was wearing clothes when he was shot."

The sheriff grinned back. "So you'd say maybe the man had a little welcome home party?"

"Quite possibly. There were semen stains in his pants. Still sticky."

I immediately saw the direction in which they were heading. "But the man could have visited a whore … and the pants could have meant he'd pleasured himself. How clean was the body, Dr. Litchfield?"

"About what you'd expect for a man who'd been on the road for some time."

"Certainly if he'd gone home – which Mrs. Neilson says did not happen – then he would have taken the time required to cleanse himself of the dirt of traveling; certainly before he … took his marital pleasure. When I was a soldier, and walking for days, I would have prized hot water even over a woman. And certainly I would have taken advantage of facilities to bathe before I intimately embraced a woman I loved."

"Perhaps so, Captain. But you weren't Jake. Despite the niceties of his house and the life he acquired when he married Lidia, those of us who knew him would agree he wasn't exactly the considerate sort." Sheriff Newell smiled. "And a man away from his wife for three years might well have been overwhelmed with passion."

I was not comfortable at the turn the conversation was taking. "Mrs. Neilson says he did not reach home. Perhaps there was another woman along the way. There are willing women in Utica, I've heard."

"Most certainly, and most willing," chuckled Dr. Litchfield. "But it'd be a bit difficult to get them to tell us who they happened to be with yesterday. Not to speak of the embarrassment to the Neilson family."

"Embarrassment, yes. But better embarrassed than accused of murder," I answered.

"We'll question the whores of Utica, of course," said the sheriff, although I suspected he'd planned to do nothing of the kind until I mentioned it.

I turned to the doctor. "Neilson wasn't wearing his uniform when we found him yesterday."

"No."

"And my understanding is that his unit is still in North Carolina. Or was a month ago."

"So I've heard; I've yet to verify that with the military authorities," said the sheriff.

"If that is so, unless he was wounded, or was granted permission for an individual leave, which would be most unusual considering the events of the past month and the paperwork required to grant such a privilege, it would appear that Corporal Neilson took leave of his unit without permission."

"Deserted," agreed Doctor Litchfield.

"Deserted. And soldiers who desert their units are not thought of highly by other soldiers or, indeed, by many civilians."

"True enough," agreed the sheriff.

"We need to find out whether any other men, particularly those who'd already served their time, and might know about Neilson's unit, were in the area where his body was found. It's possible someone was administering justice to a man who'd left his unit in time of war, wouldn't you agree?" I looked from one man to another. "Certainly that would be more credible than that a loving wife, separated from her husband for three long years, would welcome him home, and then follow him to a tavern and shoot him."

"Perhaps," acknowledged the sheriff. "I was going to look into the possibility. But at the moment we have no witnesses who saw anyone in the area where Jake's body was found."

I tried to collect my thoughts. The excitement of the moment, and the exertion of the ride to the Neilsons' house and then to town, both hit me with a wave of exhaustion and nausea. I tried to focus, but instead I felt light headed, and the room darkened. I grasped the edge of the doctor's desk.

"Aaron, sit down," he said, realizing my situation. My body was wet with sweat and I welcomed the doctor's arm, which guided me to the large chair in back of his desk. I put my head down, embarrassed that I might faint. Their voices seemed far away.

"Captain Stone will be fine in a moment," said Dr. Litchfield. "His injuries have weakened his body."

"His efforts for the Union are most appreciated, we all know," said Sheriff Newell. "His ideas about how we deal with crimes here in Hestia may not be."

"He'll be fine," said the doctor. "Yesterday, before Jake's body was found, I was out at the Livingston place with Captain Stone. Seems they'd found a man's bones in one of their fields. Stone's concerned about finding out who the fellow was, and how he got there. He thinks perhaps the man disappeared from here, and we could reunite him with his family."

"Unlikely," the sheriff snorted. "People come and go; most, to my knowledge, at their own discretion. Some don't care to return. Just this week we had a young woman reported missing. Pretty, quiet, girl. Emily North."

I raised my head, feeling somewhat better, and not wanting to have my presence ignored. "You don't think her disappearance has anything to do with Jake, or with the bones we found, for that matter?"

"So you're back to yourself. Good. And, no. I don't suspect any connection with anything. I suspect Emily had a tiff with her husband, who has a tendency to drink a bit heavily on occasion, and she's gone to stay with a friend until he cools off. Her husband is furious and anxious, especially since she's in the family way, but she'll no doubt be back soon."

Dr. Litchfield nodded. "It would be hard to hide for very long in Hestia. A man can keep secrets about himself and no one except possibly his wife is particular about what they might be. Men are men, and do what they must do. But no respectable woman has any secrets, nor wishes to be thought to have any." He opened one of his desk drawers and handed me a vial of opium tablets. "Take two of these before you get back on your horse. They'll help you get home. You've been overdoing a bit."

I hesitated. "Thank you, doctor. But I'll wait to take the tablets. My head's clear now, and I'd like it to stay that way."

"As you please," said the doctor. "You know your body and the effects of the medications. But I suggest you get yourself home. You're still weak, and I don't want any more bodies in my examination room for the moment."

Sheriff Newell had his hand on the door handle. "Take it easy, young man. Don't stress yourself with worry. You tell Mrs. Neilson and your aunt, who I suspect is in back of this representing of Jake's wife, that everything is under control. I'll inform you if we discover additional information. In the meantime I have a few details to check into before any arrests are made."

The door slammed as he left.

"Aaron, I hope you know what you've taken on," said Dr. Litchfield. "No one tells Sheriff Newell how to do his job."

Chapter 14

I rode back to Aunt Cornelia's home carefully on two accounts. First, the old bay mare I'd saddled earlier in the day was having a hard time of it by then. Despite her anxiousness to get home to her barn and oats, she could not move at a fast pace. And, besides, I still felt somewhat light headed, and knew the pills Dr. Litchfield had given me could increase that condition. I didn't want to risk embarrassing myself, or, worse, injuring myself, by falling from a horse. I needed to prove I could live a normal life, and I was beginning to accept that normal life, for me, would be one in which some remaining pain, and lasting inconvenience, would be daily challenges.

But experiencing pain is one thing; experiencing the mind drifting because of opium is something altogether different. During the year preceding this period I had developed the habit of taking a pill or two, or injecting myself with morphine, when I wanted to escape the dreariness of the limited world my injuries forced me to live in.

The medicines enabled me, in many ways, to escape from the torn body that did not yet feel like my own, and to observe myself and others from a comfortable – indeed, sometimes even an amusing - distance.

Recently, however, I'd found that when I did not choose to take the medications, my body became unreliable. I would sometimes find myself having sweats, or chills, or the faintness I had felt at Dr. Litchfield's office. I'd survived the trauma to my body, but had yet to totally overcome the trauma to my mind.

I told myself I felt faint because once again I had not eaten anything but a few bites of pastries and pudding since the day before, but in truth that was not unusual. My appetite had been lessening for some time, and the looseness of my clothing made that difficult to ignore. My body was also weaker than I cared to admit. During my three years of soldiering, despite marches and battles, sleeping on cold and wet ground, and the complete lack of cleanliness or healthy food, I'd been able to find strength even at the most dire times.

But during the past year I'd spent nearly four months in hospitals of various sorts, and then several months at home, and now with Aunt Cornelia. My recent days had been spent reading, sleeping, eating, and speaking with those who visited. Even young bodies begin to atrophy without use. Today, a day spent on horseback and in conversation, had exhausted me to the point where I was near collapse.

I watched vultures circling the woods as I approached home. After fighting ended, men on both sides of the conflict searched through battlefield smoke for wounded comrades, and whenever possible removed them to hospital tents, or at least to locations behind the lines. The living took precedence over the dead. But I'll never see a circling vulture and not remember those battlefields where vultures feasted on men we had not yet been able to bury.

I shuddered, and concentrated on the road in front of me. Pale green leaves were beginning to bud on a few tree branches. Life was continuing. It was not the first time I'd had to force myself out of thoughts of the past to focus on the living, and the present.

I determined not to share my faintness, or my concern about it, with Aunt Cornelia. She couldn't think I wasn't up to the task she'd asked of me. After speaking with Lidia Neilson I was now even more determined to prove the woman's innocence. Everyone accused of a crime in this country is innocent until proven guilty under the law, and I had no doubt that Lidia had not killed her husband. His clothing being found in her bedroom troubled me, to be sure, but the matter of the blood on the floor had been easily explained, and I was sure there would be a similar logical explanation for his knapsack.

The very location of Jake Neilson's body told me his wife could not have shot him. She'd been at home all that day, and both my aunt and Nora Burns had been with her. How could she have shot her husband at a location a half mile from her home? And if she had shot him (did Lidia Neilson even own a gun, or know how to use one?) then how could she have moved his body so far from her home? Jake was not a small man, and Lidia was a woman without the strength to lift him, much less carry him to another location. That alone would constitute reasonable doubt.

Aunt Cornelia greeted me as soon as I reached home, and, seeing I was weary (although as I had planned, I made no mention of my faintness,) called for Katie to bring a pot of tea and a plate of small sandwiches.

"Aaron, you must take care of yourself. You look pale and drawn." She poured tea, and handed it to me. "Now, sip. It will hold you until supper. Katie has a chicken just about prepared, with roasted potatoes and the apple jelly Mrs. Langdon made up last fall. Perhaps if you rest a bit you'll be up to doing supper justice, and not picking at it as you often do."

I sipped my tea and smiled at Aunt Cornelia's determination to take care of me. I actually enjoyed the experience. A woman's ministrations and tender affections can soothe some of the harshest pains and bring peace to the worst of the world's problems. In my current physical condition I could only hope some day I would be fortunate enough to have a wife who would care for me in the way I had seen Aunt Cornelia care for Uncle Henry; the way she was caring for me now.

I sat for a few minutes in silence, enjoying the warmth of the tea and the steadying sensation of food in my stomach. But after she'd clearly expressed her concern about my current state, Aunt Cornelia could wait no longer to find out about my afternoon.

"Did you see Lidia? Did you tell her you'd represent her?"

"Yes, I saw Lidia. And, yes, she agreed I would be her lawyer in this matter."

Aunt Cornelia sighed audibly, clearly relieved.

"I also met Nora Burns, and her brother Robbie. She said she was with you and Lidia yesterday."

"She was."

"You hadn't shared that with me earlier," I said. "You never mentioned there was another person at the Neilson's house."

"I thought it best Nora choose what she would tell you."

I didn't point out that in a murder investigation I needed to know all details; not just those someone chose to tell me. "Miss Burns is an interesting young woman. She is very attractive, but in different way from that of most women. Perhaps it is her short hair."

Aunt Cornelia nodded. "Nora does not feel the need to dress or arrange her hair as other young women do. She is set on making her own way, not on finding a husband. Any man interested in Nora Burns would have to have patience."

"Her brother was taking full advantage of the various food stuffs that neighbors had brought or sent with their condolences."

"He's an active boy." Aunt Cornelia smiled. "And quite mature for his years. Nora has done an excellent job of bringing him up, despite her own youth."

Seeing an opportunity to find out more, I asked casually, "Then she's taken care of him since his birth?"

"Their mother was very weak." She paused a moment. "Nora's had few conventional advantages, but she's a strong young woman. She does piece work for the garment factory in Utica. That way she can stay home and care for Robbie. And in the summer she cultivates a large garden which provides food for them for most of the year."

"Then she is poor."

"In material goods, very much so." Aunt Cornelia looked at me with an amused expression on her face. "Nora has made do with less than many, but she is not one to complain. She does what is necessary for herself and for Robbie to have what they need."

"And despite that responsibility, and a job doing stitching, she had the time to be with you and Lidia Neilson at the orphanage last week, and at the Neilsons' home this week."

"Nora has her priorities, and does what she can to help others."

"How old is she, if I may ask?"

"You're asking a number of questions about a young woman you've only met twice," said Aunt Cornelia.

"She and her brother interest me," I answered.

"Indeed. Well, Nora is twenty or twenty-one, I'd guess."

I could have asked many other questions about Nora Burns, but knew I'd reached my limit for the day. In any case, I'd determined to find out more from the young woman herself. "After my visit to the Neilsons' home, I went to see Dr. Litchfield."

My aunt's attention was immediately pulled from Nora to the doctor. "And?"

"He hadn't learned a great deal from the autopsy. Jake Neilson was shot twice, as we could have guessed when we saw him yesterday." In delicacy I did not mention the strange scratches on Jake's body. Some subjects I didn't feel comfortable discussing with any woman, even Aunt Cornelia, and sexual activity was certainly one of those.

"Sheriff Newell was also there. I told him I was going to represent Lidia Neilson."

"I'm glad. I was quite concerned about Lidia's situation before, but your involvement assures me her case is in good hands."

Aunt Cornelia then went on and chattered more than she normally does about several of her acquaintances. Over the roast chicken, with which Katie had done a credible job, we discussed possibilities for the property, depending on when the young men who might be hired would be released from their units. In this, as well as in the investigation of Jake Neilson's death, I felt for the first time that spring as though I had a role to play: that my help might make a difference to Aunt Cornelia.

I retired directly after dinner, saying quite truthfully that I was weary. I ensured a night's sleep by injecting one dose of the morphine I needed to prepare my body for a full day on Wednesday.

Sleep came quickly. But it brought with it the visions that had at first scared me, and then sometimes entertained me, as the drugs allowed me to separate myself from my body. I'd mastered the art of watching my dreams from a distance. I saw the door of my room opening. Nora Burns came in, followed by my friend Richard. I tried to ask them why they were together, but they didn't see or hear me. They embraced, and then Robbie ran in, holding a skull in his hands. He and Richard tossed the skull back and forth as though it were a ball, before the skull flew out the window. Robbie ran to the window, and was about to jump out, chasing the skull, when Nora caught him and pulled him back. Richard was gone, and Nora gave Robbie pieces of cake from a table I hadn't seen before. Somehow I knew the cake would make Robbie sick, and I tried to stop him from eating it, but no one could hear me.

I woke in a cold sweat, with my heart pounding, and actually got up and checked that both the door and window in my bedroom were closed, and no one was there.

For a long time I lay in bed, thinking through the images again. They were so clear and strong that I could smell the cake, and describe in detail what each person in my vision had been wearing.

I'd had dreams like that before when I'd taken morphine. I called them "living tableaux" to myself, because they seemed so real. When they started, back in the army hospitals, I was often convinced that they were real, and that Margaret or Mother had been at my bedside during the night, or that an army band had been playing and nurses and doctors danced through the hospital tents.

Now I knew the tableaux were not real, but they were still frightening. The visions must come from somewhere inside of me. What could they mean?

I forced myself to lie awake and think about why I'd imagined Richard and Nora and Robbie and the skull together.

I had no answers, but despite my efforts to stay awake, I did not see the dawn arrive.

Chapter 15

I was wakened by Aunt Cornelia's knocking on my bedroom door.

"Aaron? Aaron, I'm leaving for the memorial service in twenty minutes. If you're coming to the church and the parade you must get up now."

I managed to open my eyes and focus on the watch I'd left on my bedside table. It was almost nine in the morning, Wednesday, April 19. The day of the nation's memorial services for our late president. I'd almost forgotten.

I pulled on my old uniform as quickly as I could and was downstairs in time to swallow half a cup of coffee before we left. Aunt Cornelia had determined we should all attend Lincoln's memorial services, so Katie and Owen were with us as we drove to Hestia. As on Easter, we left Katie at St. Patrick's. I glanced through the crowd there, hoping to catch a glimpse of Nora and Robbie Burns, but failed to do so. We then went on to the Presbyterian Church.

The town was still decked in mourning, as were most of the parishioners. Many men were in uniform. Hestia had given, or at least loaned, many of its men to the struggle.

At the Presbyterian services four uniformed men, two of those missing legs, were using crutches. One wore a bandage over his eyes. One, who nodded at me in grim comradely greeting, was also missing an arm. And still two other young men were clearly disabled in some way as they had to be helped to their seats by members of their family. I knew those in uniform, even those without obvious injuries, still carried the scent and fear of battle with them, and would for their lifetimes. The war's cost to these men, and to their families, was enormous. And the majority of regiments had not yet been dismissed.

The Reverend spoke of the service and dedication of those who'd given their lives during the war, and spoke most movingly about President Lincoln, with special prayers for his widow and their remaining children.

At this same moment Lincoln's memorial service was being held in Washington. I hoped our country would never again have to suffer the assassination of a beloved leader. But it was a step toward national healing to know that hundreds of thousands of people throughout the Union were mourning together on this bright spring day.

Lidia Neilson was seated in her family pew, not far from where Aunt Cornelia and I were seated. Had she slept last night? Had Sheriff Newell made progress identifying anyone who might have seen Lidia's husband on the day he must have traveled through Utica and Hestia? I suspected not much had been accomplished since yesterday.

Most men connected with the police force and fire department were present at the church. They'd worked with the veterans' organizations arranging the parade scheduled to follow services.

The speed with which the event had been organized had perhaps left some details unfinished, but there was no time after the Reverend's final "A-men" to consider what might have been improved. I was immediately swept up by a group of fire department volunteers who were gathering uniformed men from various churches and accompanying us to the Hestia town hall, where the parade was both to start and finish. Sides of wagons which usually bore signs advertising "Kaufman's Meats" or "Van Hilderman's General Store," or "Miller Mercantile" were today decked in red, white, and blue bunting and every flag the town had been able to find. The theme of mourning so in evidence at the church had been dispatched with military precision and replaced by that of patriotism and the union.

Those of us in uniform were the designated heroes of the day. Ranks were deemed unimportant; privates were cheered the same as a Lieutenant Colonel, the highest ranking man I saw. At first there was an attempt to organize us by regiment, but that proved too difficult. I was not the only one who'd been enlisted in a regiment from outside central New York State, and some local companies boasted many more members than others. Without much delay about a dozen of us were asked to stand, if we could, in each wagon. I counted nine wagons, so there were over a hundred of us gathered in a town boasting a total population of under 1500, and with many men still in the ranks.

The fire fighters marched between the wagons, as did the police and several boys' organizations, and a group of women from one of the mills carrying a banner that read "THE BLESSED UNION FOREVER." A wide variety of organizations sent representatives and similar banners or signs. Every charitable and reform group boasted its own association. The Domestic Missionary Society, the Hestia Tract Society, the Ladies' Aid Society (the organization that had supported the Sanitary Commission during the war,) the Youth Abstinence Association, The Young Men's Association, The Female Moral Reform Society, the New York Mills Washingtonian Society (a fellow veteran reminded me that was a temperance group,) and triumphant members of the Hestia Anti-Slavery Society, all marched. In fact, the number of individuals in the parade sometimes dwarfed those cheering and shouting "Huzzah!" from sidewalks and windows and (from boys who had found perches aloft) trees or roofs. The shouting was accompanied by several musical groups of various percussive persuasions, most presuming to be drum and bugle corps.

All in all it was a grand parade, and one that made me proud of having done my part in the war. After the last "Hurrah!" echoed in the streets I looked for Aunt Cornelia, but failed to locate her, or Robbie or Nora.

"Captain Stone?" asked the young man who'd stood next to me in the Miller Mercantile wagon.

"Aaron," I corrected, grinning back, flush with the citizens' outpouring of patriotism and love and a feeling of closeness to my brothers in arms.

"Aaron, then," he clapped me on the back, "And I'm Eli. Come with us to the Oak Tavern. The owner has promised that today all veterans in uniform will drink the best of New York State's brews, at his expense, in celebration of the end of the war."

I accepted the invitation with alacrity, and followed Eli and his companions. On such a day a beer was an excellent idea and, in truth, I didn't relish the afternoon's ending so early.

Dozens of former soldiers pushed their way to the bar at the Oak Tavern, where, indeed, beer was pouring freely, and men were finding comrades they had fought with, and friends they had just celebrated with. My stein was soon filled, and I maneuvered my way to the entrance of the tavern, where the celebration poured into the street. Clearly the temperance societies had little influence on this block.

I leaned against one of the oak trees that gave the tavern its name, sipped my pint, and watched the men enjoying themselves and the citizens of Hestia waving their flags at us as they walked back to their homes. I knew only a few men here, and those just to nod at, but I felt comfortable in uniform, among men in uniform. I only wished

Richard could have been with us, to join first in mourning our leader's death, and then in celebrating our victory. He would have made friends more easily than I, for such was his talent, and would have been openly clapping new friends on the shoulder and making one of the many toasts raised that afternoon. I raised my stein in a silent toast to him, and to our other brothers no longer with us. From toasts I overheard, I was not the only soldier remembering lost comrades.

"I see you found yourself a brew," said my new friend Eli.

"I have indeed, thanks to you," I answered, smiling down at him, since he was several inches shorter than I was, although considerably wider. Eli's jacket was straining its buttons. He must have returned home to a wife or mother who was an excellent cook.

"I work at Van Guilderman's Mercantile. You're Cornelia Livingston's nephew, I heard."

"You heard correctly. I've been helping her out since my uncle died in January," I answered.

"And you're involved with her friend, Mrs. Neilson."

"'Involved' is a strange word to use," I replied good naturedly. "Mrs. Neilson is a friend of my aunt's, and I've agreed to help her if she should have any legal problems. She's a new widow; such times often require legal assistance."

"People are saying she did her husband in," said Eli.

"Who's saying that?" I asked. Jake had been dead only two days. I knew bad news spread quickly, but this seemed an uncommonly fast reaction.

"Everyone," Eli answered, raising his mug again. His flushed face and slightly blurred speech indicated he'd managed to be one of the first in line at the tap. "They're saying someone was bound to shoot the man eventually. Too bad the Rebs didn't take care of him first."

"Why are they saying that?" I took a small sip and determined to listen well. Gossip could provide information.

Eli leaned so close I couldn't help inhaling his sour breath. "Jake Neilson was out to make money, not friends. Everyone knew it. He married Lidia Van Patten for her house and lands and because he thought there was money there. But there wasn't; at least not enough for him."

"Many a man or woman marries at least in part for money," I said, playing the role of the naive outsider, which, indeed I was.

"And there was talk he was too friendly with Wash Loomis," Eli said.

"Wash Loomis?"

Eli looked at me blankly. "You don't know the Loomis Gang?" He lowered his voice. "The Loomis family has been stealing horses for hundreds of miles around since old George Loomis started in the 1840s. They're the best horse thieves in the East. Paint the horses, so they won't be recognized, and send them south and east on the Canal. They're rich, those Loomis boys, and no one's been able to stop 'em." Eli glanced around cautiously. "I shouldn't even be talkin' about 'em. They've been known to burn houses down with folks still inside for talkin' ill of 'em."

"Why hasn't the sheriff done anything about this?"

"It's been tried. Many times. But witnesses and law enforcers often disappear or have fatal accidents before court hearings."

"And Jake Neilson was involved with this family?"

"It's said that after Jake visited a farm the best horses seemed to disappear. No proof, you understand. I'm just sayin' what happened."

"So there are those in Hestia who aren't fond of Jake."

"Fond of! Folks hated Jake," said Eli, looking at me as though I were crazed. "Maybe his wife liked him some, but I've no proof of that. They lived off from town and she didn't come in often."

Another soldier stepped in. "Talkin' about Jake Neilson?"

"We were," I corroborated. "Eli was telling me what some folks thought of him."

"I don't know what his whole history was," said the soldier, whose red beard was beginning to be streaked with gray. "I haven't been in Hestia my whole life. But I've a cousin who served with Jake in the 117th, and we haven't heard from him in a couple of months. The last letter we got, he said he'd been wounded in the foot by a Corporal Jake Neilson because Jake hadn't liked something he said. Wrote his foot was healing, but he'd had a few days out of battle as a consequence. His wife is near sick about it, wantin' him to get home, and not knowing how he is. Not like him not to write regular, especially after being hurt. And here Jake appears, the one who caused his injury, from the same regiment, fit and dandy. My question's, where's the rest of his regiment? How'd he manage to get such an early release? And, most important, where's my cousin?"

"Maybe Jake was ill."

"He didn't look so ill, I heard, 'ceptin for those bullets in his chest," said the soldier. "If'n I'd seen him while he was still alive, I might have had some questions for him, about why he'd skedaddle and leave his brothers hungry and sick in North Carolina. To be in Hestia now he would've had to leave before the end of the war."

"True indeed. He would have left several weeks ago," I agreed. "I'm Aaron Stone, by the way."

"Jasper Field," said the red-head. "I know who you are. I saw you at Proctor's the other day. You're the one came in with Doc Litchfield." He leaned over to spit in the street. "That's what I think of Jake Nielson. Just wish I'd had the opportunity to get to 'im before someone else did. I hear it's his wife shot him."

"Why would his wife have wanted him dead?" I asked.

"Aaron here's his wife's lawyer, you should know," Eli put in.

"Better be careful what you say!"

"I never met the man, so I'm not worried to say anything," said Field. "I just know my cousin's wife's in a bad way and missing her man, and Jake Neilson's coming home didn't help her none." He looked at me. "You can quote me on that." He produced one final copious emission and turned back to the crowd.

"Jasper seems upset, don't he?" said Eli jovially. "Wonder how many others here have thoughts about Jake Neilson?"

"I wonder, too," I said. "Were there any organizations he belonged to? Any close friends I should talk to?"

Eli shrugged. "Don't know for sure. Think he attended the First Presbyterian. And seems to me he might have belonged to one of the temperance groups, and was anti-slavery. That's why he was one of the first to sign up to fight. He re-enlisted, I heard, which accounts for his being away so long."

"Somehow I hadn't pegged him as a temperance man."

"Belonging to a group don't mean you never indulge. Some of the women's groups, they're pretty strict about such things. Other groups are more liberal. Don't want to see women and children imbibing, of course. But if a man's with his friends or in his own home, then what's the danger, eh?"

Eli took a deep drink and looked at his empty pint. "Speaking of which, seems to be the time for me to get a refill." He looked at my glass, which was still half full. "Want another?"

"No, thanks. I've got a ways to go home, and I'd best be getting on."

He nodded and disappeared into the crowd.

In the past hour I'd heard two possible motives for shooting Jake. Neither of them involved his wife.

Chapter 16

Aunt Cornelia left for the orphanage in the morning, as she did most Thursdays. I had Owen saddle the older horse and headed for Lidia Neilson's home. I needed to ask her about what I'd heard at the tavern.

I knocked on her door several times before she finally answered it, formally dressed in modest mourning. Her relief was visible. I suspected she'd feared Sheriff Newell was paying her a visit. "Good morning, Aaron. You're early to be making a call, but welcome."

I walked into the parlor where we'd sat before. "I'm here on business, Lidia."

"Do you have any news?"

"Not really," I answered. "Have you heard anything more from Sheriff Newell?"

She shook her head. "No. But I've been staying close to home. If he wants me, he'll know where I am." Lidia's hands grasped the arms of her chair tightly. "I hope he allows Jake to be buried soon. I'd like to get the service over with, especially under the circumstances."

"I'll find out for you. I'll ask Dr. Litchfield," I answered, taking a small notebook out of my pocket and making a note with the pencil I found easier to handle than I did pen and ink. "I assume nothing can be done about arranging an interment until after the autopsy is officially complete, but I would think that would be over by now." I'd started making notes two days before, and I didn't want to forget any questions I needed to answer. Already the details of Jake's murder took up a third of my notebook, and included more questions than facts.

"I went to Lincoln's memorial service yesterday, but didn't stay for the parade. The sheriff and the policemen were very involved with the festivities, so I assumed they wouldn't have time to worry about Jake's murder. When I heard your rap on the door I thought it might be Sheriff Newell."

"I'm hoping he has other possibilities to check out before he comes back with more questions," I said, not wanting to discuss the scratches on Jake's body with his wife. At least not yet. There might be an explanation for those scratches other than another woman and, if so, I wanted Lidia to hear the alternative explanation first. It was hard enough for a woman to hear her husband was dead; to think he had been unfaithful first would make it even harder. Women might not expect perfection from their men, but they would certainly have no desire to discuss details of the errors of their men's ways, particularly in public.

"I want to be here to arrange for his burial," Lidia said.

She was anticipating her arrest. I wished I had more specific, more positive, news for her. "Yesterday in town I heard talk about your husband," I said. "I wanted to find out from you what might be true."

"I'll tell you what I can."

She sat as upright as though she were sitting on a Hitchcock chair, and the lines around her lips had deepened since I'd last seen her.

"You have no one to stay with you?"

"Not at the moment."

"No family?"

She shook her head. "I was an only child. Jake was my family."

"And you grew up in this house."

"My father wanted us to move to Hestia, or even to Utica; he liked the bustle of a town. But my mother loved the peace and quiet of the country. She grew roses. In another month you'll be able to see her rose garden, on the side of the house. And she loved taking care of her house." Lidia smiled softly. "When I was a child I longed for brothers and sisters, but my mother thought of this house and her gardens as her children. She loved me, certainly, but most of her time was spent in keeping her home the way she liked it."

"I assume you had servants to help with a house this size."

"A cook, sometimes. But Mother was never pleased with the way maids performed. The silver never shone brightly enough; there was dust behind the books in the bookcases. That sort of thing. And we are eleven miles from town. Not many girls want to spend their days so far in the country. Most of the time Mother and I kept the house in order ourselves."

"And then you married Jake."

"Father brought him home for dinner once; he was a business acquaintance, from Rochester. Six months later we married."

"You lived here after your marriage, with your parents."

Lidia nodded. "Mother wasn't well by then; she suffered from consumption and needed me to care for her. She died a few months after Jake and I were married. And only four months after that one of the wheels on Father's carriage somehow loosened, and he was thrown out and hit his head on a tree alongside the road. It was dreadful." She hesitated. "Jake and I both loved the house - I don't think he'd ever lived in a home like this before - and by then it seemed easier to stay than to move somewhere else."

"What did Jake do, before the war?"

"He was a factor. He'd represent anything from hops or chickens from local farmers to yards of fabrics from the mills. He'd ship them to New York, usually, although sometimes to Ohio or Binghamton, and sell them for a profit."

"He must have been away from home a lot."

"Yes."

"And you didn't mind?"

"Aaron, I really don't see what this has to do with Jake's murder."

"It may not. But I need to understand Jake's relationship to others in the community. Perhaps one of the local farmers or manufacturers felt he'd cheated them in the past. Perhaps they didn't want him coming home and starting his business again."

"It's possible, I suppose. Certainly there were some who said Jake was taking profits from those who needed it. But he was the one who risked his time, and, often, his money. He didn't take profit until everything was sold."

"Did Jake ever deal in horses?"

"He purchased anything he might be able to sell."

"Yesterday at The Oak Tavern I heard rumors Jake worked with the Loomis Gang. That he identified horses for them to steal."

For the first time that morning I saw Lidia relax. She almost laughed. "Heavens, people do find things to gossip about. Jake knew the Loomis boys. Everyone in these parts does. I even remember Wash Loomis coming here for supper once. Jake was a businessman. He did business with all sorts of people, high and low. But the horses everyone believes the Loomis gang stole? I can't believe Jake would get involved with something like that. It was too dangerous to work with that family. People ended up .." Lidia's smile faded suddenly. "They ended up dead."

"So it might be a possibility."

"I suppose so, when you think of it that way." Her hands held tight to the arms of the chair, as thought she was ensuring she wouldn't fall off. "But that was all before the war. Jake didn't discuss the details of his business dealings with me. And he's been gone three years. Would anyone still hold something against him after all that time?"

Suddenly I felt that the room was closing in. I longed to throw open one of the windows and breathe fresh air. This woman was trying to remember details about her husband's life that clearly she'd never been privy to. What woman understood what business her husband did on a day-to-day basis? If I was going to find out more about Jake I'd have to find it out somewhere else.

But I knew I had to raise one more difficult subject. "Before I go, could I bother you to show me your bedchamber? It would help me to know the way the house is designed, and see where the sheriff found the blood and knapsack."

Lidia rose, clearly more relaxed about talking about her home than about her husband. "I don't want you to imagine that every man who comes to call is entitled to see my bedroom," she said, in almost a teasing fashion.

I flushed. "Of course not. But I am your lawyer."

"Follow me," she said, walking to the stairway that rose from the middle of the hallway.

Upstairs were four chambers.

Lidia's bedchamber, which I assumed she'd shared with Jake in happier days, was in the front, over the parlor. It was a simple room, papered in a small red and green floral pattern. A high mahogany bedstead carved with Gothic designs and faces dominated the room, although there was also a small table next to the bed, a high chest of drawers, and a small green painted desk and chair near the window, much more a woman's desk than the massive furniture downstairs in the study. Perhaps Lidia wrote her letters here. Opposite the bed was a large and somewhat crude oil portrait, the sort done perhaps thirty years ago by limners who traveled the countryside and paid their way by capturing the likenesses of local families. The couple were clearly not Lidia and Jake Neilson.

"Your parents?" I asked.

"Yes. Done just after I was born," said Lidia.

"A handsome couple," I said, and looked at her. "You take after your mother."

She smiled. "So my father always said."

I wondered what Jake had felt, making love to his wife in the full view of the portrait of her parents. "Where was the blood from Robbie's nosebleed?"

"Here," she said, pulling a floral hooked rug back from the side of the bed.

I knelt down. There was a large stain on the floor, although I could not tell now whether it had been blood. I turned the rug over: the stain was duplicated there. I could not imagine a young boy bleeding so much; no wonder he was frightened.

It might be a large amount for a nosebleed, but I'd seem enough battlefield injuries to know a man shot in the chest would have bled more than a small rug could have covered.

I turned the rug back so the clean side was up.

"I've been wanting to scrub the boards and the rug, but Sheriff Newell said to leave everything as it was for now." She looked at me and bit her lip slightly. "He said it was important evidence."

"You said you'd staunched Robbie's nosebleed with a cloth. Do you still have that cloth?"

She shook her head. "Blood stains so easily. I soaked it in cold water as soon as the bleeding stopped, and then washed it."

"Of course." I looked around the room. "And Jake's knapsack was found in the wardrobe?"

She nodded. It was a simple storage wardrobe, with two shelves above, where hats were stored, and pegs along the back for clothing.

A faded man's morning coat and cloak were hanging there; the rest of the garments clearly belonged to Lidia. Beneath the wardrobe were two drawers. "The knapsack was just here, on the floor." She pointed at the corner under the morning coat. "Sheriff Newell took it with him."

"Did you see what was in it?"

"No. I was surprised to see it here at all, and didn't think to ask about its contents."

I tried to imagine a soldier returning home, weary and dirty, climbing the steps to the bedroom he'd shared with his wife. "Was Jake a very neat person?"

"No," Lidia smiled. "He was a man."

"But upon returning home after two year's absence he did not call out to you; he walked to his bedroom, and even here, he didn't toss the knapsack on the floor or perhaps even leave it in the hallway. He carefully stowed the bag in the wardrobe."

"So it appears."

"Is there any way to the second floor other than by the stairway from the front hall?"

She shook her head. "I'll show you the other bedchambers up here, so you can say you've seen the entire house."

All three of the other chambers were well decorated and apparently ready for guests. The last Lidia showed me, next to the master bedroom, smaller than the others,

was painted a pale rose color, with a white iron bedstead. It had the look of a child's room.

She looked around the room. "Jake and I were never blessed with children. This was my room as a girl, and would have been the nursery, should we ever have needed one."

She closed the door of that room. The stairway led one floor higher, to the tower of the house, but we went back down the stairs.

As we passed a tall narrow window on the landing I noticed laundry drying in back of the house. I stood there a moment, pretending to admire the view of the back gardens. For the most part they were bare, since it was still April, and frosts could still be expected.

"You must come back in two months and see the gardens," Lidia said, as she continued down the steps. "My mother was so proud of her flowers. I don't keep them up as she did – I haven't been able to find a gardener in recent years to help me – but I've grown enough vegetables for myself, and soon there will be flowers in the first garden you see there, beyond the yard." She stopped near the door to the kitchen. "I usually have a cup of tea at this time of day. Will you join me?"

"I should like that."

The kitchen ran the length of the house in the back. Lidia Neilson was clearly a capable woman; many of Mother's friends hardly knew how to heat water, and depended on their cooks for all food preparation. They would never have imagined working in a garden, any more than they would have considered entertaining a guest in their kitchen. I took note of Lidia's hands; they were red, as though she'd been scrubbing laundry. She put cups for each of us on the wide oak table and added a small plate of scones from a tin box on a smaller table near one of the windows.

"I believe these are still fresh," she said. "A woman handed them to me in church yesterday. People have been so kind."

"You must have been up early, doing laundry," I pointed out. Another skill I don't believe my mother had ever attempted, and one I hadn't noticed Aunt Cornelia doing either.

"Yes." Lidia looked down at her hands. "I'm afraid I must do everything myself here. Usually it is simple, since I have been living alone, but I had houseguests recently, as you know, and the tablecloths from the dining room, where I displayed the food that was brought to comfort me, had to be spotted and scrubbed." She smiled. "I'm keeping myself busy. If I'm busy I don't have time to think too much. And I want my home to be in order should I be removed from it suddenly."

Her voice broke as she put leaves in the teapot.

"Lidia, you understand I need to know everything about you and Jake, and your lives, if I am going to defend you."

She looked at me directly. "I've nothing to hide."

"Then why are babies' clouts drying among the tablecloths outside?"

Lidia blushed, and looked away, but she didn't hesitate. "You must be mistaken. There are no babies here."

"Nor have I seen one. But there are clouts on your line."

"Aaron, perhaps what look to you like clouts are cloths I use for … female purposes."

This time I was the one to look away. That possibility had never occurred to me, and it certainly was nothing I should be discussing with a lady.

I self-consciously glanced out the window again. Perhaps the cloths were used for the purpose she mentioned. Clouts were usually stained, but, then, so would other cloths. I wished Aunt Cornelia were there to advise me. Certainly a woman would not mistake one sort of cloth for another.

I drank my tea quickly, but for some reason I was still not convinced Lidia was telling me all of the truth. I needed some sort of confirmation. I'd seen all of the house except the oldest section, and the stable. There were no infants here. And yet Lidia was in her mid-thirties. A child would not be an impossibility.

And a child born after a husband had been at war for three years would not be easily explained. So far out in the country, it might have been possible to conceal a pregnancy. But not a child, from a returning husband.

I took another sip of the hot tea.

"Lidia, in Jake's absence, was there any other man in your life?"

"Another man in my life!" Lidia stood up, and for a moment I thought she was going to throw her half-filled teacup at me. "I have stood for your humiliating questions. I have shown you everything in this house you asked to see, and more. I have listened to your suggesting that my husband was involved in illegal, or at least immoral, activities. I will NOT sit here and listen to your accusing me of adultery."

"I know this is difficult, Lidia. But if Jake heard a rumor that you had a lover, or perhaps even a close male friend, in his absence, that could be motivation for a conflict. Either man might have been the aggressor."

"There is no other man!"

"You understand, I had to ask. And you must be prepared for Sheriff Newell to ask questions, too. All subjects are questioned in a murder investigation. People murder for love; for power; for money. All must be considered."

Lidia Neilson sat down suddenly, put her head on the table, and began to sob. "Just leave, Aaron. Leave now. I need to be alone. No more questions."

I put my hand on her shoulder for a moment, but she shuddered and moved away from my hand. I did not know what to do; emotional outbursts of hysterical women are not something I was, or am, comfortable with. I wished with all my heart that Aunt Cornelia, or some other woman, was there to provide counsel, and to talk with Lidia Neilson. She'd explained away what I'd asked, but I couldn't lose the feeling that I was not asking the right questions.

Perhaps the basis for being a good lawyer is knowing what can be asked, and when.

Clearly I had not chosen the right moment.

I stood in the kitchen and watched Lidia sob for a few minutes, completely powerless to do anything that would help her.

"Damn it, Lidia, I'm sorry for upsetting you. But I need you to answer my questions. This is not a tea party. You're involved in a murder investigation!"

She raised her tear-stained face. "I could not be more clear about what I'm involved with. And you have promised to help me. I appreciate that. But right now I need to be alone." Her words were orders. "Now!"

Chapter 17

I left the Neilson house, and turned my horse in the direction of Hestia.

Lidia had been completely unreasonable; how could she expect me to help her if she became so emotional?

Women *are* emotional, I told myself, but in a situation as serious as this, emotions had to be ignored. Perhaps I'd pressed her too hard. I'd asked her personal questions. I'd mentioned parts of life men should not mention to women.

But that was my job. It wasn't fair to imagine I would stop asking questions just because they were uncomfortable for a woman to answer.

Although if she'd truly done nothing wrong, as I was assuming, then perhaps I shouldn't have pushed her.

I wished I had another attorney to talk with; a criminal attorney who'd handled such cases in the past. Reading case law doesn't tell you how to act when a woman you are trying to help becomes hysterical, or screams, or cries.

Every time I talked with someone more questions were raised than answered. Surely this situation should be plain. A man returned home from military service, with or without leave. He was killed.

But why?

I could imagine motives, ranging from simple robbery to a lovers' quarrel to a business relationship which fell apart. But those were theoretical motives. I had no proof of any.

Did Sheriff Newell know why Jake was killed? Knowing the reason why the man was killed would surely lead to the murderer.

Could Lidia Neilson be convicted of murder without a motive? I believed her story. But, I reminded myself, I had to be prepared for what a district attorney might find. Or imagine.

With everything else on my mind I'd also forgotten to ask whether Lidia owned a gun, or knew how to handle one. That question would have to wait for another day.

My mind churned with possibilities as I rode the eleven miles to Hestia. What had seemed like a simple request from Aunt Cornelia to represent Lidia Neilson in a murder of which she could not possibly be guilty had now confused me to the point where, if I had not promised Aunt Cornelia that I would help, I might have said the situation was too complicated, and resigned from the case.

But my pride and loyalties wouldn't let me do that. At least not yet.

I needed to talk with Dr. Litchfield again, and possibly with Sheriff Newell. And Aunt Cornelia. I also resolved to become more organized. I had not been as careful as I should have been to take notes when I was speaking with people, and already I was uncertain about some details, particularly specifics of where people had been, and when.

Tonight I would sit quietly and draw up a timetable.

My shoulder ached from the horse's uneven steps down the rough road. I carefully tucked the reins loosely under the saddle, and reached into my pocket for my pills. By the time I reached the doctor's office I was more relaxed.

"Aaron; I hadn't expected to see you so soon," said Dr. Litchfield.

"How is your defense of Lidia Neilson proceeding?"

I sensed in some way he was mocking me. "Well, thank you. I stopped to see if you'd completed Jake Neilson's autopsy. Mrs. Neilson would like to be able to plan his funeral and burial."

"So far as I can say, that won't be a problem," said the doctor, indicating that I should sit. "Some coffee, perhaps? Brandy?"

Every time I'd visited the doctor he'd offered me brandy. I wondered whether brandy was on his list of medicinal products. "Yes, please. Both," I answered. "A little brandy in coffee would be just the thing."

The doctor rang a brass bell on his desk. A few moments later a young woman opened the door from the residential part of the building. "Yes, Dr. Litchfield?"

"Could you bring us two coffees, please?"

"Yes, sir." She disappeared as quickly as she had come.

"I will have to check with Sheriff Newell, of course, before I release the body to Mrs. Neilson, but I see no reason why he wouldn't agree. Clearly Jake was shot twice, and I've recorded everything I found during the autopsy."

"Would you let me know when that happens?" I asked, "Mrs. Neilson would like to have arrangements completed as soon as possible."

The inner door opened again, and the same young woman entered, this time carrying a tray with two cups of coffee. Dr. Litchfield poured a goodly draught of brandy into each cup.

"To solving Jake Neilson's murder!" he toasted, and I raised my cup in answer.

"Perhaps I should go to the sheriff's office myself this afternoon," I said, after taking a deep sip of the hot beverage. "I might be able to find out how far the investigation has proceeded."

"Don't waste your time going today," said the doctor. "I don't think they've made much progress. Yesterday the police had the memorial service and parade to oversee, and I suspect last night the jail was full of those celebrating the glorious Union victory."

I smiled. "You may be right about that."

"And at least two of his deputies have been dispatched to look for young Mrs. North. They stopped in this morning to ask whether I might know where she was."

"Mrs. North?"

"Sheriff Newell mentioned her when you were here Tuesday," said the doctor. His nose and cheeks were beginning to redden from the alcohol, and I hoped my imbibing was not as readily apparent. "She's the young woman expecting her first any day now who disappeared Saturday or Sunday. Her husband's been knocking on doors and accusing people of hiding her. He's become a bit of a nuisance in town. I believe he took one of those berths in the jail last night. Sheriff Newell promised to try to find the girl."

"She ran away?"

The doctor shrugged. "Perhaps she's gone to visit some of her people in Rome. She's been nervous about the delivery, although all was proceeding as it should."

"If she's with friends, then why should the sheriff get involved?"

"You're a lawyer, are you not? Helping a woman leave her husband is interfering in a husband's affairs and assisting a wife in violating her duty. That's grounds for charges of enticement. And the penalty for harboring runaways is $1,000 and three year's imprisonment."

"Surely someone wanting to provide solace to a young woman afraid of childbirth could be doing no wrong."

"Under New York State law, even if the woman went of her own volition, or asked for help, the person who provided the help is guilty. Husbands must be able to control their households, mustn't they?"

Dr. Litchfield added another liberal amount of brandy to his cup and took a deep swallow. "A civilized society, such as we live in, understands such restrictions."

I had not remembered such a domestic law, but I was not concentrating on family law at Columbia College. "Of course, it makes sense that a husband or wife should be aware of the other's whereabouts," I agreed.

"That a *husband* should know of his *wife's* whereabouts," corrected Dr. Litchfield. "Men must be free occasionally to engage in pursuits that we need not bother our women about, don't you agree?"

"I hadn't thought of it in quite that way," I acknowledged.

"You are not yet married!" countered the doctor. "Young Mrs. North had better come to her senses if she's avoiding her husband. She married him, and she belongs at home and in his bed."

"But what if she's come to some harm? What if she's been murdered, like Jake? Or even lost her way in some of the woods nearby? Or slipped and fell into the canal and drowned?"

"All vague possibilities, to be sure," said Dr. Litchfield. "I'm sure the deputies are investigating every angle. But my money's on the girl's wanting to get away from her husband for a time. She's young, and doesn't realize it will be just be the worse for her when she returns. Some women learn slowly."

I decided to change the subject. "The bones, Dr. Litchfield; the body found in the field last weekend. I've been somewhat distracted by the Neilson situation, but I haven't forgotten, and I still want to identify the man who was killed. For now, is it a problem for you if the bones stay here?"

"Not a bit, Aaron. I can store them in one of the plain coffins I keep in the back of my barn for such circumstances."

"I'd appreciate that. The problems of the living must come before those of the dead."

Chapter 18

I paused outside the Bradford Asylum, wondering if perhaps I should stop and ask Aunt Cornelia again how it happened she was at the Neilson home the day Jake was murdered. But I'd see her at home this evening, and the more I thought about the women who'd been with Lidia Neilson that day, the more I wanted to talk first with Nora Burns.

It wasn't an excuse to call on her, I told myself. I needed to talk with her in the course of my investigation. No further justification was needed. I urged my horse on. The Burns home was near ours, in any case, so it would not be a long excursion.

It had been a week since Owen discovered the bones in our north field, and I'd been busier during that week than I'd been in all the time since I'd arrived in Hestia. The excitement was good for my mind, I had no doubt, but my body, which had remained sedentary for far too many months, was resisting. The idea of settling into a comfortable chair, or, better yet, a bed, for the rest of the afternoon was all too tempting.

Perhaps there'd be time for that after I'd seen Nora Burns.

The closer I got to where she and her brother must live, the less exhausted I felt. I admitted to myself I wanted to see Nora, and not just to ask her about Lidia Neilson, and how it happened that she and Robbie were at the Neilson home at such a difficult time.

I passed Aunt Cornelia's house and continued west. The Burns home could not be too far beyond.

The horse had clearly wanted to stop at her stable. I encouraged her to go on, but slowed down considerably. I was tempted to swallow another tablet, or perhaps two, but resisted the urge. Maybe after I'd reached home for the night.

The wagon path to the Burns house was, as I expected, southwest of the road. At first I hesitated; I had no desire to explain my mission to someone other than Nora. Miss Burns. I mustn't slip and inappropriately call her by her first name. I hardly knew her.

As I pulled the horse to a halt I heard Robbie's voice close by. I smiled.

This was the place.

"Nora, look! I found new stones for my wall!"

I walked the horse slowly up the pitted drive. Robbie was kneeling and digging with a trowel in the corner of a garden plot perhaps a quarter acre in size; large enough to require a good deal of work, but which probably would provide enough vegetables for at least two people for a year. A wooden plow was propped nearby.

For a moment I didn't see Nora. Then she stood and stretched her arms and back. Her trim figure was outlined clearly under her soft linen bodice and skirt. She'd been weeding some large plants at the other side of the plowed area, and had pulled her long blue skirt up almost a foot and tucked it in at her waist to keep it from being soiled. I inhaled sharply. I couldn't help admiring her lower legs and ankles for the minute or so before she modestly pulled her skirt down.

"See?" Robbie called to her, pointing at three rocks he had dug out of the section where he was loosening soil.

Neither of them noticed me.

"I see," said Nora, walking toward other stones Robbie had piled in a small wagon near the edge of the garden. "Every year we plow the garden and remove the stones, and each year the Lord provides more to keep us from believing our work on earth is done." Despite her having tried to protect them, Nora's long skirts were muddy, and her hands more so. She reached over and helped Robbie lift out the largest of the stones. "We'll take these over to the house so you can put them on your wall while I'm getting dinner. After we've eaten we'll come back and dig some more."

My horse shook herself, and the noise startled Nora. She turned rapidly and looked at us.

"We have company, Robbie." She wiped her hands on her skirt and walked toward me. There was no self-consciousness in her actions, although her hair was disarranged and her attire was clearly marked with mud and sweat. Margaret would never have allowed herself to be seen in that condition. Indeed, I suspected Margaret never *was* in that condition. And yet Nora looked relaxed and natural and unashamed at doing a man's work. Her short hair swung naturally. I wondered why I'd ever admired longer hair, which was normally braided and pinned and inaccessible. I felt an uncommon urge to run my hands through Nora's hair.

Robbie ran toward me, ahead of his sister.

"You came to visit? Did you bring any cakes?" he demanded. "How do you hold the reins with only one hand?"

"I hold them very carefully," I answered as I dismounted. "And, no, I'm afraid I didn't bring any cakes. Maybe I will next time," I added, looking at his sister. "I see you're gardening."

"Yes! I'm digging a space to plant peas, and Nora is weeding rhubarb. Nora makes very good rhubarb pies and puddings."

"I'm sure she does," I agreed.

"Maybe some day she can make one for you," Robbie volunteered.

"Robbie, take your wagon up to the house and work on your wall," Nora said.

"Yes, Nora!" Robbie, released for the moment from digging, ran to get his wagon and then strained to pull it further down the path toward where I assumed their house stood.

"Robbie is building a wall around our house," Nora explained, with a smile. "He would much rather gather stones than loosen soil in the garden for peas. He seems to like you; I'm sure he'll want to show you his wall. But what is the occasion for this visit?"

"Not just a neighborly call, although I wish it were." There were several streaks of dirt across Nora's face. I longed to brush them off with my fingertips, and feel the softness of her skin. She was beautiful, and yet seemed totally unaware of her appearance.

"And so. It is business you have to discuss. I can't offer you much for refreshment but fresh water at the moment; we've been working outside most of the day," said Nora. "But I could really use a long drink. Come with me, and you can tell me the reason for your call as we walk."

"I'm preparing to answer any allegations about Lidia Neilson or her husband. I need to know every possible motivation someone might have had to hurt Jake, no matter how unreasonable it might sound. And I'm making a timeline to show exactly who was with Lidia, from Sunday after she attended church until mid Tuesday afternoon, when Jake's body was found."

Nora continued walking up the path. I followed her, leading my horse and leaving an appropriate distance between us.

"What do you need from me?"

"First, what do you know of Jake Neilson?"

She shook her head. "Very little. I hardly knew Lidia until after Jake had gone to war. I'd seen him in town, of course. Hestia is a small place. But I'd never met him." She looked directly at me. Her gray eyes were wide and clear. "The Neilsons and the Burns family were not exactly in the same social set. And he was much older than

LEA WAIT

I am. I was only seventeen when Jake enlisted. We don't even attend the same church. I'm an Irish girl, Captain Stone."

"But now you and Lidia are friends, despite being different in age and social standing."

She hesitated, but for only a moment. "Women alone find each other, for companionship."

We walked around a corner in the road and I inhaled slightly; certainly I hope Nora didn't hear me. I don't know what I expected. Aunt Cornelia had told me Nora and Robbie were not wealthy. But the building ahead of us was worlds away from either the Neilsons' home, or Aunt Cornelia's.

The small grayed clapboard one-story home was more a shack that a house. The outside walls had been repaired with boards of uneven lengths, and the entire structure could only contain one room, or perhaps two. An iron pump in the yard outside the open door was the water supply, and there were several out buildings. Two of those, a high structure designed for drying hops and a barn, were considerably larger than the house. Chickens were pecking noisily and industriously at the mud that surrounded everything.

Robbie had unloaded his wagon and was trying to balance a new stone on top of a row of rocks perhaps ten feet from the house.

He looked up as we approached him. "It's going to be a beautiful wall, isn't it?" he said. "It was my idea."

"He's been working on it for more than a month now," said Nora, proudly. "He's finished the base of the wall, all around the house, despite the mud. At first every stone he put down sunk."

"The wall will protect us from wolves," Robbie explained. "Wolves won't cross the wall, so we'll be safe inside our house."

Where had he heard about wolves? Why was he worried about them? So far as I knew they were rarely seen in New York State. Bounty hunters had killed most of them years ago. But children live in their own worlds. After I read Cooper's *The Spy* as a boy I remembered hiding in a wardrobe in my parents' bedroom to practice overhearing conversations as a patriot might to provide information about his country's enemies. I also remembered finding the wardrobe stifling and boring after two or three afternoons. Nothing exciting ever happened in my parents' bedroom.

"So far Robbie's wall has worked," Nora agreed, smiling at me. "We haven't been bothered by a single wolf." She raised her voice slightly. "When you finish putting the new stones on the wall, wash your hands and come in, Robbie. I'm going to get us some water."

The boy nodded, and concentrated on putting one stone on top of another and keeping them steady. Clearly, staying safe, and helping others to do so, was important work.

The inside of the small house was tidy, but the most positive word I could think of to describe it was "rustic." The ground floor consisted of one low-ceilinged room, with a ladder leading to a loft above it. An iron stove on the back wall served for both heating and cooking. One table and several chairs were the only furniture other than a low pallet on the side wall. Either Nora and Robbie shared it, or perhaps Robbie slept in the loft. From the outside I'd guess the space near the roof was low, and also served for drying and storing fruits, vegetables and herbs. The rough wood floor had been oiled, and was covered in part by a large braided rug, which I assumed, as with most braided rugs, contained remnants of the clothing of the occupants of the house. No doubt the history of Nora's family was braided into the blue and red and brown fabrics which had been carefully stitched, braided, wound, and then stitched again. Her feet were warmed by the worn clothing of her parents, and perhaps even her grandparents.

Several shelves held clothing, and one was filled with needles, threads, thimbles, bone and brass buttons, and floss of various hues.

Tools for the piecework Nora did for the mill.

Some mills just wove bolts of fabric, but one profitable factory in Utica took the process one step further and made ready-to-wear garments. They had been one of the suppliers of uniforms to the Union Army, and so hired as many workers as possible during the war. Seams were stitched on machines at the mill, but more delicate work had to be completed by hand. It was cheaper to let women take piecework home and return it once every week or two. Each completed garment earned pennies that allowed Nora and other women who couldn't leave children or ailing parents a way to buy what they couldn't make or grow.

Pegs near the door held several outdoor garments and a dress I recognized as the one Nora had worn the last two times I had seen her. Next to them was a crudely framed sampler embroidered with wild flowers surrounding the words "Home Sweet Home."

I wondered where their father would sleep, when he returned home. Many of the Irish lived in poor quarters, and I'd certainly seen some of the filthy overcrowded houses at Five Points on the lower east side of New York City. At least everything here was neat and clean, with the exception of the mud that anyone walking in from the yard would bring with them on a spring day such as this one.

While I was doing my best not to stare impolitely at the few furnishings in their home, Nora had pumped cool water, washed her hands and face, filled a pottery pitcher, and poured us each a glass. I sat down on one of the chairs and drank deeply. The coffee and brandy I'd shared with Dr. Litchfield, and the ride since, had left me thirsty, and the water was cool and clear.

"How did you and Lidia Neilson become friends?" I asked.

"We met through your Aunt Cornelia," Nora replied, evenly. "Lidia and I share a love of the earth, and of letting people and plants grow in peace. When we first met Lidia gardened more for beauty than for food, but the war changed that. I was able to help her design a vegetable garden, and she shared some of her flowers with me."

"And you all volunteer at the orphanage."

"Many women and children need friendship and caring. We share in doing what we can to provide for anyone who needs it."

"There are always those in need." I wondered how Nora managed to find time to sew, care for Robbie, grow food for her family, and still help out at the orphanage. Clearly she didn't sleep much. And Robbie had mentioned that she sometimes left at night. I wished I could ask her about that.

"You and Robbie were both at the Neilson home on Monday. The day Jake was killed."

"We were there. Your aunt kindly picked us up in her wagon early in the morning."

"To work on Lidia's garden?"

"In part." Nora put down her glass for a moment, walked to the door, and stood, looking out, her back to me. "Working together increases the chance of making a difference, wouldn't you agree?"

I found myself nodding, although I wasn't sure precisely what I was agreeing to.

She turned toward me, lowering her voice, as though to speak confidentially. "Don't you find being with friends, and working on a joint project, is much more rewarding than anything you can do on your own? That the more people working on a project, the easier it is for all, and the more likely you are to succeed?"

"Of course," I agreed again, without totally understanding. "Aunt Cornelia said she was sewing."

"She did some sewing," Nora agreed. "And we all took turns watching out for Robbie, of course."

"And then Robbie had his nosebleed."

"Yes. He'd been racing about the house, up and down stairs, and

I think he just got too excited. He loves stairs, since we have none here, and in Lidia's house he can run all the way up into the tower. He sometimes plays there, imagining he's a bird who can see everywhere, and fly anywhere."

"Lidia told me she's already washed the cloth used to clean Robbie up."

"Blood stains needs to be soaked as quickly as possible. I believe she did that within an hour of his nosebleed's stopping."

"And you and Robbie spent that night with Lidia, too."

"And with Cornelia. We agreed with you and Dr. Litchfield that Lidia shouldn't be alone."

"So you were there when Sheriff Newell came that evening?"

"I was at the house. But I was trying to get Robbie to sleep. It had been a very exciting day, and he was delighted to find out we were staying the night. He doesn't often sleep anywhere but home. It took him a while to calm down, and I stayed with him. Sheriff Newell had no need to speak with me, in any case."

"No; of course not."

"Come and see my wall!" Robbie called in to us, and we both stood up and walked outside.

He'd managed to balance another twelve or fourteen stones on top of the ones already in his line. I knelt down to take a closer look. "I see you used some mud to hold some of the stones in place."

Robbie nodded. "At Mrs. Neilson's house the walls have dirt in them."

"That was very smart of you to notice."

"Nora says I am very smart," Robbie acknowledged. "Next fall I'm going to school. I'm going to learn to read. Nora says some of the boys at the orphanage will be there, too, so I'll have friends."

"You know the boys at the orphanage?"

"I play at the orphanage when Nora's helping people," Robbie said seriously. "A lot of children are there. My ma's dead and Pa's been away for a long time, so I'm a little like an orphan, too."

I stood up. "I guess you are. But you have Nora."

He nodded. "She tells me what to do just like she was my real ma."

"I suppose she does," I agreed. "You're lucky to have her."

Nora listened from where she'd stopped, several feet outside the door of the house. I looked back at her, expecting her to be smiling, but instead she looked sad. It must be hard for her, I realized. She also missed having a mother and father, and she had full responsibility for an active young brother like Robbie.

"I think it's time I went home, Robbie. I thank you for showing me your wall." I turned and started down the drive toward where I'd left my horse.

"Thank you for stopping in. You're welcome, any time," said Nora.

"And I thank you, for the information and for the water," I replied. I wished I could think of an excuse for me to stay. "Robbie, if you'd like help with your wall, you come and tell me. I'd be happy to come."

"You only have one arm. How could you help?" he asked.

His answer caught me off guard. I flushed, to my embarrassment. "Perhaps I could help pull your wagon for you, if the stones were heavy," I replied.

"Perhaps," he agreed. "I'll remember that."

"Thank you." I looked back at Nora. "And thank you, Miss Burns. I hope to see you again in the near future."

"We are neighbors," she answered; an answer which was obvious, and didn't contain the encouragement I would have liked to hear.

Yet I felt certain we would meet again. In the courthouse, if not before.

Chapter 19

The noise coming from Sheriff Newell's office was enough to discourage anyone wishing to report something as minor as a neighbor's dog chasing their sheep or a vagrant sleeping in a back pew at St. Patricks'. I knew that, because the aggravated owner of the dislocated sheep and the ruddy sexton were descending the brick steps to the entrance of the Hestia Police Force Office as I was ascending them.

"Don't attempt any business in there today," advised one man, as he left.

"Place's mad enough to drive any sane man to the tavern," agreed the second, as they headed in opposite directions on the Syracuse Road.

Curiosity, as well as a need to speak with the sheriff, led me up to the high double carved wood doors. I pushed them open, and immediately understood why the other two men had chosen to deal with their problems without help from the Hestia Police.

Directly in front of me was a desk piled with papers which were being slowly searched by an ancient man with a full beard, a lined face, and an expression that said he had no concern or patience for anyone else in the room. The only one paying attention to him was a man in his twenties, dressed as a laborer, and, evident even from where I stood near the door, reeking of liquor. He was waving a pistol about in a disconcerting fashion, and threatening to, "Shoot all of you! Shoot anyone in this town who's hiding her! Damnit, I want my wife back! Doesn't anyone in Hestia give a damn about the respect a wife should give her husband! My wife is out there somewhere, and nothing's being done!"

"Calm yourself, Jonathan. I'm looking for the report. Put the gun down and take it easy," said the old man behind the desk calmly. "The report you filed is somewhere here."

While this was happening in front of me, on the left side of the room four official-looking men in blue uniforms with silver wreaths on their wide hats were shouting about, "long hours," "no extra pay," and "should have joined the Union forces; at least brothers in arms would commiserate about miserable working conditions!"

At that point Jonathan fired a shot into the ceiling, sending a cloud of plaster chips and dust falling onto the floor next to him. He turned toward the door, and saw me.

"Who the hell are you?"

"Captain Aaron Stone."

"I've never seen you before."

I watched carefully as Jonathan waved his revolver in my direction. "I'm from New York City; I'm staying with Cornelia Livingston."

He stopped for a long moment and walked up to within inches of my face. "You're the one's defending Lidia Neilson, the women that killed her husband in cold blood. If you think so much of women, maybe it's you that's taken my Em'ly. None of these police would think to question a man with money and stature. Where've you got my wife?"

"I don't know your wife." I felt my muscles tightening as I stepped back slightly, partially to escape the alcoholic stink of the man, but more so I could keep his weapon in sight.

"Well, I don't believe you!" The man leaned even closer to me, and spit decisively on my waistcoat.

Without hesitating, my arm shot out and I hit his wrist with my clenched hand, knocking his revolver to the ground.

He looked at it in disbelief. "The cripple thinks he can defend himself!" he cried, just as my right fist hit his chin. He hit my injured shoulder at the same time I smashed into his face. He stumbled backward, covering his eye, and then lunged at me. I was ready; this time I hit him just under the heart, and he went down, hitting the desk as he fell. A rain of papers followed him to the floor.

At that, one of the uniformed officers pulled Jonathan to his feet, grabbed both of the man's wrists, and held them together behind his back. Another officer had already picked up his gun.

"Jonathan North, you're drunk again, and you've become a nuisance."

Jonathan squirmed and tried to free himself, but clearly the alcohol he'd imbibed had not improved his coordination. "My wife! You've got to find Em'ly! That man could be hiding her! He's defending a husband-killer!"

"We've been looking for your wife for almost a week now," said the officer calmly. "As you well know, since you've been enjoying the hospitality of our facilities for most of those evenings." He pushed Jonathan toward the back of the room, where I could see the corner of a cell through an open door. "That man is a lawyer, and so far as I know has never even met your wife. Back with you now, and we'll talk about this after you've had a bit of a nap."

They disappeared through the door into the jail, and one of the other officers, distracted by the excitement, reached down and swept up the fallen papers, replacing them on the desk. "Here, Jones; try to keep your papers off the floor."

The old man nodded, and continued searching his stacks of documents.

The officer turned to me, nodding appreciatively. "Nice work with that right fist."

"Thank you." I felt a rush of pride and energy. I had defeated an able-bodied man. A drunk, no doubt, but a young and able man. "I'm Captain Stone; Mrs. Lidia Neilson's lawyer," I said. "I'm here to request the custody of Jake Neilson's body for burial, and to check on any progress being made in the investigation of his death."

"Yes, sir. We'll help you in any way we can." He looked me up and down, his eyes stopping on my empty sleeve. "You'll excuse the commotion." He gestured toward the area to which the other officer had escorted Jonathan North. "This has been a difficult week, as I'm sure you'll agree. Normally Hestia is a quiet town, with little need for law enforcement. In the past week we've been a bit pressed for resources."

"I heard a young woman disappeared last weekend. I assume the inebriated fellow was her husband?"

"And a nasty drunk he can be, too. Wives do sometimes take off on their own, especially when," the officer lowered his voice a bit, "their husband makes life more difficult than they're ready to handle. They learn, of course, and they do come home. Where else can they go? Usually we don't get involved. But Jonathan's not one to wait patiently. He's ready to kill us all for not finding his woman. And he might kill her, too, for causing him such trouble. We've questioned her friends and relations. No one's seen her. We're watching Dr. Litchfield's office. The young woman's in the family way, and Sheriff Newell is guessing the doctor will be the first to hear if she needs help."

"That makes sense," I agreed.

"Then President Lincoln's being assassinated, that was a tragedy, upsetting to many in town, a number of whom chose to drown their sorrow publicly and then needed assistance in finding their way home. And Jake Neilson's body being found Monday…" The officer shook his head. "A difficult week all around."

"I understand."

He stopped a moment. "Aren't you the one found a skeleton over at the Livingstons'?"

"That's right," I acknowledged. "But that body is from some time ago and not the priority that Mr. Neilson is. Mrs. Neilson would like to see her husband at rest."

"Seems to me someone already saw to that!" he grinned and then, seeing I didn't respond in like humor, added, "You'll have to see Sheriff Newell about the disposition of the body. I'll see if he's available."

I realized the two officers in the corner had been listening, so I nodded to them. "Good day."

"Not such a good one," one of the men said, "Like Frank said, the North woman's gone missing. And last week we heard two of the Loomis brothers were back in town. They've been operating south of here for some time. Aren't many horses left here. Army took all the horseflesh the gang hadn't already absconded with. Now the fighting's over down south, they're no doubt considering other ways of making their fortunes."

Eli, that young man at the Oak Tavern, had said Jake Neilson might be involved with the Loomis gang. "I've heard they're a dangerous bunch," I said.

"Can be, if you get on the wrong side of 'em," said the officer. "And anyone with a uniform is on the wrong side, unless you're their special friend." He patted his pocket. "If you know what I mean."

"Loomis boys have lawyers and judges in those pockets, too," added Frank, the officer I'd spoken with earlier. "Sheriff Newell can talk with you now, Captain Stone. He's back there." He pointed at the side of the building furthest from the cells.

Sheriff Newell's office was almost filled by a wide cherry desk that would have been impressive if it weren't for the ink and coffee stains and assorted gouges and tobacco burns. Stacks of the *Utica Register* and *Harpers Weekly* were piled on the floor next to the desk, and assorted ledgers and papers were scattered over its surface. A large iron evidence safe took up one corner of the room. Two rifles and three revolvers were piled haphazardly on a shelf in back of the desk. Through another door came the constant clicking of a telegraph machine.

"Welcome, Captain Stone. Didn't think I'd have the pleasure of your company again so soon." He sat down heavily and looked at me. "Understand you had a confrontation with one of our local citizens in the outer office. Despite the circumstances, I'd ask you to keep your temper under control. Not all of men in Hestia would be as easy to control."

"Yes, sir. I will," I replied, trying not to smile.

"I assume this visit won't take long. My schedule is full, and I'm certain you have other business to take up your time."

"I'm here, first of all, to obtain the release of Corporal Neilson's body. Dr. Litchfield tells me he's completed the autopsy."

Sheriff Newell paged through several documents on his desk, and then checked one of the ledgers. "You are correct; Dr. Litchfield has completed his examination of the body. So far as I'm concerned we can release the body to you, or to Mrs. Neilson. The only reason we'd hold the body longer would be if the lawyer for the defense – that would be you, correct, Captain Stone?"

"If Mrs. Neilson should be accused of her husband's murder. That has not happened."

"It's been a busy week, Captain Stone. In any case, if the body were released now and subsequently buried, than Dr. Litchfield's analysis would have to stand."

"He is the coroner for Hestia."

"He is. And I won't be telling you how to do your job, Captain Stone. But usually in a murder case the defendant's lawyer wants the body examined by a second doctor. Just to verify findings, you understand." Sheriff Newell's tone implied he was talking to a rank amateur in criminal situations. Which was how I felt.

Why hadn't I thought of obtaining a second medical opinion? My lack of knowledge of criminal law and courtroom procedures was not only clearly evident to me, but, unfortunately, also to this sheriff who was gathering evidence for the prosecutor's office.

"I understand. Of course I'll be contacting a medical authority in Utica to provide such a second opinion. Corporal Neilson's body will be removed from Dr. Litchfield's office within the next twenty-four hours."

"Good," said Sheriff Newell.

"I also wanted to inquire as to whether you've made any progress in tracking the whereabouts of anyone who might have seen Neilson on Sunday or Monday, before his body was found."

"No progress. We haven't had time to speak with the women in Utica and, frankly, I'm not sure of the value of such questioning. If we should establish that Jake had sought female companionship other than his wife's in the forty-eight hours before his death, what would that mean, other than Mrs. Neilson would be shamed? Frankly, I'm not sure what value there would be in finding out about Jake's choice of companions."

"I didn't mean just women. Knowing that anyone had seen him would help establish a time line so we would know when Jake got to Hestia. If he arrived Sunday, at any time, someone would have seen him. The churches were filled on Easter, and many people gathered in the afternoon to discuss Lincoln's assassination. The Syracuse Road, where Jake was found, goes right through Hestia."

"True enough. Although he wasn't found until Monday afternoon he could have traveled in the very early morning, or even at night. A man returning home after three years is bound to speed up when he reaches familiar surroundings."

"So may I assume you're continuing to make inquiries of anyone along the Syracuse Road who might have seen him."

"Yes, Captain Stone. I am. I know how to do my job, even if I don't come from New York City." The sheriff made a note; I suspected he had not yet conducted a thorough search of the twelve miles of the road between Hestia and the Neilsons' home.

"I've also heard Neilson had some contact, a few years back, with the Loomis gang. Perhaps they heard he was returning, and were afraid he would tell what he knew about their business."

"You're trying, Stone, but it won't work. A couple of the Loomis boys are back in the area, but Saturday night they were both arrested by the police in Rome for drunken and lewd behavior. Normally they'd have been released Sunday, but being as it was Easter, and knowing their history, the sheriff there sent news of their capture over the telegraph to everyone in the area, in case anyone else had outstanding warrants. As it turned out, they've just returned north from where they were operating the last couple of years, down near Binghamton, so no one here had active files on them, and they were released late Monday. Too late to be making any trouble for Jake Neilson, even if they were thinking in that direction."

I nodded. The Loomis gang might be hardened criminals, but they weren't guilty of Jake's murder.

"I'm thinking Lidia Neilson does need to get Jake buried and such, and I'll be pulling together my notes on his case early next week. So I'd advise your doctor in Utica to do a fast examination." He scribbled a note and handed the paper to me.

It was permission for Dr. Litchfield to release Jake Neilson's body to my custody. I nodded and stood. "I'll be in touch. Early next week."

Chapter 20

"Katie, you did an excellent job with the lamb tonight." I put my fork down as Katie was clearing the table. "And the rhubarb pudding was delicious." It reminded me of Robbie's declaration that Nora's rhubarb pie was the best. I hoped to test his hypothesis in the near future. Meanwhile, the dinner *had* been significantly better than Katie's usual attempts, and deserving of praise.

"Katie's been studying the copy of *Mrs. Beeton's Household Management* I bought her," said Aunt Cornelia after Katie had left the room. "Imagine an entire book of ways to cook different foods, and what to serve in what season. If there were a book like that for each profession, apprenticeship times could be cut in half! Cooking lamb with bacon, lemon and onions was a method new to me, and well worth learning. But I suspect it's not just Katie's cooking that's improved, Aaron. I think your getting out of the house has improved your appetite."

Perhaps she was right. After seeing Sheriff Newell I'd arranged with a local teamster to move Jake Neilson's body from Dr. Litchfield's office and gone with it to Utica. Instead of asking Dr. Litchfield for a recommendation to one of his medical colleagues, I'd stopped at one of the largest law firms in the city. Perhaps a bit surprised at my arrival, the firm of Bittern and Stock had recommended the services of coroner Dr. Abraham Weissman. Dr. Weissman now had custody of Jake's body, with the promise to have a second autopsy completed by Monday.

I'd then traveled back to Hestia and on to the Neilsons', where I'd promised Lidia she would have her husband's body by Monday afternoon and left her planning a service and burial for Tuesday.

I was exhausted, but pleased to have accomplished so much in one day.

While I'd been in Utica I'd obtained copies of newspapers from as far away as Albany. After the supper dishes were cleared Aunt Cornelia and I spread the papers out on the dining table. Getting caught up with national news had not been a priority in recent days, and we were both eager to find out what was happening in the world outside of Hestia.

Lincoln's killer was still at large, we read, although the Secret Service and the Army appeared in close pursuit. The assassin was assumed to be John Wilkes Booth, brother of the acclaimed actor Edwin Booth, whom I'd seen in New York City only the previous November in *Hamlet;* critics had called his performance there the definitive depiction of Shakespeare's most challenging role, and I'd agreed. That such a talented actor would have a traitor for a brother was both horrifying and fascinating, and by the number of articles in each of the papers I could see that the American public agreed. The assassin was said to be hiding near the Virginia-Maryland border, an area he'd been familiar with since childhood. I considered that particularly ironic, since so many of the bloody battles of the war had been fought near there.

"Aunt Cornelia, how do you think it happens that a family can produce two such different sons?"

"It's mysterious, isn't it," she agreed. "In the case of the Booths, of course, the whole family were actors, so they grew up in the theatre. Edwin became a great actor, perhaps the greatest. I'm sure he exceeded his family's highest expectations. John, on the other hand, was clearly less adept, and began dabbling in politics. It can't be chance that his attempt to take the president's life took place in a theatre. Perhaps he saw the assassination of Lincoln as his greatest role. Not even his famous brother got the attention John has now attained through notoriety. From the articles we've read, it appears he didn't attempt to disguise himself during the actual assassination, even if he is in hiding now."

"You're right. He wanted people to know he was responsible for killing the president. Perhaps he even saw the act as something to be proud of."

"We all see the world through different eyes. Even if we grow up in similar families, in similar places, our experiences are never the same."

"And yet in some families the generations follow the same occupation. The Loomis family, about whom I've been hearing this week, are criminals. The Booths are actors. My father is a lawyer, and so am I."

"All true. And yet you and your father may not practice the same kind of law. Edwin and John Booth certainly will be both be remembered, but for acting out very different scenes."

That April evening was a pleasant one. The spring light lingered until almost eight o'clock, and I enjoyed being able to see outside rather than being limited by the artificial light of an oil lamp or lantern. In the distance we could hear the vibratos of spring peepers calling to their mates. Katie brought us additional coffee, and, although I wished I could add a bit of brandy to mine, I did not mention the idea. Despite her surprising call for cognac last Saturday morning, I knew my aunt was a temperance society member.

"Aunt Cornelia, I still don't understand why you rose so early last

Monday, went to the Burns house to get Nora and Robbie, and then went to Lidia Neilson's home."

"I told you, we were doing some sewing."

"Yes. And Nora told me she and Lidia discussed gardening. But why leave before dawn to begin such activities? Sewing can hardly be done until the sun is up, and certainly discussion of gardening does not need to happen before dawn."

"There are differences between men and women, Aaron. We women don't expect you to understand our purposes, any more than I can understand why so many young men ended Wednesday's parade at the tavern. Or in the town jail, sleeping off their indulgences."

"And in most circumstances I would not question you, Aunt Cornelia, nor the actions of any woman. You're right. I do not fully appreciate many interests or activities of the gentler sex. But when I'm trying to gather information to defend someone accused of murder, I need to know as much as possible about her, and her friends and family as I can. I need to have a comprehensive view of who she is, and why she might or might not have murdered her husband."

Aunt Cornelia hesitated only a moment before replaying. "Lidia, Nora and I often work together, to help women and children."

"You volunteer at the orphanage."

"Yes. And sometimes our work, or our planning for that work, takes us to other places. We need to talk quietly, to assess needs, and make decisions as to what we can do that will most benefit those we would like to help."

"So you have meetings, like the one I interrupted when you were at the orphanage last week."

"Correct. And sometimes it's difficult to plan times we can be together. Nora has her piecework to do for the mill, Robbie to care for, and must grow and prepare all the food for their home. Lidia has had only herself to rely on to support her home and gardens. I am blessed with monetary resources, and Owen and Katie, and now you, to depend on, so my time is more flexible than theirs. We often meet at hours others may think odd, but that fit all of our schedules best."

"I see." I didn't see. I'd spoken with Lidia Neilson, Nora Burns, and now with Aunt Cornelia, who had always, so far as I knew, been open and honest with me. While each woman had answered my questions, and none had contradicted each other, I still felt I did not truly know what had brought them together as friends. And, specifically, I did not know what they had been doing at the Neilson's home on the day Jake Neilson was murdered.

I shook my head slightly and smiled at myself. I was a man. Clearly I did not understand the situation completely. It was no doubt something innocent; something that might have been very clear if I'd spent my childhood years with miniature tea sets and dolls and embroidery needles instead of with trains and toy soldiers and blocks. Or, I amended, if I'd spent time at the temperance and social reform and abolitionist meetings I knew Aunt Cornelia, and quite possibly her friends, had attended in the past.

"I'm getting weary," Aunt Cornelia announced. "I believe I'll go upstairs now. I shall see you in the morning."

I stood up as she left. "I'll finish my coffee, and perhaps look at the Binghamton paper."

In the ten days since Owen had found the skeleton in the north field my life had changed completely. For the first time since the Wilderness Campaign, I was of use to others. I had a purpose.

Chapter 21

Saturday morning Aunt Cornelia and I were enjoying a bit of toast and sliced cold lamb from the evening before when the bell by the front door began ringing. Since we weren't expecting guests, and Katie was in the kitchen, far from the front of the house, I went to see who it was.

"Captain Stone! Has anyone here seen Robbie?" Nora Burns stood on our piazza, her blue skirt damp and torn in two places and her hair disheveled.

"I haven't; I'll check with Owen and Katie," I answered. "What's wrong? Come in."

"When I woke up this morning he was gone," Nora explained. Aunt Cornelia joined us, waved Nora into the dining room and poured her a cup of coffee.

"Thank you, Cornelia," Nora answered, taking a fast sip of the hot beverage. "Robbie's been missing at least two hours. I can't think where he's gone to. I've checked every inch of our property, and thought he might have come here for some reason. Perhaps to ask Captain Stone's help with his wall."

"I saw Robbie in our north field about a week ago," I said. "It was early in the morning. Maybe he's gone there again. I'll check."

Nora looked at me. "And you didn't tell me?"

"He seemed fine. He headed home after we'd chatted a bit."

Nora looked at me in dismayed anger.

Aunt Cornelia interrupted. "Nora, you come with me. We'll get Katie and Owen and search all the buildings here. There are lots of places a small boy could hide."

"But why?" Nora's tears were brimming. "Why would he run away?"

"Did you argue?"

"Robbie wanted to work on his wall last night, and I wanted him to get to sleep. He was mad at me, but there was no reason for him to run away!"

"He may not have run away; he may just have wandered. Young boys do that. Aaron, go over to the north field and look near where you saw Robbie before."

"I'll check the path between his house and the field," I said, pulling on a light jacket.

"You know the path between our house and the north field?" Nora spoke quietly, but there was another tone in her voice.

"Robbie took it the couple of times I've seen him there."

"You've seen him in the field more than once, then?"

"Twice, actually. He was fine, both times. I'm going to look now, and I'll meet you back here." I hesitated a moment. "If you find him, ring one of the cowbells in the barn. The sound will tell me I needn't search further."

I left Aunt Cornelia explaining the situation to Katie; with four people searching I had no doubt they'd be able to check all the Livingston buildings.

Why had Nora been upset that I knew about the path? It had probably been there since her father had rented the field for hops growing. Over the past four years it had grown over, so was harder to find, but even in the past it would have only been wide enough for a narrow cart.

I pushed brambles out of my way as I headed toward the field. The path on our property hadn't been kept up either. All too quickly nature took over what people had cultivated or trimmed. The Wilderness had been damp and overgrown and muddy, a little like this, but with more grasses and low bushes. Here trees had forced the lower foliage out by cutting off the light. Spring was taking its time, but even in the week since I'd walked this path the budding leaves had begun to open and the grasses were a lighter, brighter, green. I stumbled on a rock. Perhaps that was why Robbie had wandered. He hadn't run away. He was searching for rocks for his wall.

I hesitated; maybe I should pick that one up. But it would be difficult to balance with one hand; better to find Robbie and then tell him about it. Maybe we could get the rock together, later. I smiled to myself. Robbie and his wall to keep out wolves!

I stood on a stump at the edge of the field and looked over the field. The wind had dried the land somewhat in the past week. It wasn't the quagmire it had been when we'd removed the body. But my boots were already wet through. I should have asked Katie to put another layer of tallow on them after they'd been soaked. "Robbie!" I called, "Robbie! Are you out here?"

Could he have fallen? Hit his head? He was only four, after all.

I walked down the center of the field, calling his name every few minutes. The canal was at the end of the field; I didn't want to think about that danger to a small boy.

I followed the tracks we'd made with the wagon, heading toward where Robbie had known the bones were buried, trying to avoid stepping on the remains of the dead animals I'd noted last week. A vulture circled overhead. I hoped he was only preying on dead animals.

"Robbie!" The boy must be here; I felt it. And yet if he could hear my voice, why didn't he answer? He might be angry with his sister, but that hadn't anything to do with me.

I crisscrossed the field several times, trampling grasses and branches and the detritus of the flooding, and then decided to follow the path to the Burns home. Perhaps Robbie had become hungry or thirsty and had already returned home.

It appeared no one but Robbie had followed that trail for several years; it was more overgrown than the path from our house to the field. The boy had probably climbed over the fallen branches or even gone under them. I found the way more difficult to navigate. Most days I felt quite comfortable; proud, in fact, of all I could manage with only one arm. But moments like this reminded me I was not as capable of physical work as I'd been before the amputation, despite the blows I'd managed to deliver at the police station. I determinedly pushed branches out of my way with my right arm, and kept calling.

"Robbie! This is Captain Stone!"

The only answer was the occasional mocking caw of a crow, or the blurred sound of the wings of a startled song sparrow or purple finch.

To my left the sun shone through empty branches onto a willow tree blown down by winter storms; its roots were exposed, and raised into the light.

"Robbie! Robbie!"

The path ended at the main road, almost directly opposite the narrow drive to the Burns' home. I started to run.

"Robbie!"

I was sure I'd find him at any moment. Most likely he was sitting on the granite horse block outside his house wondering where his sister was, and why she hadn't prepared breakfast for him. Or he'd wandered into the woods to find new rocks for his wall, and had already returned with them.

But the horse block was empty, and a quick look around the small house proved Robbie was not working on his wall, although I did note he'd added several dozen rocks to it since I'd last seen him.

The door to the house had been left open, no doubt in Nora's frightened search. She'd also left doors to the other buildings open, so I decided to check them, too.

"Robbie! Where are you!"

The barn contained only two stalls and a pile of winter hay not yet consumed. Chickens squawked as I ran through them to check the privy; it was empty. Nora's horse was in a small fenced area connected to the barn, and didn't look concerned about her missing master or mistress.

The woodshed must also have housed Mr. Burns' workroom; it contained a workbench with a number of tools neatly cleaned and organized on the wall around it. Axes, saws, shovels, and garden tools stored on the opposite wall all appeared in order. There were no wardrobes or smaller rooms where anyone could hide, although half the building was designed to store dry wood for the winter. Perhaps when it filled the room it could have fallen on a small boy. But this was April, and although the sweet smell of dried wood was still strong, the pile of maple, birch, and beech wood that would have fed the stove all winter was almost gone. This was the time of year to fell trees and start drying wood for next winter.

The only other out building was the newest of the group: an oasthouse, a two story structure designed for drying hops. Mr. Burns had rented Uncle Henry's field to grow hops - he would have needed an oasthouse. Inside the building I could still smell the peppery aroma of hops dried here before they were taken to market in Utica or Rome.

The building was clean, and showed no trace of the hops that had no doubt supported this family, as they supported many New York State families. I was about to leave when I noticed a shadow near the back wall that seemed to be coming from a space where there were no windows, in back of the press.

I walked toward the corner. The back wall did not touch the side wall. When I pushed, the back wall easily slid sideways, revealing a small, hidden, room.

I stood for a moment and looked, not sure what I was seeing. Inside were a half dozen sleeping pallets, two of them on the floor, and others stacked in the corner. An empty tin pitcher and glasses were on a low table with two traveling lanterns filled with oil. A pile of blankets and quilts lay on the corner of one of the pallets, bandages and liniments were arranged on a shelf on the far wall, and an assortment of old garments hung on pegs near the door. A covered chamber pot was in the corner opposite the pallets.

The room was not decorated in any conventional way, but someone had drawn a topographical map of central New York State on one wall. It detailed the roads from Utica to Syracuse, including the Erie Canal, Oneida Lake, the Oswego Canal and Lake Ontario.

The air in the room was stuffy, as though it had been closed off for a long time. It had no windows. Perhaps Nora had moved the door slightly while she was looking for her brother, and then not closed it tightly again. If the entrance had been closed this room would have been invisible.

I closed the door; whatever the purpose of the room, it was clearly not meant to be seen.

I headed back down the path to the road, and then to the north field. Had anyone found Robbie? I hadn't checked the most dangerous spot of all.

The canal.

Chapter 22

I don't remember how I got back to the north field; I must have pushed myself over and through prickles and thistles and branches I'd been careful to avoid on the way toward the Burns' house, because my shirt was torn and my hand bleeding by the time I reached the field.

I called again. "Robbie!"

Then I ran toward the canal.

Although most said the Erie Canal bordered the Livingston property, that wasn't entirely accurate. The north field was surrounded by the often-repaired snake rail fencing Uncle Henry put up years ago, when traffic on the canal was at its peak. This stretch of the canal, from Utica to Rome, had been one of the first completed, in 1819. The zigzagged fence railing was not just to mark the border between the state-owned property next to the canal from private property. It also provided a barrier should canalers try to stop in an area not designated as a loading site.

Which they had quite possibly done if the body in the north field had come from the canal.

As a boy I'd watched the draft horses clop-clopping their slow way along the towpath on the side of the canal, pulling the barges, which carried freight, and the packets, which carried passengers.

Families lived on the canal boats; men and women and children, rough folks who coped with every sort of element, natural and human, and whose jobs were never done. Once they'd reached the end of the canal at Albany or Lake Erie they turned around and went back. I used to envy boys lucky enough to drive horses along the towpath. The adventures they must have had! Living on New York City's Gramercy Park seemed very dull compared to a world where you met trappers and traders and horse thieves. Beef, lumber, wool and flour went east; settlers went west. Gamblers, merchants, politicians, peddlers, and travelers of all sorts went in both directions.

The days I remembered were in the late thirties and early forties, when the canal had already passed its peak; the steam railroad at Albany had headed west in 1831 and after that few people wanted to be slowed down by traveling on a crowded and old-fashioned packet boat. The canal had been widened to forty feet to allow more traffic, but now scows and barges were pulled by mules, not by horses. The Army had needed the north's horses.

Fencing near the canal had been heavily damaged by the spring's flooding; it would be one of the first things on the list for repair when we were able to hire some men. But since the waters had taken most of the fence down, and in some places totally removed, I had no problem getting through to the towpath.

Robbie would have had no problem either. My mind pictured him slipping into the canal; stretching to hold on to the soft earth that made up the sides; calling for help that didn't come; sinking lower; unable to swim or catch his breath. I imagined his small body floating, mixed with the flotsam and jetsam that was a part of the stinking canal waters.

My heart beat faster. How could parents stand losing a child? How would Nora deal with losing her brother? "Robbie!" I looked up and down the ten-foot wide path. Most of the potholes and rocks created by winter storms and spring thaws had been filled in and tramped down; canal traffic had to move, and no one wanted their mule or driver to break a leg or slip from the towpath to the canal.

How could I return to Nora without Robbie?

"Robbie!" No one was in sight, and no traffic was on the canal right now. I walked for perhaps fifteen minutes in each direction on the curving path, calling out for the boy, and looking for any change in the wall of the towpath that would indicate someone had slipped into the water. The only sign of life was a muskrat who watched me for a long moment, and then dove below the surface of the canal.

Nothing indicated a boy had been there.

Finally I climbed back through the fence into our field and headed toward the house. I'd been gone at least an hour. Maybe Nora had already found Robbie, and I'd been too far away to hear the cowbell.

I called one more time. "Robbie!

"Captain Stone! Captain Stone!"

I turned, and there, to my incredible relief, was Robbie, crawling through the fence from the towpath in back of me. "Robbie!" I ran toward him and, to both our surprise, swept him up in my arm and hugged him. "Where have you been? Your sister has been so worried about you. And so have I."

"I was having an adventure! I couldn't sleep, so I came to the field to see if I could find any more bodies, but I didn't find any. And then I heard voices, so I went down to the canal to look. There were two boys there, bigger than me, and they had a mule that was pulling a boat!" Robbie looked at me as though he had just seen a unicorn.

"The mule was really big! His name was Sam. I followed the boys and Sam and the boys said I could have a ride on the mule, for just a little while. I was on top of Sam! And we were pulling the boat, right along in the water! I was so high off the ground! I could see everything! I was as tall as the trees!"

Robbie took a breath. "But then the boys' dad called out from the boat and said they'd better get me down from there. I slipped a little, the mule was so wet. He'd been sweating, the boys said, because I was so heavy. And then I ran back and here I am!" Robbie looked up at me and grinned. "I'm back!"

"So you are," I replied, holding his hand tightly. "Thank goodness. And now we have to find your sister and tell her all about that adventure. She was very worried about you, Robbie."

"But I'm fine!" he said, hopping along next to me as I hurried us both back toward the house. "I'd like to see those boys again. One was named Isaac and one was Ben. They live on a boat on the canal!"

"I'm sure they were fine boys," I answered, thinking of my own brother Ben, who'd died when he was twelve. "But you can't just run off and not tell anyone where you've gone."

We made it through the path back to our barnyard in faster time than I'd thought possible. "Nora! Aunt Cornelia!" I called out!

"I'm back!" yelled Robbie.

Within minutes Robbie was being swept up by his sister and covered with kisses and hugs. Aunt Cornelia and Katie and Owen all looked greatly relieved. They'd searched our house from attic to cellar and then had done likewise with all the buildings, and with the south field, which had had been left fallow, but not flooded.

Katie made a platter of lamb slices and cheeses and slices of bread and poured a tall glass of milk, and we all settled around the large pine kitchen table where Robbie gulped the milk between telling his sister and my aunt all about his adventure.

I sat back and watched them, as they moved from scared to horrified, to delighted with Robbie's explanation of his "'venture", both trying very hard to be stern with him. Robbie's red hair bounced, and his face was smudged with dirt, but he gobbled the lamb and cheese and bread and clearly loved the attention he was getting.

Then, gradually, he began to slow down. All of a sudden he went over to Nora's chair and climbed on her lap, snuggled in, and fell asleep. For a moment I envied his comfort with her.

"Why don't we put him on the bed in my room?" suggested Katie, who'd been listening from a corner of the kitchen. "It's just off the kitchen, and you'll be able to hear him should he make any noise."

Nora stood up, cradling Robbie, and followed Katie into the small room.

"I'll make you up some tea and buttered bread, to go with what young Robbie's left," Katie organized when she returned, wiping up the crumbs from Robbie's meal. "Go on into the dining room. and I'll bring in plates and napkins and such soon enough."

Amused at Katie's taking charge, Aunt Cornelia and I allowed ourselves to be dispatched. Our coffee cups were still sitting on the table from our interrupted breakfast, although Katie made short work of switching them to thin white porcelain tea cups decorated with gold rims, including one for Nora, and adding matching plates and napkins. By the time Nora joined us in the dining room water for tea was boiling on the stove and we were set for a simple nooning meal after an unexpectedly exhausting morning.

"Robbie's asleep," said Nora. "Thank you both again for everything. I don't know what I would have done if Robbie hadn't returned."

Her eyes were full as she looked from one of us to the other.

Aunt Cornelia reached over and patted her hand. "Now then, you eat, and by the time Robbie wakes you'll both be ready to go home and have some quiet time. What a day you've had, for sure!"

"Nora," I said without thinking, for I had called her that in my mind, "I mean, Miss Burns."

"Nora, for sure it is," she answered. "After all you've done. In public it can be Miss Burns, for courtesy's sake. But here, Nora will do fine."

"Thank you," I looked at her red hair, gleaming in the sun that shone through the windows, and so like Robbie's, and I wished she could stay here, and not go back to that ramshackle home where she had to pull a living out of the ground and do piecework for a mill. "And if we are friends, I hope you won't mind my asking you something."

"Cornelia, your nephew here seems a nice enough sort, but have you noticed he always has a question or two to ask." Nora shook her head, but her eyes were bright.

"He does. You're right," said Aunt Cornelia. "But there's no law says you have to answer them all, you know."

"You might as well ask, then, and I'll decide whether your question is worth answering, Captain Stone," Nora said. For the first time I sensed she was flirting with me, and I hoped my questions wouldn't spoil the mood. But I was too curious not to ask.

"It's Aaron, please, if I may call you Nora. This morning, when I was looking for Robbie, I took the path from our north field to your home, to see if he'd returned there, or had fallen along the way. When I was at your home, I noticed you'd left the doors of your outbuildings open, so I checked them, too, to be sure your young man wasn't hiding anywhere."

Aunt Cornelia put down her cup of tea.

"I can understand your doing so," said Nora. "When a child is missing the normal rules of privacy can be ignored, I think."

"Thank you for saying that. Because I saw something I didn't understand, and I have a suspicion it was not intended to be seen."

At that Nora also put down her cup, and her open smile became more cautious. "And what would that have been?"

"A room hidden behind a sliding wall in your oasthouse," I said. "It was partially open, and I looked in."

No one said anything.

"I suspected it was a private area, so I slid the door closed tightly before I left," I assured her. "But I wondered – who lives in that room? Or, in any case, lived there?"

Aunt Cornelia was the one to break the silence. "Nora, it's time. We have to share some of our secrets with Aaron." She stood up. "Why don't you both come with me?"

Chapter 23

"Are you sure? After all this time? We've been so careful." Nora looked at Aunt Cornelia doubtfully.

"He's my nephew, and he's defending Lidia. We'll just tell him what our families used to do. It's better Aaron know than that he question. Or that he question the wrong person, in the wrong place."

Nora nodded hesitantly.

We followed Aunt Cornelia through the kitchen, where Katie was checking a bubbling pot, and out the back door. I assumed my aunt was looking for a place we wouldn't be overheard, but I had no idea why.

Outside, Aunt Cornelia spoke softly, but firmly. "Owen went into town to get some supplies after we all knew Robbie was safe, so we don't have to worry about him." She walked casually, pointing out the new sprouts of grasses, and a few spring flowers by the buildings, but gradually led us around the barn, and past two other out buildings, and then back toward the house, walking toward the far side of the house, not the back. If Katie had been watching us from the kitchen windows we were now out of her sight.

Aunt Cornelia glanced around, and then turned and walked straight back toward the north side of the house, where a bulkhead door led to the root cellar. What was all this secrecy about a root cellar? All families had them. She took a key from her pocket and unlocked, and then threw open the door of the bulkhead. Nora and I followed her down the steps. At the bottom, she lit a lantern from a match in the tinderbox next to it.

The room was as I remembered it from my childhood, although the space was emptier than it had been when I'd helped carry barrels of apples and potatoes down the stairs during summers fifteen years before. Now it was April, and the room awaited food from the coming season's harvest. A few braids of onions and garlic still hung from the low ceiling next to now-sparse bunches of herbs, and stalks of dried shell beans. The west side of the room was edged by bins of sand storing turnips, parsnips, beets and carrots. Shelves of squashes, cabbages, and pumpkins were in the back. Several covered barrels in the corner reminded me that salted pork and beef were also stored for the winter, and a hogshead of molasses was next to them. Boxes of walnuts would be somewhere on a shelf, and knitted bags of dried berries. The Livingston home was close enough to the village so before the war some supplies had been purchased, but I assumed that recently few had been available. No matter the year, in winter months transportation was uncertain and even families in town stored enough food for their households for weeks, if not months.

A startled field mouse scurried across the floor in front of us.

Why had Aunt Cornelia brought Nora and I to an area common to all country homes? Why was this a secret? Why, indeed, would any room be a secret?

But what was the hidden room in the Burns' oasthouse?

Aunt Cornelia walked in back of some of the crude shelving holding vegetables and called softly, "Nora! Help me?"

I followed them and watched as the two women moved a pile of empty wooden crates stacked loosely in a corner of the room. The slats were far enough apart to allow air to reach stored vegetables or fruit; now the crates were littered with leaves and stems that showed they'd been used for produce during the past winter and were awaiting this year's produce.

"I can help with that," I said without thinking, but then realized I couldn't move the crates on my own. They were large and heavy enough to require two arms.

"I've done this many times, Aaron," said Aunt Cornelia. "It makes less noise to lift the crates than drag them. If we do it this way we ensure no one inside the house can hear. Henry and I tested it several times over the years."

Her words didn't ease my embarrassment. Such a simple physical task, and I couldn't help. The two women quickly and quietly moved perhaps a dozen crates, while my frustration mounted. Clearly they were involved in activities of which I was unaware … activities they hadn't felt comfortable sharing with me, at least until now. And it wasn't something just the women had done. Uncle Henry had also been involved.

Was it my disability that had kept them from telling me? Did they realize I would be of no help, so they had protected my pride by not letting me know?

My mind tumbled with anger and outrage. "Isn't there anything I can help with? If I can't be a part of whatever this is we're doing, why tell me?"

Nora shook her head at me and frowned. "If we didn't trust you, you wouldn't be here now."

"There are only three people in New York State who know about this room," Aunt Cornelia said quietly, pushing on a wall of empty shelves that had been hidden by the crates. "The three of us standing here. Henry knew, but he's gone. And Nora's right. We didn't have to show you."

She picked up her lantern and held it in front of her.

In back of the shelves was a room similar to the one I'd seen at the Burns home. A stack of pallets. Bedding. A table with a lantern and pitcher. A bucket. A chamber pot. And wall pegs draped with men's and women's clothing.

Aunt Cornelia let me look for a moment and then silently moved the wall back in place. She and Nora quickly replaced the empty crates. Within a minute or two there was no sign of the room concealed in the corner of the root cellar.

She blew the wick of the lantern out, and we walked back outdoors, closing the heavy wooden bulkhead door in back of us and locking it.

No one said anything. Aunt Cornelia removed a small kitchen knife from her pocket and cut several branches from a nearby bush. When we reached the kitchen she handed them to Katie. "I needed to stretch a bit, so we've been walking about the yard. I've picked some forsythia; would you put it in some water for me? It should bloom within a few days."

"Certainly, Mrs. Livingston," Katie smiled. "Yellow's the color of spring, for sure. Robbie's still sleeping soundly. Haven't heard a peep from the lad."

We sat in silence in the parlor for a few minutes. These two women had entrusted me with information. But I didn't understand what I'd been shown. Clearly, it was very important to them. Neither Nora nor Aunt Cornelia were smiling, and I sensed they were nervous about my reaction.

Was I too simple to understand? There were hidden rooms at both the Burns house and here. Rooms these two women felt kept deep secrets. Rooms that did not appear to have been used recently, but which could be quickly utilized. Rooms that had been created, concealed, and maintained for some purpose unknown to me.

"Aaron, do you understand what we've showed you?"

"I've seen hidden rooms in both of your homes. But, I confess, I don't know their purpose."

Nora and Aunt Cornelia exchanged looks.

Aunt Cornelia was the one to answer, her voice low. "We in central New York State are proud to live in a part of our nation which has always been open to innovative thinking. One of the first conferences supporting women's rights was held in Seneca Falls, almost twenty years ago. Temperance societies are active throughout upstate New York, and have been since early in the century. Religions have started here – Joseph Smith founded the Church of the Latter Day Saints in Fayette. The Perfectionists are headquartered not far away, in Oneida. The Adventists began here. The Fox Sisters, the first of the spiritualists, came from Rochester. Many supporters of John Brown were from this area."

"Northern and central New York State have long been known as locations where free thinkers were common, and often welcome," I agreed. "But what has that to do with what you've showed me today?"

"You've always known that Uncle Henry and I were abolitionists, have you not?"

Suddenly it all fell into place. "You and Uncle Henry – and your family, Nora – provided safe houses. Secret rooms. For escaping slaves?"

"Exactly," said Aunt Cornelia. "Located along the canal, as we were, we were close to many people needing help. Some were traveling in ones, or twos; others in small groups. Most were heading north and west, toward Canada. We worked with other abolitionists to help them reach Oneida Lake, and then on to Lake Ontario, where there were ways to get across to freedom. Some helped on the canal; others on land."

"And you did this, despite the penalties that you would have paid under the conditions of the Fugitive Slave Act if anyone had known?"

"We did," Aunt Cornelia continued. "It was the right thing to do. Over the years we were successful in helping many. But we always kept our identities a secret. Henry and I knew about the Burns' room, and they ours. And Henry and I knew of a house owned by an African family in Utica that was safe, and a canaler who would hide one or two people on his line boat. But those were the only contacts we knew. We sent people on one step at a time." She hesitated. "Not everyone wanted to help those escaping their masters. A family in Rome was burned in their home for helping. The fewer people who knew those involved the better."

"But since January 1, 1863, when the Emancipation Proclamation was made law, there has been no need for such escape routes," I put in.

"And we're all thankful for that, praise the Lord and President Lincoln, and all of you who fought for the Union. But the rooms you've seen today remain secret, since there are still those who, despite the laws, blame slaves for the war, and are angry with those of us who helped them. Many of those Americans, especially the immigrant Irish, fear freed blacks will take their jobs, and resent those of us who help the slaves."

"Not all of us Irish feel that way," Nora assured me quickly. But it's best if we keep our secrets, as we always have."

"And now you will do so as well," said Aunt Cornelia.

That was a command; not a question. But I had no reason to betray their confidence. I agreed readily, as I looked from one of the women to the other. "I'm very proud to know you both. Nora, I assume your father built your safe room?"

"He did," Nora answered. "Back in the early fifties, about the time life was getting worse for many. I was Robbie's age then, so I don't remember much about building them, except that sometimes I wasn't allowed into the oasthouse. When I was older I brought food to some of our guests, washed their clothes and aired their bedding when there was enough time, and listened to their stories. I'll never forget taking warm water to a girl about my age – perhaps twelve – whose back was a web of raised scars. Her name was Cilla. She told me one night she'd refused to tell her owner where her mother was. The man had raped and beaten her." Nora looked down, and her voice shook as she remembered. "Later her mother was sold. Cilla and her father had traveled north from Virginia. They were trying to get to Canada." She looked at both of us. "I think of her often. I hope she made it."

Aunt Cornelia reached out and touched Nora's hand. "It wasn't easy, hearing the stories. But it reminded us how important the work was. Those people had the courage to journey this far, risking their lives for their hope of freedom. Henry and I built our cellar room back in 1845. It was here when you visited as a boy, Aaron. It was a project Henry and I shared; something we both believed in and did together. There were moments when it was frightening, but one of the mainstays of our marriage was our fight for a way of life we both believed in." Aunt Cornelia smiled.

"Not all battles are between soldiers," Nora added. "And not all wars have been won. That is why we continue trying to help women and children who have been victims."

"Victims of the war, yes," Aunt Cornelia added quickly. "Many tragedies have occurred because husbands and fathers were not there to help. Women have been left with no money to pay mortgages; farms have failed; children have been left fatherless. The past is always with us."

"And that's the work that you do at the Bradford Asylum," I said. "Of course. All part of the same active caring you've been doing for years. I'm honored to know both of you ladies. I'm impressed with what you have done, and are doing."

"You're helping too, said Aunt Cornelia. "By helping Lidia. Because she is one of us."

"Did she also shelter fugitive slaves?" I asked.

There was a pause. "No; Lidia never sheltered slaves. But she works with us now."

Chapter 24

After learning about the safe rooms, and the dangerous work done by Aunt Cornelia and even by a gentle young woman like Nora Burns, I spent Sunday thinking about the many tasks I could no longer complete alone, and generally feeling useless and full of renewed self-pity. I didn't help the feeling by telling Aunt Cornelia I hadn't slept and didn't feel well enough to attend church. She was sympathetic, had Katie bring me tea and toast, and said she'd pray for me. I most likely needed those prayers. I stayed home and followed the tea by injecting a larger dose of morphine than I was used to.

My afternoon was spent partially in dozing, floating above my room and imagining myself able to do anything, from moving rocks for Robbie to saving whole families of slaves, to making love to an unending line of beautiful women. None of those activities, of course, hinted at the reality that I was still without one arm, and would continue to be so. My anger would rise through my visions, like a wooden raft rising through tumultuous seas. I could not tie it down, or stop it. No matter how helpful or courageous or adventurous I might be, I could not replace that arm, in my eyes, nor in the eyes of anyone else.

I was angry at the war, which had taken so much from me, and at myself, for setting my dreams so much higher than my damaged body's current state would allow me to achieve, and at Aunt Cornelia and Nora, because they'd accomplished so much, even though they were only women.

I refused dinner, even knowing that made me appear as rational as a sulking child to Aunt Cornelia, but I could not face her. She'd risked her life to save the lives of others. She treated her accomplishment with calm and serenity. As did Nora Burns. And they both took for granted that their courage could change at least parts of the world.

I could not move a single empty crate.

How could a capable and independent woman like Nora ever care about a disabled incompetent?

I took more morphine Sunday night, and suffered for it. I spent the night back in that Army hospital, where a nurse who looked like Nora cared for me. The ground under the cots in the tent were running with blood, and every few minutes Nora would raise her blood soaked skirt and petticoat so that I could see her tempting legs and thighs, as she wrung the blood out. Somewhere outside the tent I heard Richard laughing, and my father telling me to get off my cot and start acting like a man. Everywhere I looked the faces I saw were of comrades who'd died in arms.

By Monday morning I'd endured hours of sweating and nightmares, my eyes were red, and my stomach was twisting as though I'd swallowed a snake.

Nevertheless I forced myself to get out of my room. I'd committed myself. I had to go to Utica to get the results of Jake Neilson's autopsy, and then take his body to his widow.

Fortified with coffee, plain toast, and several opium tablets, and with Owen's help in harnessing the horse to the farm wagon, I started glumly on the twelve miles to Utica. By the time I'd reached the outskirts of town I'd pulled myself together enough to detour around

Slaughterhouse Basin, for my stomach's sake, and took the most direct route – Lafayette Street and Bleecker Street, and then past the Court House, around Chanceller Square, and on to Dr. Weissman's office.

True to his word, he saw me immediately.

"Captain Stone," he said, ushering me into a small dark room lit by two oil lamps. "I thank you for the opportunity to examine Corporal Neilson's body. I assume you'll want a formal report written up for possible use in court?"

Two framed certificates hung on the wall over his desk. One proclaimed that Dr. Abraham Weissman was a member of the New York State Medical Society, and another that he was a member of the American Medical Society. I wondered why I hadn't seen similar declarations on Dr. Litchfield's walls. "Yes; thank you. Although I might also have to call you to testify," I warned him.

"Murder cases are usually tried before the Court of Oyer and Terminer," he said. "It meets every three months, either here in Utica at the Courthouse on John Street, or in Rome, at the Courthouse there, as I'm sure you know. So as long as I know in advance, it won't be a problem for me to be present."

I nodded as though he was just reminding me of commonly known information. I was already impressed with Dr. Weissman; Dr. Litchfield, although friendly enough, had not mentioned preparing a formal report.

"Since Corporal Neilson's death was a week ago, his organs are not in ideal condition, you understand, but I believe I was able to analyze his situation adequately."

"I assume there was no question about the cause of death?"

"Clearly two gunshots to his chest, made from perhaps six to ten feet away. They destroyed most of the chest cavity."

"From a rifle? Or a musket?"

"A revolver. One of the bullets must have fallen out, perhaps as Neilson was carried to the tavern, as I understand was done, or perhaps during the previous autopsy. But I did find one remaining bullet. It appears to be from a .44. I've put the bullet in an envelope and attached it to my report."

"Did you find anything else that might be helpful?"

"I assume Corporal Neilson had seen combat."

"Yes."

"He had several small scars from wounds. What appears to be a bayonet cut is on his right arm. It had healed irregularly but would not have interfered with his use of the arm. A wound in his left thigh had not totally healed and was slightly infected. I would guess that injury was several months old. The bullet was still in the thigh, which delayed the healing and was the cause of the infection. He'd been caring for the wound, but it would have caused him pain when he walked. I would not be surprised if he'd been using a cane of some sort. He would certainly have been limping. If he'd been my patient I would have advised him to have the wound opened again, cleaned, and the bullet removed. But many soldiers continue on with their work after they've been wounded, and I suspect that is what Neilson did."

"Would the bullet wound have been serious enough for him to be released from his unit?"

"It's possible," Dr. Weissman said thoughtfully. "It would have depended on his regiment. Some officers would have dismissed any injury less than total disability as one to be endured. But the war was coming to a close when Neilson was wounded. A sympathetic officer could have sent him home. Neilson also had musket calluses on his right hand, so he had not been long away from using his. Did he have a weapon with him when he died?"

"Not that I know of," I replied. If Jake was wounded, that would explain why he was here, and not in North Carolina with his regiment. I needed to know what had been in his knapsack

"He had some minor scars on his back, and at some time in the past his nose had been broken. But none of those injuries appeared recent. He did have recent scratches on his back and upper arms. They could have been caused by walking through areas where bushes and low hanging branches had hit him, if he weren't wearing a shirt, although this time of year that would be unlikely. I'd guess the scratches were made by fingernails Not his own; the locations would have been too hard for him to reach."

"Could they have been made during lovemaking?"

"Possibly. Or they could have been defensive scratches, made by someone he was attempting to assault."

"You have written all of that in your report."

"I have," Dr. Weissman said.

"Did you find anything else that could tell us what Jake Neilson was doing in the last several days of his life? Particularly, of course, during his last hours."

"His pubic area was contaminated by both semen and urine," continued Dr. Weissman. "Frankly, the man had not bathed in some time, so his body was covered with layered dirt and sweat. His feet were callused as though he'd been walking a long distance, and had done so for some time. No blisters; just calluses. Typical of a soldier, I might add. The only other thing I can tell you is that his last meal was barley and bean soup with bread, and he'd ingested enough whiskey so the odor was still evident when I opened his stomach. I would say the whiskey and beans had been consumed within two hours of his death." The doctor closed his report and handed it to me.

"I thank you very much. You've given me some additional information to work with."

"I understand his wife is being accused of killing him?"

"So far she's the only identified suspect."

"That is an unfortunate scenario. A Union soldier who returned home, walking painfully for possibly hundreds of miles, only to be met by a vengeful wife. The question would be what the motive could be."

"That indeed is the issue," I agreed.

"I wish you the best of luck. If I can be of further help, you know where to find me." Dr. Weissman paused, and looked at me. "May I ask you a personal question, Captain Stone? One unrelated to this case?"

"Certainly," I agreed.

"I assume your arm was amputated during the war."

"Yes," I answered, wondering if Dr. Weissman would ask to look at the stump. A number of doctors had. It was not a pretty sight, but I was no longer embarrassed to bare my body in front of a medical professional. "It was done in Virginia, a little over a year ago."

"And I assume you were given morphine for the pain, then, and since."

"Yes. And opium." I wondered how he knew.

Dr. Weissman spoke quietly, but looked directly at me. "Your eyes tell me you've used the drugs recently. And I know what a godsend painkillers are to patients suffering the kind of injuries you endured. But you're clearly an intelligent man, and I think you should know that studies are beginning to be done in Europe indicating prolonged use of the sort of opiates you are using can make users more and more dependent on them and can, over time, damage both the body and the mind."

"Doctors have always told me there is no harm in relieving pain."

"That is indeed what we have always thought. But the use of pain medications of this sort, particularly of morphine, is new in the

United States, and we have no studies of what their long-term effects might be. Captain Stone, you know your own body, and what it can endure, better than any one of my profession can. But in my practice I am beginning to see men wounded during the war who are using morphine and opium when their wounds should no longer require it. I wanted to make you aware that, should at some time you be one of those men, there could be unforeseen, and possibly dire, consequences."

I'd privately wondered about some of the effects of the medications, especially of the morphine, and thanked him for his advice and counsel. But the vial of opium pills in my pocket was not my first concern that day.

I delivered Jake Neilson to his widow by two in the afternoon.

The funeral was held at the First Presbyterian Church at ten o'clock Tuesday morning, with burial immediately following in the graveyard adjoining the church.

Sheriff Newell wasted no time.

As Lidia Neilson was leaving the churchyard she was arrested for the murder of her husband and taken to the Hestia Jailhouse.

Chapter 25

"How could you arrest Mrs. Neilson so abruptly, in the presence of her friends and neighbors, on such an occasion?" I slammed my fist into Sheriff Newell's desk. "Have you no consideration for a lady? No honor?"

"I do as I'm ordered," Newell shrugged. "We found no evidence implicating anyone other than Mrs. Neilson in her husband's death. I managed to hold the district attorney off until Jake was duly prayed over and buried. But then he wanted her in jail, where he could question her, and where we can be sure she will not disappear."

I knew all of that, of course. I just wasn't ready to deal with a female client imprisoned for murder and being locked behind iron bars in a small country jail within sight of the drunks and petty thieves usually held there. I had already seen Jonathan White, sober this time, but still protesting the absence of his wife, in the entryway of the building. He'd wisely ignored me.

I hated that Lidia was a witness to such scenes. And that Nora and Aunt Cornelia were planning to bring her clean clothes and private items and bedding. They would also see the rowdies and riffraff who were the usual inhabitants of local jails.

But their errand was necessary. The bedding in this jail clearly was not changed between prisoners, and was filthy with every type of human emission I could imagine. Certainly it was inappropriate for any decent woman to sleep upon. I'd followed Sheriff Newell and Lidia to the jail and watched as she was led to a cell and the iron door locked behind her. Lidia, dressed in funeral attire, had showed no emotion. I sensed she was relieved that the possibility of arrest had finally become a reality.

"Which district attorney has been assigned the case? I am going to have to see him."

"Jenkins. Albion Jenkins," said Sheriff Newell. "He has an office three blocks down on the right. He handles most Hestia cases requiring a district attorney."

"When will the case go to court?"

"You'll have to talk with Jenkins about that. Circuit's due in Utica in a couple of weeks. I suspect he'd like to cross this situation off his calendar now rather than wait until the session three months from now."

"Does he have all your records regarding the case?"

"He does. For any copies you need you'll have to speak with him."

I nodded. "And Mr. Neilson's knapsack?"

"He has that, too."

"May I speak with my client for a moment?"

Newell shrugged. "Suit yourself. But she stays in her cell."

Lidia Neilson was seated on the edge of the low pallet that served as a bed for prisoners in the Hestia jail. At least it was not on the floor. I hoped Lidia's clothing or hair didn't become infested with any insects while she was waiting for Nora and Cornelia. I tried not to notice the slops bucket in the corner of the cell, but it was difficult to ignore the reek of the entire area.

"How are you?" I asked.

"No longer worried about when I might be arrested," she answered, with a half smile, getting up and walking to her side of the barred wall.

"I'm going to see the district attorney this afternoon. If Albion Jenkins comes to talk with you, be straightforward, but don't volunteer any information. If you think of anything that might help your case, save it to tell me."

"I understand." She reached down, unpinned a broach from the bodice of her dress, and handed it to me through the bars. "Would you keep this safe for me?"

The broach was a typical mourning pin; a circle of gold braided around ebony bars, surrounding a glass through which I could see intertwined braids of hair.

"Yours and Jake's?" I asked.

"No; my parents'. It seemed right to wear it to the funeral, since I mourn them, too. But I've heard personal items of value disappear in jails."

I nodded and put it in my pocket. "I'll keep it safe for you. Before I see the district attorney, can you think of anything else I should know about the day Jake was killed?"

Lidia hesitated a moment. "No. There's nothing you need to know."

"Are you absolutely sure?"

"I didn't kill my husband."

"I believe you. I just wish there was another suspect. A jury will want to know why Jake was killed, and how, and the answers to those questions will lead to who killed him." I paused a moment. "I kept forgetting to ask you, Lidia. Do you own a gun?"

"Two rifles are in the house. Jake used them for hunting, before the war. They're in his study, in the sideboard."

"Do you know how to shoot?"

"I've seen it done. I live in the country, Aaron. But I've never used a gun. I've never been hunting. Certainly I've never killed anyone."

The doctors had agreed Jake was killed by bullets from a revolver.

But I didn't want to leave anything to chance. "Would you mind if I went to your home? I'd like to see if those rifles are still there, or if there's anything else I can find which might convince the court of your innocence."

"You've already seen my home. But you're welcome to look at it again if you think it would help."

I nodded. "Thank you. I'll try to stop to see you tomorrow. Try to relax, and I'll get you out of here as soon as I can."

"I know you will. I'm grateful."

I left the Hestia Jail and went to find Albion Jenkins.

Mr. Jenkins' office was the most elegant I'd seen so far in Hestia. He and another lawyer had spaces on either side of a small building which, from the outside, could have been just another brown brick home. Perhaps it had originally been built to house a family and later converted to offices.

The entrance hall was wide, and served as the anteroom for both attorneys. Two clerks had desks there, and acted as gate keepers, appointment makers, and, based on my experience in law offices and the number of law books in the bookcases surrounding the hall, researchers for the men they served.

"I am Captain Aaron Stone, Esquire, late of the Army of the Republic," I said, drumming up every credential I could think of. "I represent Mrs. Lidia Neilson, and would like to speak with Albion Jenkins as soon as possible."

"Mr. Jenkins is not here at present," said one of the clerks. "Perhaps I can set an appointment for you?"

"Do you know whether he has all of the records concerning Mrs. Neilson's case."

"So far as I know, he does," replied the clerk. "Of course, I can't speak officially without his permission."

"Of course. Perhaps I could make an appointment for later this afternoon?"

"I'm sorry, but Mr. Jenkins is in his Utica office today. He should be here tomorrow; he's going to arrange the transfer of a prisoner from the jail here to the one in Utica. Would you be able to see him at eleven tomorrow morning?"

"Eleven will do," I replied, putting my hat back on. "May I ask if the prisoner to be moved is Lidia Neilson?"

"It is."

At least after that Lidia would not have to be in a jail where everyone knew her. But Utica was twelve miles away. That was a substantial distance to travel for anyone visiting her. Including me. "I'll be back at eleven in the morning, then."

That afternoon felt like spring; the air was soft. In a sheltered spot close to one home I saw the first fire pinks of the season; foot high plants covered with deep crimson blossoms, balanced with long thin dark green leaves around the base. I stopped to admire the dark red blooms; they were brighter, but still close to the hair color Nora and Robbie shared. Just thinking of them made me feel better. I'd seen them that morning at the funeral and cemetery, but wished I had an excuse to visit them later today.

My pocket watch told me it was only two in the afternoon. I decided to get a light meal at the Oak Tavern before heading back to Aunt Cornelia's home. I needed time to plan my next course of action.

The tavern smelled of stale beer, tobacco, oil lamps and soot. The typically dark ceiling seemed the style in such establishments and no doubt helped the patrons stay warm in the long winter months, as did the two large fireplaces.

A tasty bowl of hare stew, a plate of bread, and a glass of beer were soon in front of me, and I was enjoying the food and drink when I sensed someone at my elbow.

"Aaron! Good to see you again!" My young friend Eli, from the day of the parade, had recognized me. Judging by the color in his cheeks I suspected he'd been enjoying the liquid offerings of the tavern for some time.

"And you, Eli," I answered.

"May I join you? I've eaten, but I could stand another brew."

"You're welcome," I answered. "I won't be staying long, but I'd enjoy the company."

Eli pulled over another chair and grinned. "So, how is your case going? The one about Jake Neilson."

"No news," I said. I didn't need to broadcast Lidia's arrest to someone I'd only met once before, and who clearly enjoyed gossip.

"I heard they arrested Mrs. Neilson." Eli bent toward me, breathing over my stew. "They say she'll hang."

My mistake: to assume not everyone in Hestia knew exactly what was happening to everyone else.

"No one's convicted of murder without motive, Eli. In this case, there is none."

"That's not what I hear. When a man's beaten his wife as often as Jake has, I'd think that would be a motive."

"Where did you hear that?" I asked calmly, although my mind was racing. Could that be true? Why had no one, including Lidia, told me Jake abused his wife?

"It's known generally," Eli responded, taking a deep drink from his stein. "'Course, he'd been away so long, no one's thought about it in a while. But he was known to pack a punch, especially after he hoisted a few, if you know what I mean!" Eli raised his glass, so I'd be sure not to miss his meaning. "As they say, no man can treat a woman like that unless she's married to him. But Jake'd been married for a fearsome long time. No one thought much about it till he turned up dead."

"But folks have been talking about it since?"

"Just yesterday Sheriff Newell and Dr. Litchfield were sitting at this very table, and I heard them say as Jake probably had it coming. They just figured he'd have been home longer before Lidia was up to doing anything about it."

Chapter 26

I excused myself as soon as I'd finished my stew and went directly to Dr. Litchfield's office.

"Did Jake Neilson abuse Lidia? Do you know of any times he hurt her?"

Dr. Litchfield put up his hand as though to put a space between us. "Aaron, what goes on within the marital relationship is confidential."

"You were her doctor! If she were hurt, you would know about it!"

"Not necessarily. Unless someone breaks a bone or such most don't seek out a doctor. Especially when going to a doctor might mean letting people know they can't handle a private domestic situation. If a woman is married, Aaron, she belongs to her husband. You're a lawyer; you know. Under the law a married couple is one entity. That's one of the reasons those foolish women looking to get the vote will fail. A married couple is one legal unit. They should get one vote."

"But violence within marriage can't be ignored!"

"Murder certainly shouldn't be," Dr. Litchfield agreed.

"So Jake did hit Lidia."

Dr. Litchfield shrugged. "I always assumed it was when he'd had a bit too much at the tavern. She did lose three children in pregnancies, though, as I think of it. One was because she fell downstairs. I don't remember the explanations for the other losses. Sometimes God has reasons none of us can understand."

"Why didn't you tell me this before?"

"You didn't ask. And I believe disagreements within marriages should be between husband and wife. Even if Lidia did have some rough days with Jake in the past, he'd been away for three years, and she had no reason to kill him."

"But that's exactly what she did have. If living with Jake meant living with pain —someone who might push her downstairs when she was pregnant – if that actually happened, Dr. Litchfield – then maybe three years of living without pain would be enough motivation to want to remain living in peace."

"You're getting overly excited, Aaron. Lidia's situation wasn't unique."

"Did you discuss this with Sheriff Newell over lunch at the Oak Tavern yesterday?"

"It's possible."

"Then you gave him exactly what he needed to tell the district attorney to arrest Lidia. She's at the jail right now, in a disgustingly filthy cell, charged with the murder of her husband."

"No other suspects have been found, have they?" Dr. Litchfield lit his pipe. "Aaron, you never know what a person, even a woman, might do. There was a woman over in West Turin a few years back. Had a husband and five children. Husband decided they should sell their farm and move west. Within a few days of telling his neighbors that decision he started to suffer severe stomach pains. After his death it was proved his wife had poisoned him with arsenic. Just because she didn't want him to sell the house she'd grown up in." Dr. Litchfield shook his head. "She was still in jail last I heard. Women are emotional creatures, Aaron. The only thing you can count on is that you'll never know what they'll take it into their heads to do."

"Do you believe Lidia Neilson shot her husband?"

"Can't seem to find anyone else who might have done it, can you? Seems as reasonable an explanation as any."

"Those men at Proctor's Tavern said he was at least a half mile from the Neilson's home. Is it reasonable to assume that Lidia Neilson, a woman in her thirties, chased her husband out of the house, followed him for half a mile, and then shot him? Especially since they hadn't seen each other in almost three years. There's no sense to it!"

"What sense is there to anyone else's shooting him?"

I took a deep breath and tried to be logical. Factual. "What proof do you have that Jake hurt Lidia in the past?"

"The three children she couldn't carry to term. Well, one might have been a natural miscarriage. But that fall down the stairs might not have been an accident. And another time your Aunt Cornelia brought Mrs. Neilson to my office because a cut on the back of her head was bleeding badly, and I found her abdomen and arms covered with blue and green bruises. She lost a child that time, too."

"How did she explain the bruises and cut?"

"She said she'd slipped and fallen on the kitchen floor."

"Why didn't Jake bring her in?"

"She said he was out of town. But the bruises just didn't look right to me; they weren't in the places they would normally be if someone fell. Plus, the bruises were on the front of her body; the cut was on the back." Dr. Litchfield shrugged. "Two or three other times I was out near their home and stopped in and Lidia's face was bruised. She didn't leave her house much after her parents died. She always had an excuse for her injuries; said she was clumsy. But I didn't remember her bruising so easily when her parents were still alive."

"Couldn't you do anything about it?"

"Aaron, she was married. She was the property of her husband. And she never said he hurt her. Never."

"And if the district attorney asks you to testify?"

"Then I'll tell him, and the jury, what I think. I think Jake Neilson hurt his wife. It will be up to the jury to decide whether she shot him or not. I don't know that she did. But I can imagine a woman might be angry enough to shoot someone like Jake."

Chapter 27

I struggled to contain my anger at the day's events.

The morning had started with the relief of Jake Neilson's funeral and burial, but then had quickly headed into circles of nightmares with Lidia's arrest and imprisonment. And now Sheriff Newell had essentially washed his hands of the case. That had been bad enough, but now I'd found out that Lidia might actually have had a motivation to kill Jake, that both Sheriff Newell and Dr. Litchfield had believed that all along - and that no one, including Lidia herself, had thought to mention it to me.

I started walking home. Aunt Cornelia, Nora, Robbie and I had taken the carriage to the funeral, but after Lidia's arrest the others had gone to the Neilson's home to retrieve some comforts for Lidia. I was on my own.

I wouldn't be able to see the district attorney until tomorrow. I kicked a stone off the roadway. It hit a fence surrounding someone's yard and bounced back onto the road. My toes hurt, but the stone had only moved a few feet from where it had started.

I'd believed Lidia was innocent. Had I been naïve? If she were innocent, I now had an uphill battle to prove it, since neither the sheriff nor I had found any possible other suspects. Had I been conned into having faith in Lidia?

Clearly Aunt Cornelia and Nora believed in her. And a man's role, my role, was to protect women, not allow them to be mistakenly indicted for murder, or, worse yet, convicted. So far I'd failed. Lidia'd been arrested.

The most elegant sections of Hestia were lined with tall elm trees that in summer provided umbrellas of shade over the streets and homes, but were now just beginning to bud. The pale green colors reminded me of springs in other places. Even in the midst of rugged marches and the horror of battles there had been spring.

There was always hope, I reminded myself; always new beginnings.

In war I'd grown used to seeing good men killed for no reason other than they were under orders. I understood that, It was war. But I couldn't accept that an innocent woman could be imprisoned, or even hung, for a crime she didn't commit. I hadn't fought for a world in which that could happen.

Strangers I passed on the street assumed the faces of friends I'd known and loved as brothers during the war. Richard, whose body had never been found, but who I had no doubt was in a mass grave in Gettysburg. Jonathan Strong, who'd died in agony of the intestinal problems that had affected us all. Russell Whitney, who ran ahead of his regiment and drew fire so others could gain ground. Fritz Shoener, the best sharpshooter I knew, until he himself became the victim of a Confederate rifle. Randy Van Tassell, who'd re-enlisted and told jokes around the campfire even after having being wounded four times, promising that if he were killed he'd come back to haunt the man who pulled the trigger. I wondered if somewhere in the south there was a soldier in gray who still saw Randy's shape behind every tree.

I hoped there was. Although if dead soldiers became ghosts, there were regiments of them in Maryland, Virginia, the Carolinas ...The cawing of three dark crows, calling to each other and diving between the trees brought me back to the pitted road and the realities of today. It was Tuesday, April 25, 1865. The war was officially over; even if not all the regiments had been released. The newly united country was moving on. President Johnson was promising there would never be another war between the states.

I was walking down a rural road in upstate New York, fighting a battle to save a woman from being convicted of the murder of her husband. A soldier who'd survived the war, but not his homecoming. I couldn't believe his wife had killed him. But what other explanation was there? So far I'd failed to find one.

And there was still no rationale for those bones Owen had found in the north field.

I'd accepted violent death for a cause. I could not accept violent death which served no purpose.

Robbie Burns was the one to greet me at home. He ran toward me, clearly delighted to see me. "You came home! We've had a big day."

How could anyone not smile back at a child?

"We went to church and then they buried Mr. Neilson. They buried him in a box."

"Yes."

"Not like the man buried in the field."

I reached down and managed to pick Robbie up in my right arm and give him a big hug. He didn't seem to mind at all and his hug back made the world seem brighter. I couldn't remember the last time someone had hugged me. We sat together on the piazza steps.

"No. The man in the field wasn't buried in a box. A box for a dead person is called a coffin, Robbie."

"Why wasn't the man in the field in a coffin?"

"Maybe not enough people loved him to care about burying him well."

Robbie thought for a moment. "Nora loves me. If I died she'd make sure I was in a coffin box, wouldn't she?"

I had to resist hugging him again. "I'm sure she would, Robbie. But you don't have to think about dying for a long time."

"Soldiers died in the war, though. They were older than me, but not old, like Mr. Bitterman at the dry goods store. He has a gray beard and no teeth and he walks with two canes."

"That's right. The war was very hard. Many young men died."

Robbie looked very somber. "And the war took your arm."

"Yes. But the rest of me is fine." I reached over and tickled him. "See? My right arm and fingers work very well."

He doubled over with giggles. Then he looked at me seriously. "My ma died. And my pa is a soldier. Is my pa going to die, too?"

"I don't know, Robbie," I answered honestly. "But you and Nora have each other. That's very important."

"Yes," he nodded. "I don't remember Pa. He left a long time ago, before I was born. I'd like to see him. But I have friends. You're my friend."

"I'd like to be, Robbie. I'd like that very much." I wondered if I could find out where Robbie's father was, and if he were still alive. My friend George Watkins had been working at the Union Army headquarters in Washington the last time I'd heard from him. Perhaps he could check records of New York State regiments.

"Me, too." He sat for a moment and then grinned at me. "You said you'd help pull the wagon with rocks for my wall."

I laughed. "I could do that. And I will. I promise. But not today. It's getting late, and we've all had a long day. Is your sister inside now?"

He nodded. "She's with Mrs. Livingston. We went to Mrs. Neilson's house and then took some things to the jail, and then came here. The jail is where they put bad people."

"Yes."

"I don't think Mrs. Neilson is bad, though. She makes good molasses cookies, and she gives me hugs and doesn't yell at me." Robbie thought for a few minutes. "Nora said people think Mrs. Neilson killed Mr. Neilson."

"Yes."

"But she didn't. He left the house and he was alive and walking." Robbie bent over to whisper. "But he wasn't walking good. I think his leg hurt."

I looked at him. "Did someone tell you that, Robbie?"

"No! Nora said not to talk about Mr. Neilson. Sometimes we play pretend games. She said to pretend I never saw him."

"But you did see him."

"He ate lunch with me in the kitchen." Robbie whispered even lower. "He was dirty, and he smelled. But Nora said I shouldn't say that, and I shouldn't talk to him. So I went over to the big side of the house. There are lots of stairs to climb there."

"I remember."

"That's when my nose started to bleed. It bled a lot." Robbie looked down. "I'm a big boy, but I got scared anyway. Nora came and helped the blood stop."

"Did you see Mr. Neilson then?"

"He was yelling downstairs. I didn't want to see him."

"Then what did you do?"

"I went up to the tower. My nose wasn't bleeding much then. I like to look out the windows in the tower. I can see everything. I'm almost in the clouds."

"What did you see, Robbie?"

"I saw robins building a nest in the maple tree in the garden, and three clouds that looked like horses running, and Mr. Neilson walking away."

"Did anyone go with Mr. Neilson?"

"No. Just him. Then I went downstairs. No one was yelling anymore, and I wanted a molasses cookie. I told you Mrs. Neilson makes good molasses cookies."

I hesitated a moment. But I couldn't believe Robbie would lie.

"Robbie, do you remember what you and Mr. Neilson had for lunch?"

Robbie sat still for a moment. "Soup. Soup with beans and peas and little white things in it." He looked up at me. "It was good!"

Dr. Weissman had said Jake Neilson had eaten bean and barley soup not long before he'd died.

Chapter 28

The front door opened in back of us. "Aaron! I'm glad you're home. Did you talk with the district attorney? Lidia said you were going to try to." Aunt Cornelia looked exhausted.

"No; he was in Utica. I have an appointment to see him tomorrow morning. He plans to move Lidia to the prison in Utica, closer to his office, and to the courthouse."

"Can't you keep her in Hestia, nearer to her friends?"

"I can try, but I'm not sure I'll be able to do that. I'll know more tomorrow."

Nora came out onto the porch. "Robbie, I think it's time we went home. We have to get you some supper. Tomorrow will be a good day to plant peas."

"Can Captain Stone come home with us?" Robbie reached out and took my hand and looked up at his sister. "He's my friend."

"Captain Stone has had a busy day."

"I'd be happy to walk home with you both," I volunteered. "If you don't mind, Nora. I won't stay, but I could see you to your door."

"How nice of you, Aaron, to volunteer," said Aunt Cornelia, approvingly. "Supper here won't be ready for at least two hours. Nora, it will do you good to talk with someone closer to your age than an old lady like me or a child."

"I'm not a child!" Robbie protested, understanding at once. "I'm four!"

"And you're not an old lady, Cornelia," added Nora. "But thank you for your company, Aaron."

We set off together; Robbie walked between us, holding one of our hands in each of his.

"This is fun!" he said. "Today I have two people. Two people walking to my house!"

"I promised Robbie I'd come and help him with his wall one day soon," I told Nora.

"Not the wall," Robbie corrected. "I can build the wall. Help me with the wagon. It gets heavy."

"You're right. Help with the wagon," I agreed.

"You'll be welcome," said Nora. She was wearing the dark dress she'd put on for the funeral and burial. It fit her a little closer than the dresses I'd seen her in before. Most women had a mourning dress in the back of their wardrobes for such occasions, and perhaps she hadn't worn hers in several years. "We don't get many visitors out here in the country. Robbie's enjoyed your company."

"As I have been pleased to get to know both of you." I looked at Nora sidewise, but she stared straight ahead, although her face flushed a little.

"Can you come tomorrow, Captain Stone? Can you come tomorrow to help with the wagon?"

"Not tomorrow, I'm afraid. I have to do some work in town for Mrs. Neilson. But soon. I promise. Soon."

I didn't believe Robbie had lied to me about the soup or about seeing Mr. Neilson leave. But if Jake had been at his home, and then left on his own, why had all three women in the house lied about his presence? I wanted to be sure about the details before I questioned any of them, and I wouldn't ask Nora in front of Robbie. He'd clearly spoken to me in confidence.

I sighed. A four-year old boy was my only witness, and he hadn't seen anyone hurt Jake Neilson. He'd only seen him eating bean and barley soup.

"Aaron?"

Had Nora asked me a question before? I looked at her.

"You're in another world. Will you see Lidia tomorrow?"

"It's possible. I'll try."

"I heard you say they were going to move her to Utica. Would you tell her Cornelia and I will try to visit her at the end of the week? I don't want to take Robbie to Utica tomorrow with all the crowds."

"Crowds?"

"Surely you haven't forgotten? Tomorrow is April 26; President Lincoln's funeral train is stopping in Utica tomorrow in mid-afternoon. People will be gathering from a hundred miles around."

"I *had* forgotten." I wondered if District Attorney Jenkins would be heading back to Utica at noon tomorrow. If so, then our discussion would be a short one.

"I'd thought of taking Robbie," Nora went on, "But he's had enough of death in the past week. It would be better if we just stay at home and get those early peas in the garden. Right, Robbie? Maybe we'll have peas in time for the Fourth of July."

Robbie nodded. "I like peas. And I've got almost all the rocks out of that part of the garden, so we can put in the row and the sticks for them to grow on. Can we tie the sticks with pieces of colored yarn, Nora?"

"Later in the season, when the peas begin to grow, we'll do that." Nora turned to me. "I save small lengths of yarn all year for us to use in training our climbing vegetables during the summer. The brightly colored ties make the garden look gay."

"I know! It's hair time, right Nora?"

"It is. I'm glad you reminded me."

I shook my head, not comprehending, when she looked at me.

"All year Robbie and I collect the ends of our hair when we trim it, and the ends of ribbons and very short pieces of yarn and sometimes scraps of fabric too small to sew with and we put them in a special box."

"Let me tell, Nora!" said Robbie. "Then in the spring we take all the yarn and ribbons and curls and put them on branches of the low trees and the bushes near our house!"

"And then what happens?" I said, wondering what purpose this strange spring ritual served.

"The birds come and take the hair and ribbons and cloth away and use it for their nests, silly!" said Robbie. "We watch and sometimes we see a nest with a piece of red yarn in it."

"One year we even found an empty sparrow's nest in the fall. The baby birds had grown up, but the nest was lined with red curls," said Nora. "It's a tradition; Mother did it with me when I was little, and now Robbie and I do it."

I thought of sparrows and blue jays and cardinals living in nests lined with Nora's hair, and the vision pleased me more than I could have imagined. "Those birds are lucky to have such soft nests," I said. I wondered if Nora would ever grow her hair like other women did. I was now used to her look, and the way her face was framed by her shorn tresses. Most women who had, for some reason, to endure hair that short for some period of time would hide it under a cap or hat. Nora's hair moved with her as she walked and talked.

Seeing her, I now thought women who braided and threaded and pinned their hair looked unnatural.

"Robbie says he doesn't remember his father. He must have been gone a long time."

Nora hesitated a moment. "I told you, he enlisted right after the war started."

"He's never even written me a letter, or sent me a birthday present," said Robbie. "Hans, at the orphanage, said Pa's probably dead. That's what happened to his father. Hans and his mother and brother didn't get any more letters, and then they heard his father had been killed. At Gettysburg," Robbie added. "A lot of people died there. Maybe my pa died there, too."

Gettysburg. Echoing cannons and flashing bayonets, and charging horses, and bodies, everywhere. Richard, and so many others, gone. It had been a bright sunny day, like this one. So far away. And yet never far from my mind.

"Did you hear about Gettysburg?" asked Robbie.

"Yes. I was there," I said.

"Did you see Pa there? Or Hans' father?"

"I saw many brave men."

"That's enough questions, Robbie," said Nora. We were at the entrance to the cart trail to their home. "Aaron, it was kind of you to come so far with us, but I think now you should go home. I'm sure Cornelia would like to speak with you about today, and about the future."

"I'm going to work on my wall!" said Robbie, dropping our hands and running the rest of the way.

I looked at Nora. She was so beautiful, and so innocent. And so many horrible things had happened in my world and in hers. I wanted to comfort her; to let her know I was her friend as well as Robbie's. I took a step toward her, but she backed away from me, like a doe startled in the woods.

"Remember to give Lidia my message," she said. "I'll visit her at the end of the week. Thank you again for walking with us." She turned, and followed Robbie up the path.

I watched until the path curved, and her figure was hidden by the trees.

Chapter 29

"I need to know, Aunt Cornelia. Did Jake Neilson ever hit Lidia?"

"Only the two people in a marriage really know what happens within it." Aunt Cornelia's voice was calm, but her knuckles whitened as she sipped her tea after dinner in the parlor. "What makes you ask?"

"Because Dr. Litchfield told me he thinks Jake was a wife-beater, and he also told Sheriff Newell," I answered bluntly. "And if Albion Jenkins can prove Jake beat Lidia, that would be a reason for her to kill him. It wouldn't make the murder justified, but it could convince a jury she did it."

"They hadn't even seen each other in three years."

"Perhaps. I have a witness who says they saw each other the day of Jake's murder."

Aunt Cornelia started to speak, but I put my hand up. "I know you said he wasn't at their house. And I want to believe you didn't lie to me. But now I'm not so sure. Even if he was at his house, I need to know whether he was a threat to Lidia, now or in the past. I haven't found anyone else who had a motive to kill him, and Sheriff Newell and the district attorney haven't found anyone else either. If they had, Lidia wouldn't have been arrested."

"Have you spoken with Lidia about this?" I couldn't help noting Aunt Cornelia wasn't dealing with the issue of whether she and Nora and Lidia had lied about Jake's reaching home the day he was killed.

"No. I talked with Dr. Litchfield after I saw Lidia today. I will ask her, though, as soon as I can see her again. I need to see the district attorney first. I have to get some idea of what he knows, and find out what was in the duffle bag Jake left at home. Something there might give us a clue as to what he was thinking."

"Talk with Lidia," said Aunt Cornelia. "I know Jake wasn't an easy man to live with, but many men are not. I was blessed with your Uncle Henry, and sometimes it's hard for me to understand what difficult times many women have. I have known some women for whom marriage was a state of bondage, not of protection."

"'Bondage?' Isn't that an unusually strong word?"

"Not for the situations those women found themselves in. Women marry young, often without knowing the man they are committed to well, or before understanding all that is demanded of women within marriage."

My expression must have told her I doubted that.

"I'm not just talking about the naïve young woman who doesn't understand the needs of men in the marriage bed, Aaron. Although that is certainly one of the initial shocks for many of them."

I flushed. Aunt Cornelia had always been unusually honest and forthcoming with me, but the delicate nature of this conversation was reaching the edge of decency. And yet I needed to hear what she was saying.

"Some men are kind at first. But others are unduly rough. Perhaps they want to demonstrate their power, or they lack understanding of the female nature and constitution. I suspect some men are themselves embarrassed at the physical nature of marriage, or they truly don't know how to treat their wives because their only physical experiences with women have been with those who are paid to submit and provide services."

"Aunt Cornelia," I blurted in embarrassment and consternation, "How can you say that about men? You've often said Uncle Henry was a fine man."

"And so he was, and I a lucky woman. But women talk with other women, Aaron, and we have eyes. We often see what men do not in the relationships of those we care about. I'm sure there are connections and alliances, particularly those between men, which we do not fully understand. But I've been a member of organizations supporting the rights of women for many years, and I've heard many women's stories. We've finally changed some laws. Here in New York State women can now own property. Even married women can own property without the consent and management of their husbands. But that is a very new situation. Until the past few years women *were* the property of their husbands in New York, and the law saw them as one entity – one body, as it were. And that body was not the woman's. A man had total rights to the body of his wife, and if he felt she needed chastisement, or if he wanted to bed her, then the law said he could do as he wished. She had no recourse; no power to say no. Many judges still feel the law should be interpreted that way."

"The law has never allowed a man to maim or kill his wife!"

"The difference between rational and deserved punishment and abuse is sometimes a thin one. Certainly, you are correct. The law does not say a man can kill his wife. But the courts are much more understanding of a man who kills his wife than of a woman who might kill her husband. I don't know all the legal cases that you do, Aaron, but I've heard of many cases in which a woman died at the hands of her husband and the crime was excused, or seen as the fault of the woman because she didn't behave in ways society considers proper for a wife."

"I'll allow that some men are very strong, and perhaps guilty of using too much force. Such is the nature of man – to do battle, and to react physically. Women are smaller; weaker; more delicate in sensibilities. Women do not translate passions into physical violence as men do."

"Aaron, you still have a lot to learn. But to get back to this specific case, I believe Jake Neilson was a man who might have hit his wife, especially when he was intemperate, or angry."

"Dr. Litchfield implied that Lidia and Jake had no children because he caused her to miscarry at least once, if not twice."

Aunt Cornelia shook her head. "I don't know what Lidia will feel comfortable sharing with you."

"She seemed very welcoming to Robbie when I saw them together. I imagine that she would have wanted her own children. That would be natural."

"Lidia cares a great deal about children, and about young mothers. She shows that in her work with Nora and me at the orphanage. It's one of the tragedies of her life that she's never carried a child of her own to term."

"This is another question which is embarrassing, Aunt Cornelia," I said.

"Go ahead. If your dear mother were here I am sure she would want me to answer whatever you needed to know."

I was less positive than my aunt about that; nor was I at all sure I could have asked Mother the questions I was beginning to feel at least a little more comfortable asking Aunt Cornelia.

"When I was at Lidia's home last week I noticed the laundry she'd done, hanging in her yard."

"Yes?"

"I thought she had hung an infant's clouts on the line, and I asked her about them."

Aunt Cornelia froze slightly as she listened to me. I could almost see the openness of her expression closing down. "Yes?"

"I had the idea that she might have had a lover; perhaps even a child; and that Jake had come home to find such a situation, perhaps providing a motive for the man involved to kill him."

All the tension in Aunt Cornelia's body disappeared; she was clearly amused by my theory. "And you asked Lidia whether she had a lover?"

"I did. She assured me she did not."

"Indeed. I suspect you caught Lidia quite off guard with your imagination."

"I suppose I did. But I was trying to find a motive for Jake's killing, as I am still."

"I assume she also assured you that she did not have a love child."

"She did. And I believed her. But there were those cloths on the line. She said they were the cloths a woman uses … monthly. I am a grown man, Aunt Cornelia, but I did not grow up in close proximity to any women, in that sense." This was getting more and more difficult. Finally I just blurted out, "Do a woman's cloths look like clouts?"

Aunt Cornelia clearly was not only not offended; she was amused. "I would not be surprised, given your lack of experience both with babies and with the intimate details of young women's lives, that you could confuse the two. Is that answer complete enough?"

"Yes; yes, it is fine," I said. "And I think I've covered enough discomforting topics for this evening."

"I hope you're still glad you decided to represent Lidia, Aaron."

"I am not sorry, for my own sake. But I hope I can do what you and Lidia and Nora expect me to do, and convince a jury that Lidia is innocent. I do not believe Lidia killed her husband. But the more details I find, the more difficult her defense is becoming."

Aunt Cornelia reached over and patted my hand reassuringly, as she might a child's. "You're doing fine, Aaron. I'm proud of you. The situation is not simple, and you are doing your best. That is all any of us hope for."

I nodded, as I headed upstairs to bed, where I swallowed several opium pills to help me relax, despite Dr. Weissman's concerns.

I knew Lidia, at least, hoped for a lot more than my best. She hoped for a verdict of not guilty.

And until then she, a decent woman, was sleeping in a jail with no privacy, and scoundrels of the town as companions.

Chapter 30

District Attorney Albion Jenkins' office was far from the elegant and intimidating room I'd imagined. In fact, it was almost empty. A few amateurish watercolors of local scenes hung on the wall, and the only furniture was a plain maple table that served as a desk and several ladder-backed chairs for clients.

There was no clutter; no books; very few papers. Jenkins' clerk, whose hallway desk was almost invisible beneath the piles of papers and boxes marked "evidence," clearly screened paperwork and kept Mr. Albion's world in order.

The district attorney himself, however, presented a less than pristine appearance. His mustache had been trimmed disturbingly off-center, and a trace of the eggs he'd consumed, perhaps for breakfast that morning, or perhaps for breakfast two weeks ago, added a spot of color to his cravat.

He greeted me as I entered his office. "Captain Stone, and my adversary in the Neilson case, I believe." He came around his desk and offered his right hand, while his eyes focused a moment too long on the area that should have been filled by my left arm. His handshake was firm and he smiled. "I don't believe we've met before; welcome to Oneida County."

"Thank you, sir. I'm glad to be here. I spent summers in Hestia as a child, but had not been here in ten years before this spring."

"Sheriff Newell told me you had family in the area."

"Cornelia Livingston, my mother's sister, lives five miles northwest of town; her husband Henry died a few months ago and I came to see if I could help her through her loss."

"A difficult time. And I'd heard you were injured." He glanced again at my shoulder.

"The Wilderness campaign, about a year ago." It was refreshing to deal with a man, crooked mustache or none, who did not hedge his questions out of politeness. "Did you serve?"

"No. I planned to, but my wife was adamantly opposed to my enlisting, and her father paid someone to take my place. Not something I'm proud of, but I was able to continue serving the people here at home." He smiled at me. "And my wife and I are still on good terms, and have lively two year old twins, Mary and Sarah. They've become the center of our family and are no doubt a direct result of my serving, as it were, on the home front. You completed your legal training before the war?"

"I attended Columbia College in New York City, where my parents live, and passed my examinations with Judge Clemens there before I enlisted in '61."

"I'm a Yale man, myself," Jenkins said, sitting on the edge of his desk and gesturing for me to sit in one of the chairs. "Then clerked with Judge Sandhurst in Albany, in the late 50s. Moved to Utica after I passed my examinations because my wife's family was here. So you haven't had much chance to practice."

"No. But I'm eager to do so." It would not be to my advantage to share that not only was this my first criminal trial, but that most of my studies had been in civil law.

"I assume you know Mrs. Neilson's case will be tried by the Court of Oyer and Terminer in Utica. Since most of my work is there, I only visit Hestia occasionally. I have small offices here and in Rome. Mrs. Neilson will be moved to the prison in Utica, most likely tomorrow. She was scheduled to be transferred today, but with President Lincoln's body coming through the city this afternoon it seemed prudent for most of the law enforcement officers in Utica to concentrate on the crowds and any problems they might create. I would expect more than the usual number of ruffians and hooligans will appear for the spectacle, and without police presence they might well turn respectful mourning into an occasion the more temperate citizens of Utica would not care to remember."

"I understand. That also gives me a little more time to talk with her myself close to home."

"Good. I realize the jail here is crude, and that is particularly difficult for a woman, especially a cultured lady like Mrs. Neilson. I did speak with her this morning, and assured her that the facilities in Utica, although far from the home she is used to, should at least be more comfortable than where she is now."

"Thank you."

"From my discussion with her I assume Mrs. Neilson will be pleading her innocence."

"That is correct."

"Do you have your list of witnesses finalized?"

"No; and you?" I wondered whether Robbie Burns would be considered a credible witness at four years old. He was the only one so far who had given me strong information about Jake Neilson's health and whereabouts on the day of the murder. Nora and Aunt Cornelia, of course, would have to be called. But I wasn't yet sure how much they would help. And of course Dr. Weissman would testify.

"Again, not as yet. It is still early; we will, of course, be in touch as we prepare for court."

"I understand you have Corporal Neilson's knapsack; the one found in the wardrobe in his bedroom."

"Yes. Sheriff Newell turned it over to me."

"Since anything in it might be used in court, I would like to see it."

"I assumed that. I have it here." He pointed behind his desk.

"I assume the sheriff and your clerk have established an inventory of items found inside?"

"Yes. It's here on the desk, if you'd like to check it over, and I've already had a copy made for you. Why don't you look through the knapsack and the list while I speak with my clerk about documentation necessary for another case? Make yourself at home, and I'll check with you in a quarter hour or so."

"Thank you." Jenkins was clearly not only meeting the requirements of his profession, he was anticipating my needs. It was too early to say whether this was because he was trying to win my friendship, or whether he was only pretending to do so. We would soon be adversaries, so I decided to reserve judgment, and take advantage of whatever information I could obtain in the meantime.

The pungent odor of sweat and dirt rose from the knapsack. The clothing within was not clean, and perhaps had not been for months. Not unusual for a soldier.

I looked though the bag, checking the inventory list to make sure everything had been catalogued. Jake Neilson had carried a limited number of items home. Depending on the circumstances under which he left his regiment, he might have walked a good part of the way from North Carolina and had not over-burdened himself.

Two pairs of well-worn socks; one hunting knife; a soiled handkerchief; a packet of letters tied with string. I glanced at the envelopes. Most, but not all, appeared to be from Lidia. Perhaps their contents would better illuminate the relationship between Lidia and Jake. I set them aside.

Two worn blankets such as soldiers slept on, or under, or wrapped around themselves in the cold. A canteen decorated with a crude sketch of the Confederate flag, no doubt taken for use or as a souvenir from a prisoner of war or dead Rebel soldier. A tin cup, fork and spoon. A razor, dulled with use. A havelock, worn under one's hat to protect the neck from becoming scorched from the sun. Few soldiers had managed to obtain one; perhaps Lidia had sent it to Jake. Crumbs that indicated the bag had once contained hardtack. A cartridge box containing half a dozen bullets for a Colt .44 revolver. A powder flask. A small canister of percussion caps. Three silver spoons, wrapped in a filthy linen napkin embroidered with a J that might have been used as a bandage; it was stained with dried blood. Perhaps Jake's regiment had "liberated" a wealthy plantation, and he considered the spoons his spoils. It had happened with more than spoons.

I had just finished re-wrapping the silver when Jenkins returned. "Anything out of order?"

"No; all looks as it is on the inventory. His .44 wasn't in the knapsack?" Most Union soldiers used the 1860 Colt .44 revolver; its walnut grip and brass trigger guard were so familiar my fingers automatically moved to the position they'd assume to hold it.

"I asked my clerk the same question. Only the cartridges, as you saw." Jenkins looked at me for a moment as though he expected me to ask another question, but I didn't. All I could think of was Dr. Weissman's determination that Jake Neilson had been killed by a .44 revolver. Men who were not soldiers could certainly have owned a .44. But soldiers, or former soldiers, would be most likely to be familiar with one. Why would a soldier have bothered to travel with a powder flask and cartridges, but without a gun?

"I'd like permission to borrow the letters, to read them."

"As you can see, my clerk recorded their dates and who they were from on the list. I haven't read them myself yet. But you're welcome to take them. So long as they get back to my office by, let's say, next Monday, so I have a chance to read them, too."

"Monday is the first of May," I realized out loud. "It has been a long April."

"For the country, it has indeed. But within days Lincoln will have gone to his final rest, and, we can hope, his assassin will be captured." Jenkins' tone was weary.

"Have you heard anything of that in the past several days?" I certainly had not had time to find, much less read, a newspaper.

"Just that the search had been narrowed to a few areas in Virginia and Maryland where that scum Booth had ties."

"Let us hope the chase will soon be at an end. The murder must not go unpunished."

Jenkins looked at me, as we both realized more than one death was on our minds. "No murder should."

Jake's letters in my pocket, I walked to the jail, intending to talk with Lidia. But before I spoke with her I had one other errand.

"I'd like to send a telegram," I told the young man in the telegraph office. "Can you get one off for me this afternoon?"

"Not much business today; most folks have gone to Utica to pay their respects." He looked longingly toward the door. "Wish I'd been able to go, too. That mourning train would be something to remember."

"You're right; it would be," I agreed. "I'd like a telegram sent to Mr. George Watkins at Army headquarters in Washington, D.C. From Captain Aaron Stone." I looked at the young man again. "Captain Aaron Stone Esquire." Perhaps that would get more attention. The revision of my name didn't seem to impress him.

"Write down what you want me to send."

I hesitated a moment and then wrote,

"Dear George. Time to call in that favor! Need current status of soldiers Corporal Jacob Neilson and (?) William Burns, both of Hestia, New York. Reply needed as soon as possible. Best wishes, Aaron."

I wanted confirmation of Jake's status, despite Dr. Weissman's assumption that he had been wounded and sent home. And I wanted to be able to tell Robbie and Nora something about their father.

George would have access to the federal records. Everyone knew they were not complete, and would not be perhaps for months, until both armies exchanged records of prisoners and burials, and regiments still in remote areas were heard from. But if the information were known now, George would be able to find it for me. I hoped he could find it quickly.

Lidia was sitting dejectedly on the cot in her cell. She looked up when she heard me ask for her.

"Aaron! Any news?"

"I've talked with Albion Jenkins, and he says most likely you'll be transferred to the prison in Utica tomorrow," I told her. "He said to tell you the facilities there should be more comfortable."

She nodded. "So he informed me this morning. I can hardly think the facilities could be worse." She gestured at the man snoring drunkenly in the next cell, fully visible to anyone who walked by, as, I realized, Lidia was when she was in her cell. No privacy at all. Perhaps the most difficult situation of all for a woman.

"Nora asked me to tell you she and Cornelia would try to get to Utica later this week to see you."

"That is kind of her. Yesterday they brought me some sheets, soap and a few other personal items."

"Is there anything else you need?"

"You can get me released."

"You've got a trial for murder ahead of you. I don't think I'll be able to get you released before then."

Lidia's face fell. "I had hoped."

"Lidia, I have to ask you. Did Jake ever hit you?"

She looked startled. "Why would you ask that?"

"Dr. Litchfield told Sheriff Newell that Jake had been rough; that you may have lost at least one child because of his actions. That he pushed you down the stairs, and that you were often seen with bruises and cuts."

Lidia hesitated. "When Jake had too much to drink, he could be difficult. That is true. But what relevance has that now?"

"Because if Jake hurt you frequently during your marriage that could give you a motive to kill him. Perhaps you were afraid that once he was home he would hurt you again."

"Jake wasn't an easy man. You'll hear that from others, I'm sure. But it doesn't matter to anyone else but me whether he injured me or not. Aaron, I didn't kill Jake. If I tell you how Jake hit me, and pushed me down the stairs once, then the jury will be even more convinced that I killed him. Am I right?"

"It's possible."

"Then Jake never hurt me. I don't want the humiliation of talking about it in open court in any case. Under the law a man has the right to treat his wife as she deserves, and most men on the jury or bench would assume any punishment I received was warranted by my behavior." She was silent a moment, and then looked directly at me. "If people believe I killed Jake then it won't matter why I did it. You'll have to convince them that someone else murdered my husband. You'll have to!"

Chapter 31

It was late afternoon by the time I reached Lidia's home; my horse was weary, and I had been sorely tempted to head for Aunt Cornelia's home rather than take the Syracuse Road eleven miles west.

I passed Proctor's Tavern, where newly budded forsythia surrounded the dooryard. Dr. Litchfield and I had been there a little less than ten days before in hopes of saving Jake Neilson's life. Instead we'd proceeded to his home, to inform his widow of the death.

Half a mile further down the road I paused to look at the spot on the road where we'd been told Jake's body was found. Spring grasses there had already turned green.

Dr. Weissman had estimated the assailant was only a few feet away when the shots were fired. Jake would have seen the person who shot him, and perhaps stumbled backward a foot or two before collapsing. There was now no sign of a struggle, if indeed there had ever been. I suspected Jake's murderer was someone known to him. Perhaps he had not felt threatened until the revolver was revealed. I wondered again where his own gun was.

The Neilson house stood, silent and calm, as though nothing of consequence had happened there. A pair of goldfinches were twittering near an evergreen bush to the side of the drive as I dismounted. I let my horse drink at the wooden horse trough at the far side of the drive and then tied him to the horse block.

I checked the study first. Lidia had said the only guns in the house were stored there. As she had described, there were two rifles in the cabinet. I carefully checked the rest of the cabinet, and the drawers in the desk and did not find a revolver, or any other type of weapon.

I had neither time, nor need, to examine every paper on the cluttered desk, but I did see bills from a Hestia feed store and a mercantile establishment. Nothing of note. No calendars or diaries or journals of any type. Books on botanical subjects and animal husbandry were on the top of the desk, in addition to a pile of *Harper's Weeklys* from the past year. Many families of soldiers saved copies of *Harper's* to share with their men when they returned, and as a record of the conflict. Perhaps Lidia was doing the same.

I walked up the stairs to see the tower where Robbie had said he'd been when he'd seen Jake Neilson leaving. The tower was empty, and larger than I'd assumed. Eight vertical panes surrounded a large enclosed cupola whose floor was inlaid with diamond shaped pieces of wood. The windows were low enough to the floor so even a child Robbie's height could see out. I wondered why Lidia had never put a comfortable chair, or a writing desk, in this room. It seemed a perfect place for a retreat.

Robbie could certainly have seen someone in the drive below; the actual front doorway was blocked by the roof, but most of the drive near the house was visible, although the Syracuse Road itself was hidden by trees. To one side of the house were the roofs of the barns and out buildings, and in the back, the gardens. In the summer and fall the view of the surrounding hills would be breathtaking. The tower would also provide a dramatic view of thunderstorms in summer months, and snow storms in winter. On the far side of the house was the old building that had been the original house. Lidia had not included that on the tour of her home she had given me, most likely because that area of the home was not being actively used, but I resolved to walk through it before I left.

I took one more look from the tower. Robbie could definitely have seen what he said he had.

The bedclothes on Lidia's bed had been pulled off; perhaps that had been the easiest way for Nora and Aunt Cornelia to get the sheet and blanket she had needed in jail. One of the drawers in the wardrobe was slightly askew; nothing inside seemed out of place, so I closed it again. All seemed in order.

As a last possibility, I looked in Lidia's small desk. There, indeed, was a pile of letters. I opened the top one and glanced through it. The note was brief, but it had been sent from Jake in February, and told of his unit's capture of Fort Fisher. Jake was clearly proud of their accomplishments, as he should have been, and only mentioned in passing that he had been slightly wounded. No sentimental thoughts of home or affections were included, but neither were words indicating any enmity between Lidia and Jake. This must be the last letter she'd received from him. It had likely arrived in mid to late March, if not after. Mail deliveries were notoriously slow, and this letter had been written and posted in North Carolina.

I replaced it in the desk. Nothing in it hinted that Jake would be returning home soon. In my pocket were her letters to him. Perhaps they would prove more fruitful.

The house appeared undisturbed. I walked through the kitchen where Lidia and I had shared a pot of tea and into a short hallway leading to the original part of the building.

The kitchen of the main house might originally have been an outbuilding for the smaller, older house. Wealthy homeowners often built kitchens away from their living rooms, to remove smells and congestion from more dignified rooms.

The older house appeared to once have consisted of four rooms:

the classic colonial living room, dining room, parlor, and kitchen, all of which were also used for sleeping in the late eighteenth century and early part of this. Indeed, I suspected many of the poorer homes in Hestia still followed this model, as I thought of Nora's home, where she and Robbie shared one room, used for all purposes.

Today doors to all four rooms were closed. The first had become a pantry, lined with shelves partially filled with jars of sauces and berries and jellies and vegetables. It was almost May; most preserved goods would have been eaten during the winter. Bins of grains and root vegetables in sand were stored here. The room reminded me of Aunt Cornelia's root cellar.

I smiled, as I realized this space differed from Aunt Cornelia's in the most important way: it did not contain a secret room.

Next to the pantry was a spinning room, equipped with two spinning wheels. A medium sized loom in the corner stood empty. Not many women of today spun or wove, but perhaps Lidia's mother or grandmother had done so, and she'd left this room as they had arranged it.

The room furthest from the house as it was used today was arranged as a bedroom. Perhaps the room had been used by a maid or cook? It was considerably larger than the room Katie slept in, but was appropriately far from the living quarters of others in the home.

Heavier drapes that I had seen in the rest of the house hung on the windows, so no one outside would have been able to see even the light from the candle on the night stand. I looked closer; the candle had been burned recently enough so the tallow dripped on the brass candleholder had not been cleaned off. There was no dust on the drippings, which normally attracted dirt and dust.

As I looked closer I saw a hole several inches wide in the plaster wall above the nightstand. Someone had thrown something against the wall, or had hit it with their fist, and the spot had not been painted over or repaired. Plaster dust and a small chip of blue china lay on the floor underneath the mark. Whatever happened had happened recently.

A line of wooden pegs on the wall held a number of dresses, petticoats and cloaks, as though their owner had just stepped out for the afternoon. No one had mentioned anyone but Lidia's living at this house recently, and yet this bedroom was not only fully equipped, but appeared to have been occupied not long ago. The stenciled pine chest at the foot of the bed was full of quilts, woven blankets, sheets, and a pile of cloths like those I'd seen drying in Lidia's yard. They still looked like stained infant's clouts, but perhaps the stains were blood. Under the cloths were worn and mended sheets, which were clearly stained with blood.

The red painted commode held a blue washbasin and matching chamber pot, but no pitcher. I compared the blue china chip I'd found in back of the bed with the basin. It was the same color and thickness.

Perhaps this room had been used by a maid. Stained sheets were not unusual in a household, and would be given to a member of the staff to use. But the Neilson home had not had a maid in some time; I remembered Dr. Litchfield saying so. This room was clean and dusted, and the candle had been used recently. And fabric was not easy to come by, especially during the war years. Why would someone have left what appeared to be usable clothing here?

I walked around the room again and frowned. What had this room been used for?

There was one last room, clearly used for storage, filled with pieces of broken chairs and assorted other wooden furniture, a broken spinning wheel, and crates of household goods. Two carpets were rolled up in a corner. A basket near the door held the pieces of the heavy pitcher that matched the washbasin in the bedroom. Perhaps

Lidia had hoped to repair it. I left the trunks and moth-eaten sofa alone, and went back to the bedroom.

Here there was no sliding wall. But was this another hidden bedroom?

Chapter 32

Owen had taken one of the old guns from the barn and gone shooting that Wednesday; as a result, dinner was pigeon stewed with bacon, butter, parsley and port wine. I couldn't help but remember the times pigeons had served as dinner in camp. We'd relished the flavor without the enhancements of bacon and port wine, and didn't mind picking the buckshot out of our mouths with our fingers. A soldier wouldn't have wasted wine on a pigeon, I smiled to myself. Such a treasure would have been savored by sipping. Or drunk by some, in an attempt to forget the agonies of the day. Katie's recipe certainly enhanced the flavor of the birds.

Aunt Cornelia and I praised the dish, and complimented her on the cold lemon pudding served over sponge cake which followed. Katie glowed with pride.

"You were right about her cooking," I said to my aunt later.

"I've found most young people, given the right training and encouragement, can make enormous progress," agreed Aunt Cornelia. "I've seen too many people dismiss those who have grown up in environments where they haven't been exposed to a wide variety of skills and possibilities. Katie appears to enjoy cooking now that she has mastered the basics, and if we encourage her will no doubt continue to improve."

"Aunt Cornelia, this afternoon I went to the Neilson's house, with Lidia's permission, to see if her rifles were still in place, and whether or not I could find a .44 revolver. Dr. Weissman is ready to testify that a .44 was the weapon that killed Jake."

"Did you find such a revolver?"

"No. But I found something else that perhaps you can explain."

"Yes?"

"You and Nora told me that while you both had provided safe houses for escaping slaves, the Neilsons had not participated in such activities."

"Neither of them were involved, nor, so far as I know, were they even aware of the efforts of some of us to help slaves reach Canada."

"In the Neilson house there is a bedroom on the first floor that is outfitted in ways similar to the safe room in your root cellar, and in the Burns' oasthouse. It looks as though it has been used recently. There is a dent in the plaster where a heavy china pitcher hit the wall; I found a chip from the pitcher under the bed, along with plaster dust. The rest of the pitcher was in pieces in a storeroom."

"You were very observant."

"Aunt Cornelia, you were at Lidia's house the day of the murder. What really happened there?"

The room was silent for several long minutes.

The Aunt Cornelia spoke. "Aaron, Nora and I had hoped not to have to take you into our confidence, but it is clear we need to trust you with our lives, as well as Lidia's." She took a breath and then continued. "But I dare not speak without allowing at least two of us involved to be present. Not doing so would be betraying a confidence. Go to the Burns house and ask Nora to join us. I will ask Katie to watch Robbie. Tell Nora I feel this is absolutely necessary, and that I hope she agrees with me."

"What is this about?"

"I will not say more until Nora is here," said Aunt Cornelia, standing as though to dismiss me. "Get Nora, and then, if she agrees, we will tell you."

Chapter 33

Robbie was already sleeping when I arrived at the Burns house.

"Aunt Cornelia asked me to get you; she wants to tell me something, but won't do it without your agreement," I said, knowing how ignorant I sounded.

Nora shook her head slightly. "I'm not sure I want to do this."

"I could carry Robbie," I suggested, although I realized he would be heavy to balance and carry in my one arm.

"Robbie's used to my sometimes going out while he is sleeping," said Nora. "I won't be gone long, and he's a heavy sleeper." She carefully lit an oil lantern with the flame from the lamp on her table, and turned down the lamp. "If Cornelia needs me, then I will come."

We walked together down the rough drive to the roadway. Neither of us said anything. In the distance an owl cried, and then a horse whinnied. Perhaps it was one of Lidia's. Owen had brought her team to our barn so he could care for them while she was away.

Nora stumbled over a rough place in the road, and I reached out and touched her arm lightly, to steady her. For a moment she pulled away, but then she relaxed, and left my hand where it was. I wanted to put my arms around her, to hold her, to let her know that whatever was happening, I could be trusted. But for the moment even her allowing me to guide her slightly with my hand was enough. I could forget the reason we were together and wished our journey had been as far as Hestia or Utica, rather than just down the road to Aunt Cornelia's house.

As we approached Aunt Cornelia's house Nora moved away. The moment was over.

A mahogany tray holding a teapot, cups and saucers, sugar, milk, and a small plate holding slices of the sponge cake we had enjoyed for dinner was on the parlor table. Aunt Cornelia poured, as she apologized to Nora for having bothered her this late in the evening. "Are you certain Robbie will be all right?"

"He had a busy day; he'll sleep well," Nora replied, adding a teaspoon of sugar to her tea. "We planted thirty feet of peas today, and weeded the rhubarb and asparagus."

"Did he work on his wall?" I asked, thinking of Robbie's serious expression as he planned his project.

"He found some more rocks in the garden, and filled his wagon with them," said Nora. "He said you'd come to help him pull the wagon up to our house."

"I promised to do that," I agreed. "Perhaps tomorrow morning, before I do anything else."

Aunt Cornelia interrupted our casual conversation. "Nora, Aaron visited Lidia's home today. He found the first floor bedroom, and the broken pitcher."

Nora put down her teacup. "And?"

I spoke up. "I know Jake ate bean and barley soup an hour or two before he died. The autopsy determined that. Bean and barley soup is what you both told me you ate for your nooning meal the day of the murder. It's proof Jake was at home Monday before he was killed."

Nora looked from me to Aunt Cornelia and then back at me. "Lidia didn't kill Jake. Your job is to prove her innocent, Aaron.

That's all!" Nora's eyes flashed and the color in her cheeks deepened. "Why are all these details important?"

"They're important because we lied, Nora," said Aunt Cornelia, leaning toward the young woman. "We told Aaron and Sheriff Newell we were with Lidia all Monday, and that Jake did not come home. We can explain the blood on the floor. But Jake's knapsack was in the wardrobe, and now they have proof he joined us for a meal. They'll know we lied about not seeing him."

"That doesn't mean Lidia killed him!"

"No; of course not. Aaron understands that." Aunt Cornelia shot me a serious glance, and I nodded back. "But it undermines our credibility. We had a reason for not being truthful; we were protecting someone, and we were protecting ourselves. But to a judge it will look as though we were lying to protect Lidia. If this all comes out in court it will appear we were covering up a crime."

"We were," said Nora, softly. "It just wasn't the crime they think it was. If we tell the truth we could end up in jail along with Lidia. Plus, all our work would be undone."

"That's why I wanted you to come here tonight to discuss this. I believe we have to tell Aaron what happened."

"And trust he will not tell others?" Nora looked at me as though she would sooner trust one of Robbie's wolves.

"And hope he will not have to tell others," correctly Aunt Cornelia gently. "It's already known that Jake was abusive to Lidia. In many minds that could give her a reason to kill him."

As the women talked, ignoring my presence, I felt increasingly uncomfortable. What were they trying to hide? How could I promise not to tell others something that they were implying was illegal?

But this was Nora, and Aunt Cornelia. What could they have done that was so wrong?

Nora turned to me. "Aaron, Cornelia and I were at the Neilson's home that Monday. We did lie to you. Can't you just accept that we had a very good reason not to tell the truth, and not press us for details? Anyone's knowing why we were there could put us in jeopardy. You could end up with three clients to defend." She focused on my aunt. "Cornelia, if we tell Aaron we'll have broken the vows we took and put everyone involved at risk. And it would end the work we've been doing."

"I know, Nora." Aunt Cornelia sat back in her chair and looked from her distraught friend to me and then back again. "I'm hoping; trusting; that if Aaron knows the reason for our not telling him our mission, he'll feel a part of our work and will keep our secret."

"He's a man! And a lawyer!" Nora spoke as though those two identifiers clearly defined a devil; certainly, that were not descriptors of anyone who could be trusted. Then she turned to me. "Aaron, can you honestly tell us you will keep what we tell you secret?"

"My Henry kept our trust," Cornelia reminded her.

"And he's the only man who knew!" added Nora.

I raised my hand in protest. "How can I honestly promise to protect a secret I do not know? We're here because I'm trying to protect Lidia. Does your secret have anything to do with Jake's murder?"

Nora and Aunt Cornelia exchanged glances

"Not directly, Aaron. But it's responsible for Jake's leaving his home that day and walking toward Proctor's Tavern. It's why Lidia and Jake argued."

"Did Lidia follow him when he left?"

"No!" said Nora. "We didn't lie about that. Lidia never left her home that day."

"If Jake and Lidia argued, that could be seen as another reason for her to murder him."

"Lidia did not kill Jake!" Nora's voice was raw with frustration.

"To prove she did not we have to at least eliminate any motivation, or find someone else with both reason and opportunity. So far I haven't been able to find such a person." I shook my head. "All I can make sense of from this conversation is that you were both with Lidia that day; that you shared a meal with Jake; that Lidia and Jake quarreled; and that the quarrel was related to the reason you were all together."

Aunt Cornelia nodded. "Exactly, Jake. And if you knew the true reason for our being at the Neilson's that day then you'd understand why we were reluctant to say that Jake had come home. We were worried about our friend, and thought it would be better to just say we were with her Monday. Which was, of course, true."

Nora looked at Cornelia. "We've said too much already. You're right. We have to tell him. I only hope we're making the right decision."

Chapter 34

"Women have always looked to each other for friendship, Aaron. But after the war started and so many men enlisted we learned to lean on each other even more than in the past. Many women were alone, or only with their children, and had to do not only their own work, but chores that had been done by their men. If extra hands were needed they looked to each other for help. Many also took on jobs at the mills, the mercantiles, and wherever else they could find them. Army privates were promised sixteen dollars a month, but they were seldom paid on a regular basis. Often their families didn't see a paycheck for six months or more. Women had to provide, or their families would starve." Aunt Cornelia stopped for a moment, and Nora continued the story.

"One day early in the war your aunt kindly brought over some milk and eggs so Robbie and I would not be without. Robbie was just beginning to walk. Cornelia had an idea that changed the way I thought about myself, and about what I could do in the world."

Aunt Cornelia added, "I shared with Nora that I'd been speaking with a young woman, Sophie Austin, at the church, where we were rolling bandages for the soldiers. It was a warm day and many of us had pushed up our sleeves. Sophie refused to do so. We joked with her about being too modest, and as I reached over to help her loosen her sleeves I saw her arms were covered with blue and green bruises. Later I spoke with her privately. She cried as she told me that shortly after her marriage a year before her husband had hit her because the stew she'd made for dinner was cold. He'd spent the evening at the tavern and returned late, and she'd let the stew cool rather than burn it. After that he regularly punished her for such behavior. He hadn't enlisted at first, so she was still in danger. I was appalled, Aaron. Sophie was so young and so scared. She'd run away once, to her parents. Her mother had cried and hugged her, but her father took her back to her husband and told her she must be a good and obedient wife. That a man treated his wife as she deserved, and that she had made her bed." Aunt Cornelia shook her head. "Sophie confided she'd thought of slicing her wrists, or hanging herself with her apron strings. She didn't think she could go on living such a nightmare."

Nora added, "We decided to help Sophie, but we couldn't tell her what we planned until we determined what could be done. We had the safe rooms, which we had kept secret, fearing the strong feelings of anti-abolitionists. We quietly contacted other women we knew who'd helped slaves to escape and asked if they'd be willing to help women in domestic bondage. Many of them agreed to help, especially since their husbands were at war, and their decisions were their own. They contacted other women *they* knew. We protected the privacy of everyone in the same way we had when we were helping slaves, so each of us knew only a few others, but there were many willing to help."

Cornelia picked up the story. "Indeed, a number of women we contacted asked for assistance for friends or acquaintances. And as word spread, despite our efforts to remain secret, women volunteered to help who had not been involved with slaves, but who heard of our mission. Lidia Neilson was one of those. She'd survived difficulties with her own husband, and saw our work as a way to help others who were younger, and had more possibilities."

The two women smiled at each other. I sensed this was the first time they'd told their story. I listened, alternately proud of what they'd done, and appalled that they had needed to do it. Had any of the men who'd served with me treated their women in the ways Nora and Cornelia were describing? Most, I felt, could not have. But there were a few of whom I could believe such behavior.

"We were almost ready to talk with Sophie. We planned that she should be the first woman to escape her husband through our contacts. We were so excited that our plan was ready to be tested. We were convinced it would work." Cornelia sighed. "The day before I was to call on Sophie and explain our plan, she drowned in a creek near her home." Cornelia shook her head. "There was no proof of any wrong doing, but I couldn't help thinking that either she'd been killed by her husband, or had ended her own life. Our help had not come soon enough."

"Sophie's death became our impetus. It pushed us to work quickly to provide a way for women to escape situations they couldn't control," said Nora. "During the past several years we've helped over three dozen women, some with their children, get to safety. Many of the women came from the east or south, and by the time they reached Hestia they were beyond the searches of their husbands or fathers. Some went on to Canada, on the same routes the slaves had taken. Some went west, where they could change their names and begin again, or where they had friends or relatives who'd shelter them. We were helping those who don't own their own lives to be free. Just the same as before."

"But the danger to you ladies is great." I looked from one of the women to the other. "Dr. Litchfield was talking about such situations just the other day. As with the Fugitive Slave Act which condemned anyone who helped a slave escape from his master, those who help a woman to leave her husband are guilty of enticement, interfering in a husband's affairs, and assisting a wife in violating wifely duty. There are heavy fines and prison terms for harboring runaways. I couldn't believe the penalties were so great."

Nora and Aunt Cornelia looked at each other quickly.

"Why was he talking about such a topic at all?" asked Aunt Cornelia, too casually.

"A young pregnant woman in town disappeared perhaps ten days ago," I answered. "I saw her husband at the jail twice; he was distraught, and drunk, and demanding that the sheriff's department find her. Everyone assumed she'd run away."

I looked from Aunt Cornelia to Nora as the truth came to me. "You. She ran to you. You were helping Emily North leave her husband," I said quietly.

Nora nodded. "Emily came to me several weeks ago. She'd heard I'd helped women like her. I listened, and met with her several times to be sure she really wanted to take the necessary risks for herself and her child." She looked at me, her eyes steady. "Many women need help, but not all admit it, or can accept it. They have to be strong enough both to know they have to leave, and to do it." She paused. "Emily was married when she was sixteen; she had no family and no property. Her husband had threatened both her and the child, saying she wouldn't be able to work as hard after the child was born. At three different times he hit her in the stomach, hoping she'd lose the baby. Cornelia and I met Emily early Monday morning and took her to Lidia's home. It was difficult; she went into labor shortly after we got there, but she insisted on staying with us. She wanted a new life for her child and herself."

"That's why you left so early that Monday morning," I said to Aunt Cornelia, with new recognition of where their story matched information and questions I already had. "And why you took the wagon."

"We knew Emily was close to her time and might need help. As it turned out, we were right. Without the wagon we could not have taken her."

"What about Robbie? Was he with you?"

"I went back for Robbie after Emily was safely with Lidia and Cornelia. He thought we were visiting a neighbor. He never saw Emily. We told him we were sewing and couldn't be disturbed. We took turns watching Robbie and caring for Emily." Nora paused. "Luckily, it was an easy labor. She gave birth to a little girl in the middle of the morning." She smiled at Cornelia. "A beautiful little girl. Emily named her Amy, because she would be beloved. But of course Emily didn't have the strength to travel to her next stop right away."

"And Jake arrived at about noon," I put in, eager to hear the rest of the story. I didn't know if it would help or hinder Lidia's case, but I wanted to know what had happened. "He found Emily?"

"The door banged open, and Jake just walked in. He didn't expect anyone but Lidia to be there, of course. As it happened, Lidia was with Emily and Amy just then. Robbie and I and Cornelia were in the kitchen, heating soup." Nora paused. "Jake was limping, his hair was long and uncombed, and he was badly in need of a bath and a shave. I almost spilled the soup when I saw him. I thought he might be a gypsy, or one of those boatmen who've gone crazy and wander near the canal."

"You did fine, Nora," said Aunt Cornelia. "Of course, Nora had never met Jake, so she had no idea who he was. I knew it was Jake, but I had no idea what he would do. I just said, 'Mr. Neilson! Lidia will be so surprised to see you! I'll get her for you,' and went to the room Emily was using, quickly explained what had happened, and got Lidia. We were all focused on keeping Jake away from Emily. We had no doubt that if he knew she was there he would turn us all in to the sheriff, she and little Amy would be forced to go back to her husband, and we would all be imprisoned. We couldn't let that happen."

"'What the hell is this in my kitchen? Where's my wife and my welcome home?'" Jake looked at me, and at Robbie, and at the dishes we had out, but I didn't have time to introduce myself. In truth, I don't think Jake cared who we were." Nora shook her head. "He crossed the floor when he saw Lidia and grabbed her. She was very calm, considering the situation. She kissed him lightly on the cheek and pushed him away a little. 'You need a bath,' she laughed. 'Of course you're welcome home! I just didn't expect you for months! Why don't I go and draw you a bath. Or perhaps you'd like some bean and barley soup. You must be hungry after your journey.'

"'I don't need no bath. I need you to rid my house of these people. I need food, and whiskey, and the comforts of home.' He sat down heavily and pulled off a boot that was worn through in three places. The smell of his rank feet, black from mud and sweat and rotten leather, filled the room."

"'I'll get you some whiskey,' Lidia said, 'But I have only a little.' She poured him a drink. He pulled her onto his lap, in front of us all, as she put the glass on the table."

"The whole scene is so clear in my mind. I kept hoping Amy wouldn't cry; that Robbie, who was watching with wide eyes, wouldn't say anything wrong. That Lidia would somehow be able to control what Jake said and thought. I knew in the past he'd been a trouble to her when he'd been drinking, and it was clear the whisky she poured for him was not his first of the day." Cornelia's shoulders tensed with memory as she told the story.

"'My Lidia! Prettier than ever, that's what you are. Not every soldier has someone waiting for them like my Lidia.'

"'You've already had whiskey," Lidia said, struggling to get up.

"About then I sent Robbie to play outside," said Nora. "It was bad enough he'd seen a man like Jake. I didn't want him seeing what might come next."

"'Haven't you missed me? Don't you want me, wife?'

Jake's filthy clothes and hair crushed against Lidia's body, as he pinned her to him.

"Lidia kept her head, through all of this. 'You go up to our room,' she said, 'You take the whiskey up there, and I'll bring warm water, and scrub your back for you, and your hair. Make you presentable and comfortable.'

"'I don't want no bath. I want you!' He winked as he tore the front of Lidia's dress down to her waist and grabbed onto her breasts, hard. He bent his head and bit her right nipple until it bled." Aunt Cornelia's voice was strained.

I could only imagine how scared all the women had been.

"Lidia didn't make a sound. We all knew she was thinking of Emily, and Amy, and hoping somehow Jake wouldn't find out about them.

"'Let's go upstairs, Jake,' Lidia gasped, 'To our room. Our bed. You're embarrassing me in front of our neighbors.' She tried to hold her dress together, but Jake had his hands inside the bodice, and there was no way she could conceal herself.

"'They're just women. Maybe they'd like to join us? Especially the young one.' Jake leered at Nora. 'You want the bed, do you, wife?' Jake stood up, dragging Lidia with him out of the kitchen and toward the stairway. He pushed her ahead of him, and she tripped, hitting her face on the wooden stairs. Jake pulled her to her feet and dragged her up the stairs.

Nora's voice was shaking slightly as she spoke. "We didn't know what to do. I ran to Emily and explained. I pulled the drapes closed in her room and closed the door. She promised to try to keep the baby quiet, under the quilts. We heard Jake and Lidia upstairs. It was clear what was happening. But we couldn't stop it. I hoped he'd had enough whiskey so that after having his homecoming, as he termed it, he'd fall asleep and perhaps we could get Emily out, into the wagon. Maybe take her to my house. The jouncing of the wagon would not be good for her, but we needed to keep her presence unknown."

"That was the plan we decided on. It was all predicated on the possibility that Jake would sleep for a while. As long as he was awake we didn't dare move Emily. After about a half hour Jake came downstairs, no cleaner than before, and demanded soup, which we gave him. Lidia came down shortly thereafter, pale, and in a different dress than the one Jake had ripped, but in control of herself, so much as she could be. Robbie came back in, ate his soup quietly, by some miracle did not ask questions, and then went somewhere else in the house. At that moment I didn't pay attention."

"Then, suddenly, the baby cried. Emily tried to stifle it, we could tell, but a baby's cry can't be mistaken.

"'What in hell is that?' Jake roared. He got up and slammed open the door to the pantry, and then the other doors, until he found Emily, cowering in bed. 'And who is this?'

"'A friend, Jake, come quickly to bed with her infant and here for a short time.' Lidia tried to explain.

"He looked at us, as we had all followed him. 'Why isn't she with her husband?'

"No one answered. 'What's your name, girl?'

"'Emily,' she answered, as she hadn't prepared herself to answer with another name.

"'Emily is my guest for a day. She'll be leaving very soon,' Lidia assured Jake. 'You won't even know she's here.'

'I surely can tell she's here now, though,' he bellowed. 'She and that mewling thing next to her. I want them out of my house.'

"Please, Jake, just for a few hours. She isn't well enough to travel yet,' begged Lidia. 'I'll make sure she leaves later today.'

At that Jake picked up the pitcher from the commode, near the door and threw it at the bed, where it showered Emily and the baby with plaster and broken china. 'I'm master of my own house, and I say I want them gone now! This is not the homecoming a man should have – women and children filling the house that should be his alone. I'm going to a place they'll have whiskey, and men to appreciate the cruelties I've endured, and I'm going to tell the world what this house is like, full of women and babies, and how you've treated me.'

"At that moment Robbie screamed from upstairs; his nose had started to bleed heavily. Nora ran upstairs, and found him in Lidia's bedroom, bedclothes scattered on the floor, and his nose bleeding as though it would never stop. She took a cloth to staunch the blood, and get him calmed down.

"Jake continued his tirade for a few minutes, and then slammed the front door and left. Lidia grabbed Jake's knapsack and took it upstairs, throwing it into the wardrobe. Nora straightened the bedclothes, and Lidia pulled the rug over the blood that had stained the floor. By then Robbie had disappeared, most likely to the tower where he liked to sit. Nora fetched him back and they lay down a bit, thinking Robbie could use a nap, and was used to Nora's being with him.

"I went to Emily and got her calmed down," said Aunt Cornelia, "I told her we would have to move her to Nora's home, soon, perhaps within the hour. But it did appear Jake would be gone for a while, so we had a little time to plan and ready the wagon. Lidia and I began gathering quilts to layer in the wagon. Nora and Robbie were still upstairs resting when you and Dr. Litchfield arrived, Aaron, to tell Lidia of Jake's death."

She paused. "Of course, our major concern was that Jake would do as he'd promised and tell the men at the tavern of coming home and finding all of us, and a woman named Emily, at his home. The others would no doubt know immediately that it was Emily North. She'd only been missing a few hours then, but there are a limited number of Emilys in Hestia who are young and pregnant. Hearing that Emily was at our home, no doubt one or more of the men would tell the sheriff, who would come to get her, and would also arrest Nora and Lidia and I for having helped her to leave her husband."

Nora smiled, as though reliving the moment of relief. "As soon as you and Dr. Litchfield left, Lidia and Cornelia came to tell me. That someone had shot Jake was like a miracle. We could leave Emily where she was for the night. Lidia would be safe," Nora shook her head at the recollection. "And we would not be arrested, and could continue our work. It never occurred to any of us that Lidia would be accused of Jake's murder. After all, she'd never left the house. She was with us the whole time."

Chapter 35

We were both silent as I walked with Nora back to her home that night. She looked exhausted, but I hoped she trusted me, and was relieved to have told her story.

But, in truth, I diddn't know what she was thinking.

My mind was full of fury, and what an Army chaplain had once called the "chaotic darkness of the soul." How could people be so cruel to one another? On the battlefield, the war had been the excuse. We were fighting for our families, our country, our way of life.

Although soldiers on the other side were also fighting for their families; their country; their way of life. If groups of educated men in the Congress and the military ranks could not reach agreements without bloodshed, then perhaps it was understandable that simple men and women could not live together in peace.

No family is perfect. My parents had their differences with each other, and I with them. But our differences meant raised voices, not raised fists. I'd always known, intellectually, that there was violence within some families. But I'd dismissed such possibilities as unusual, and generally only occurring in families that were poor or uneducated or in some other way damaged.

The conversation that evening had made it clear that violence within the home; within the place that should be safest for all; was

this house. Father believed in freedom and opportunity. He often spoke of being enslaved by the English in Ireland. He believed all men should be free.

"My parents were not blessed with children, which for the Irish is almost a sin. They'd lost their families, or had left them, and they had a great desire to create a new family in this world where they'd started over. When my mother became pregnant with me at the age of thirty-seven, she rejoiced. God had answered her prayers. Hers would not be a barren marriage."

Nora's voice was soft and low, and acquired a slight Irish lilt I hadn't noticed before.

"I was born a healthy babe, but my birth took my mother's strength. She was a kind woman; a caring mother; but also a woman who needed much care herself. Her heart was weak, doctors told my father. She would not live long. She would certainly never bear another child.

"Because she was weak, I had to be strong. I took on many of mother's chores, hauling water, keeping the stove burning and making soup when I was younger than Robbie is now. I cared for Mother, and as I grew older I helped Father when I could. I believed in abolition, as he did, and I often helped cook and bring food and water and such for our guests in the oasthouse.

"I was young, but I was trusted, and proud to be so. Because no one expected a young girl, sometimes I was the one who led the escaping slaves to their next destination. I also carried messages to and from my father and Cornelia and Henry Livingston, who were engaged in the same cause."

"So that's how you came to know my aunt so well."

"Yes. In part." The night was dark, but I could see Nora's silhouette well enough to know she was hugging herself tightly.

"My father had his faults. He was often angry with my mother and with me, and even with God. He cursed my mother's weakness, and felt I was to blame for it. He was angry with those who were rich, especially the English who'd caused the great hunger in his homeland, and also with the plantation owners, because they, too, were exploiting the poor and the enslaved. As I grew older I began to understand that my father's work in helping slaves to escape was at least partially the result of his hatred of their masters. By helping laborers get to Canada, he was undermining the system that supported rich landowners in the south, much as his people had escaped overseas landlords in Ireland.

"As I grew older, he also saw me as God's replacement for the duties my mother could no longer perform. Despite her objections, and mine, when I was twelve my father began taking me to his bed, and treating me as he had his wife."

It was all I could do not to cry out in anger and pain at the horror of Nora's story. But she continued.

"Such behavior is not as unusual as some might think. I did not choose the role I was put in, but I accepted it, and I cared for my mother, and did as I could for my father. It was the way of our life. I felt the burden of such responsibilities was mine alone.

"When I was fifteen one of our guests in the oasthouse was a woman named Annie. I'd brought her water to bathe in, but I had no other clothing to offer, although her dress was stained and torn.

"Father sent me, as he had many other times, to Cornelia's house, to see if she could find a dress suitable for Annie to wear for the rest of her journey. I remember every detail from that night. Your aunt gave me a flowered skirt and a blouse and shawl for Annie. The shawl was red, and I remember thinking it would become Annie well.

"I went directly to the oasthouse room, to give her the clothing. As I got closer to the building I heard muffled screams. I was scared; I thought perhaps someone had found our safe house, and was hurting Annie. I dropped the clothing, grabbed a wooden log from the woodpile outside the house, and ran in.

"My father was on top of Annie, doing to her what he had done to me so many times. She was fighting him, trying to push him off, and biting the hand he held over her mouth to stop the screaming I'd heard.

"It was as though I was in a trance. The anger and pain of all the years came into my hands and arms, and I hit my father with that log. I hit him over and over again, until he stopped hurting Annie."

The woods were silent.

"Annie helped me wrap Father in an old quilt we kept in the oasthouse. That night we tried to carry him to the canal, but it was too far, and we were afraid he would be found. We buried him in the soft plowed earth of the Livingston's north field and I got Annie to her next safe house. I told my mother what had happened, and we prayed together. One month later I gave birth to Robbie. My mother died the month after that."

The horror of the silence was stifling.

"Robbie and I stayed here. Folks believe he's my brother, and that my father enlisted. Only Cornelia, who helped me with his birth, knows the truth." Nora turned and looked at me. "And now you know. And you must never tell anyone else. Especially Robbie."

I reached out, and this time she came into my arms. I stroked her hair, and I said nothing. She had said it all.

Chapter 36

That night I slept very little, despite my pills. My mind was filled with women. Women running; screaming; climbing, all trying to escape from something unseen. A line of women, holding their skirts out and joining hands and skirts with other women, so they formed a fence; a wall that I couldn't see over, no matter how I tried. A woman in a deep hole, digging farther still, throwing white stones out of the hole. Stones that all became skulls.

A dozen times I saw Nora being raped, and I tried to get to her, to rescue her, to kill the man who hurt her, but she was too far away.

At some time during that long night an early thunderstorm hit Hestia and, in my head, the thunder became cannon fire.

I was thankful to see the dawn. Night was finally over. I could begin a new day.

I'd promised Robbie I'd help pull his wagon, and this was not a week to go back on a promise. Aunt Cornelia merely nodded when I told her where I was going.

Robbie was already out and digging in the garden when I got there. I waved to Nora, who was working further back in the plot. She acted as though nothing had changed in her world, despite mine having turned upside down. "Good morning! What are you planting today?" I asked Robbie.

"I'm not planting; I'm just digging," said Robbie, as though what he was doing should have been obvious. "We'll plant beans here. You have to loosen the ground after the winter and take out the sticks and stones before you plant."

"I can see that," I said. "And when will you plant the beans?"

"When the moon is full, of course." Robbie looked at me as though I clearly knew nothing about beans. He was right.

"I came to pull your wagon for you."

"I don't need your help now; Nora pulled it for me."

"I promised."

"I know." Robbie shrugged a little and glanced at the woman he thought was his sister, still a ways over the field. "But Nora said you might not come. She did it."

I'd been entrusted with secrets. What I did with those secrets was still to be seen. "I'll talk with Nora. And I'm glad your stones are where you need them. But if I promise to come, then I will."

Robbie looked at me seriously. "Truly?"

"Truly."

He smiled at me. "I'll have more stones in the wagon other days."

"Then I'll be back." I wouldn't let anything get in the way. Robbie needed to be able to depend on someone other than Nora. But was that person me? What if I went back to New York City? I'd just be another person who disappeared, like his father, who he'd never met.

Nora was leaning on an iron fork, forcing it deep into the ground, and then bringing up the moist dark soil and turning it over. I could see the piles of stones and thick roots she'd removed and flung to a pile on the side of the garden. Her bodice was dark with sweat, and her skirts were pinned up as they had been when I'd seen her in the garden before. She wore old boots; they looked large for her feet. Perhaps they'd been her father's. A flame of anger ran through my body as I thought of him, and what he'd done. The sun shone on her hair, damp with sweat, so it gleamed like a helmet. She didn't stop her work when I approached.

"I came to help Robbie with his wagon, as I promised."

"I wasn't sure you'd come. I didn't want him to be disappointed."

"I wouldn't disappoint him, Nora."

She stopped and looked at me. "You heard last night. Not everything is as it seems."

"True enough. But that doesn't mean everything is worse. It might be better."

"Perhaps in some worlds." Nora put her foot on the fork and pushed down again. "What are you going to do now?"

"I have paperwork to complete. Then I'm going to Hestia, and on to Utica. I'm hoping to see Lidia before she's moved to the prison in Utica this morning. I'm going to see the district attorney."

"Tell Lidia I'll try to visit her tomorrow."

"I'll tell her."

Nora looked at me, her eyes shadowed, as though she didn't trust what they might see. "Will you tell her what we told you?"

"I'm not sure. If I need to do that, may I?"

"We placed our trust in you. You must be careful not to say anything that might be overheard."

"I understand."

"For Emily's sake. She's safe now. Away."

"I assumed she was."

Nora nodded. "You know where Robbie and I will be if you need to see us. But there's no reason to come here." She looked at me, defiantly. "What I told you last night was in confidence."

"I understand."

"Perhaps it would be better if you went away."

"What if I want to be here?"

She hesitated a moment, and then pushed the fork down into the soil again. "We will be at home."

I raised my hat to her, and then left, waving to Robbie as I went. I felt as though I were the one on trial. And I wasn't sure what the verdict would be.

By the time I got home Cornelia had left for the orphanage. Of course; this was a Thursday.

Katie brought me my usual coffee, and a raisin scone that I complemented her on, while I settled in to read the letters that had been in Jake's knapsack.

Most were from Lidia, and all were posted in those special envelopes printed with small patriotic designs and sold by the postal service to raise funds for the war. I glanced through them, but they added nothing to my picture of Lidia and Jake and their relationship. Most were brief notes wishing Jake well, sharing local news, and describing what Lidia was doing in the garden. One note mentioned she was volunteering one afternoon at the orphanage, but there was nothing to hint at the work she was doing with Nora and Cornelia, nor were their names ever mentioned. There was nothing to indicate that Jake and Lidia were anything but a comfortably married couple; she wrote that she missed him, and wished him to return safely and soon. Nothing in any of the notes hinted at abuse, or even at a difficult relationship. The very fact that she had written to him every two weeks, and that he'd kept her letters for at least the past six months, seemed a sign of a strong marriage. Many soldiers had waited in vain for letters from home, from wives they assured me were literate and loving.

Jake's letters to Lidia had been similar in tone. Factual, caring, and appropriate.

I turned to the three letters that were not in what I now recognized as Lidia's handwriting.

One was from a man named Malcolm Arthur, who must have been a distant cousin of Lidia's. He mentioned visiting Hestia and seeing her, and thanked Jake for his wife's hospitality. He reported Lidia was doing well, although she'd lost some weight, and that their house was looking a bit worse for age. If the war continued, than perhaps he, this Malcolm Arthur, would return and do some of the necessary repairs to help Lidia and Jake out. The letter was short and to the point, and there was nothing in it uncomplimentary to Lidia, or to her relationship with her husband.

The second, from Rev. Pinkston, at the First Presbyterian Church, was basically a several page homily on the importance of service to God and one's country. I suspected the reverend had copied the same letter out and sent it to every member of his congregation serving in the army. I was surprised Jake had kept it; if I'd received such a letter when I was on the battlefield I would have crumpled it up and used it to start a cook fire. Paper was precious in camp.

I'd almost given up the possibility that one of the letters would provide me with any help when I opened the last envelope.

To my surprise, its author was someone I had met: Jasper Field, the angry young man who'd been in the Oak Tavern after the parade. The one who'd told me Jake had served with his cousin.

Dear Jake Neilson,

We ain't heard nothing from my cousin who is in the 117ᵗʰ with you. He's Frank Field, and his wife has been waitin' for him, and is pretty upset you can believe. Last she heard from Frank he said you'd hurt him in the foot, so we figure you'll know how he is, and maybe why he hasn't written to his wife that he loves. If the reason he don't write is anything to do with the injury you caused him, then don't think about coming back to Hestia.

Jasper Field

I read the letter several times, and then copied it over for my notes before I left for Hestia.

Chapter 37

The Hestia police station was full of civilians and police, all talking loudly and intensely. Lidia Neilson had been taken to Utica by the time I arrived.

"Aaron Stone?" the young man from the telegraph office to whom I talked the day before waved at me as though we were old friends. "Just got in the reply to your message." He handed me a folded sheet of pale blue paper. "Lucky it got through. With all the news today the lines have been clicking since early morning. My hand's exhausted just writing it all down."

"Thank you," I said, pocketing the message. "What's all the news about?"

"You haven't heard? They got him! Happened last night. That John Wilkes Booth, the actor who shot President Lincoln? He's dead. Cheated us out of a trial, that fellow."

"Where was he?"

"Hiding in a barn near Port Royal, Virginia, like the coward he was. The Sixteenth New York found him and set fire to the barn; that rousted him. Some reports say they shot him; other reports say he shot himself. But he's dead, for sure. Shot through the head they say. And it was New York boys that got him." The young telegraph operator looked as proud as if he himself had been among them.

"That's surely good news for the country," I said. I made my way back through the crowd, realizing now that the death of John Wilkes Booth was the subject of most conversations.

Glad as I was to know the dastardly assassin was dead, I couldn't help but think it would have been more American if he'd been given a trial. But the feelings of the country being as high as they were, Booth probably wouldn't have lived to see a trial in any case. I wondered, too, what his brother Edwin, the great actor, was suffering now, as he contemplated the fate of his brother, and of his country. Perhaps he wondered if he could have influenced his brother and changed history. Or perhaps he was just relieved to have the curtain fall on the drama that had been his brother's, and get on with his own life.

Outside the building, I opened the telegraph.

Aaron Stone, Hestia, NY:
   Corporal Jacob Neilson of Hestia, served 117th New York;
   wounded North Carolina after Fort Fisher; discharged late
   March, 1865. Williams Burns of Hestia, no record enlistment.
   Best wishes, George.

So Jake had been injured and sent home, as Dr. Weissman had speculated. And, of course, there was no record that William Burns had enlisted. It seemed weeks before that I had naively thought I could find out information for Robbie and Nora about their father.

I rode to Utica. I needed to return Jake's letters to his knapsack, and I needed to talk with Albion Jenkins.

The Utica office of Albion Jenkins, Esquire, was considerably more impressive than his office in Hestia. Here he shared an elegant building with several other lawyers just down the street from both the courthouse and the prison. In contrast to the small house in Hestia, clearly this location had been originally designed for offices.

Jenkins' mahogany paneled suite, marked by a brass plate on the door, was on the first floor. Its reception area was arranged to project power and influence. Upon entering the room I faced a massive desk carved with geometric patterns that end in corner columns topped by grotesque faces similar to those on gargoyles. Were they to represent the sinned, or the sinners? A dozen straight-backed chairs lined the walls, giving the impression that Mr. Jenkins was an extremely busy man, who might easily have up to a dozen supplicants awaiting an audience with him.

The walls were hung with oil paintings of British hunting scenes which added to the authority and pretense of the room, although they didn't embrace the American spirit or reflect the interests or needs of most of those I expected would sit in these chairs nervously waiting for Jenkins to honor them with his presence. Today the chairs were empty.

I rang the brass bell on the desk. In truth I rang it twice, and was about ready to open the door to the next room without invitation when it opened in front of me.

"Yes?" To my surprise, it was Mr. Jenkins himself. Given the importance of the reception area, I'd assumed there would be a regiment of minions delegated to delaying anyone who had the audacity to visit Albion Jenkins, Esquire.

But Jenkins was the same cheerful fellow I'd spoken with only the day before.

"I didn't think I'd be seeing you again quite so soon," he greeted me. "Come in; come in. My new quarters here are not quite in order, but I anticipate they will be soon enough. I've only had this position two months."

We walked through another room lined with mahogany

bookcases, their empty shelves filling the walls from floor to ceiling. A half-dozen crates, most likely full of law books, were stacked in one corner. "I'll have to purchase two or three desks, and then find clerks to sit at them," Jenkins informed me. "When our soldiers come home I anticipate having my choice of bright young men happy to work with me to test the limits of the law and prosecute those who break it, and my current clerk in Hestia will be joining me here by the end of the month."

The third room was his actual office. Jenkins' desk was prominently located at an angle facing the door, and a table in the corner was covered with papers and heavy leather books of laws, their pages marked by dozens of yellow papers, perhaps marking relevant cases. Jake Neilson's knapsack was on the floor under the table.

"Mr. Jenkins," I began, but he interrupted me.

"Albion. Save the 'Mr. Jenkins' for court. I hope we'll have many cases to work, together or across the table, in the future. I'm glad to see another young lawyer settle in the area. Too many of the legal and judicial sorts here are mired in place, and have been so for decades, if not generations. After the hardships of the war we need new minds. New thinking. Our world has changed, and we must find ways to change with it. Within our legal system, of course," he added.

I didn't contradict him. My future was too uncertain to commit to either remaining in the area, or leaving it. For the moment I felt comfortable dealing with the district attorney on a personal level. "Albion, then. I need to be blunt. I spent last evening going over the case you have against my client, Lidia Neilson, and I wanted you to know I'm going to propose, officially, of course, that the case be dropped for lack of evidence."

"I realize the evidence is slim, Aaron, but Sheriff Newell told me he has no other suspects, and there is motivation. Jake Neilson was known to be a wife beater."

"With your permission," I began. "I've spoken with Lidia and with her friend, Cornelia Livingston, my aunt, who is respected throughout Hestia. Both of them deny any abuse other than a few normal tussles between man and wife. Dr. Litchfield has suggested abuse, but even he has no proof, other than that Lidia Neilson lost three babies before their birth, which is sad, but not criminal, and that she bruised easily. Certainly she is not the only woman in the area whose skin is sensitive."

"Perhaps," said Albion, looking at me closely.

I continued, "Lidia did not expect her husband to return home from the war as early as he did; indeed, she did not even know he'd been wounded. A letter I found in the desk in their bedroom dated six weeks ago doesn't mention his injury. She was, of course, delighted when he did return, and, in addition to her statements, two other respectable women of Hestia, my aunt Cornelia, and Miss Nora Burns, can testify he arrived home at noon on Monday, April 17, finding them all in his home. They all agree that he arrived home, ate a meal, and then he and his wife retired to their bedroom for a more *private* homecoming."

"Excuse me, Aaron, but I believe all three women in question have stated that they did not see Jake Neilson that day."

"They did. And all three are prepared to recant their statements. They were frightened when they heard Jake had been killed, and were afraid Lidia would be accused, the victim of false gossip. Which is, indeed, what happened. All three will also testify they saw Jake Neilson leave his home after his meal, saying he wanted to celebrate his homecoming with some drink, and there was not adequate whiskey in the house. That was the last time Lidia Neilson saw her husband. Indeed, I happened to be in the company of Dr. Litchfield when he told Mrs. Neilson of her husband's death, and I know of the shock she evidenced, hearing such a thing when she had welcomed him home only hours before."

"And I assume you have an explanation for the blood found in the Neilsons' bedroom?"

"I do. A young boy who was in the house when Jake Neilson returned home, four year old Robbie Burns, had a nosebleed in that room, and the result was the blood stain Sheriff Newell found on the floor. Robbie, with the innocence and honesty of childhood, confirmed that for me, as did his sister, Miss Burns, and my aunt and Mrs. Neilson." His *mother*, Miss Burns, my mind told me. But no one else could know that, for the sakes of both Nora and Robbie.

"But someone shot Jake Neilson. Who would you propose as the murderer?"

"It is not my responsibility to collect evidence pointing at anyone else. My responsibility is to clear an innocent widow of charges that she killed her beloved husband, with no cause or witnesses. Indeed, there are respected witnesses who can testify that at the time of her husband's death she was in her own home, with friends, far from the location where he was shot. But," I reached into the deep side pocket of my jacket, "last night I read through the letters found in Jake Neilson's knapsack, which your clerk very carefully inventoried before you loaned them to me yesterday." I handed the letters to Albion. "Among these letters you will find no indication that the Neilson's marriage was anything but amicable. But I ask that you pay particular attention to the letter from a Jasper Field, a young man in Hestia. In it he accuses Jake Neilson of wounding, possibly killing, his cousin, and threatens Neilson, should he return to Hestia."

I looked directly at the district attorney. "That man, Jasper Field, was at Proctor's Tavern, only half a mile from where Jake Neilson's body was found, when the body was brought there. I don't know if Field was responsible for Neilson's death. But he was angry with him, had threatened him, was nearby and under the weather with drink at the time of the death."

"Will Miss Burns and Mrs. Livingston go to my office in Hestia and write out their statements, and have them witnessed by my clerk?"

"I am certain I can arrange that."

"I will talk with Mrs. Neilson and have her statement witnessed at the prison here."

"I would like to visit her this afternoon. Would you have any objection to that?"

"She has a right to see her attorney at any time. Tell her I will most likely stop to see her after I have the statements of Miss Burns and Mrs. Livingston in hand."

"And?"

"And I see no reason to sustain the charges under the circumstances. If the other ladies had come forward earlier, perhaps we could have avoided all of this." He looked down at the letters, now on his desk. "And I will read through the letters, with special attention to the one from Mr. Field. It appears Sheriff Newell and his police need to investigate this business a bit further."

"Thank you, Albion."

"And I thank you, Aaron. Assuming all is as you say, then I anticipate apologizing to the widow Neilson for our reaching a mistaken conclusion too early in the investigation. Unless other information comes to light, I agree that we don't have a case against her. Why waste the time and money of the citizens of New York and increase the embarrassment of a respected lady when there is no evidence of her committing a crime?"

Chapter 38

I stopped at the prison and explained to Lidia what was happening; she understood immediately what Nora and Cornelia had told me, and what use I was making of the information.

Friday morning Nora and Aunt Cornelia went to the district attorney's office in Hestia and made their statements.

By Friday evening, Lidia was home. Aunt Cornelia hosted a celebratory dinner for all of us, at which no one mentioned Jake, or Emily, or what the difference was between a whole and a partial truth. I'd been convinced of Lidia's innocence from the beginning, and I was still convinced of it. Was Jasper Field guilty or innocent? I didn't know. But, as Albion Jenkins would have said, that was up to Sheriff Newell to investigate, and, based on further information, a prosecution would go forward. Or would not.

We toasted each other, and freedom, and the law, with cups of good tea, as Robbie played on the floor with black and white stones that he arranged in different patterns.

Despite Aunt Cornelia's invitation to spend the night, Lidia, most particularly, wanted to be home and sleeping in her own bed after her experience in two jails within a week. Owen drove her home in the carriage, and I offered to walk with Nora and Robbie, as was becoming my pleasant habit.

The night was clear, with a thin crescent moon and two lanterns to light our way. Robbie stayed close to us both, sometimes clinging to Nora's skirt, and plainly exhausted.

"You know your efforts are very much appreciated," said Nora, as we made our way up the way to her home. "I had my doubts about telling you about our work, but Cornelia was right. You listened, and you arranged everything. Thank goodness Lidia is now on her way home."

"Lidia should not be imprisoned for a crime that Jasper Field, or perhaps someone else, committed. Of course, I'm very aware that if Jake had not been murdered then I might be trying to get all of you ladies out of jail," I smiled, joking a bit.

"And Emily North might be back with her husband," said Nora, not smiling. "What happened was best for everyone. Even Jake."

I was a bit surprised at her being so adamant. The harshness of battle was still too close for me to discuss death without emotion. Even if a man was not a perfect husband, did he deserve to die? That was a much harder question than whether an innocent woman deserved to be freed.

"Robbie will fall asleep as soon as we're home, but would you like to visit for a short time? I made a rhubarb pie early this morning."

"Robbie recommended your rhubarb pies highly," I agreed. "I would very much like to sample a piece."

At their home Nora put Robbie on the pallet and covered him with a quilt. He was asleep before she'd gotten the pie down from a shelf and sliced pieces for each of us.

"Robbie was right. Your pie is excellent," I said, very much enjoying both the pie and the company.

"I'm glad you think so." We sat and ate in silence for a few minutes. "Will you be returning to New York City soon?" she asked suddenly.

"I don't know," I answered truthfully. "Albion Jenkins assumed I'd establish a legal practice nearby. These past days have shown me there's a need for men who can investigate and defend people who are unjustly accused."

"There are many such," Nora said. "And many others, like those of us helping women like Emily North, bending the law in pursuit of righteous causes."

"I've seen that," I agreed. "Although each case must be examined on its own merit. Laws are put in place to keep order, and can not be ignored without some risk to society."

"But if society sits back and allows people to be hurt, then society is not right," she said earnestly. "It is necessary to protect the innocent, even if the law does not provide for such actions."

"Six months ago I would never have conceded the truth of that," I admitted, "I'm beginning to agree that you're correct. But I still believe people can not take law into their own hands."

"Not even when it's clear the law is not punishing someone who hurts innocent victims?" Nora leaned forward to emphasize her point. Her hair gleamed in the lantern light.

I reached out and touched it lightly, expecting her to move away from me. She did not.

"Laws must be changed, then," I continued, stroking her soft hair lightly. With one of my fingers I moved a strand of hair behind her ear. "Men who want to live in a fair society must fight to change laws that don't protect the weak and innocent." I removed my hand, not wanting to pressure Nora in any way. "With everything that has happened in the past two days, I forgot to tell you. I telegraphed a friend of mine who works in the War Department in Washington to ask about Jake, and I also asked him if there were any records of your father's war service."

"Why did you do that?" Nora moved back. I could not have touched her now if 'd wanted to.

"I did it before you told me your story the other night. Robbie said he'd never heard from his father, and you said he'd been gone since before Robbie was born. I thought I might be able to find out what regiment he was in, and whether he'd be wounded, or imprisoned, or even when he might return to you."

"You shouldn't have done that. You know he won't return."

"I meant no harm; I made the request before you told me what happened."

"Even so, it wasn't necessary, and wasn't your concern." Nora stood up. "I'm thirsty after the sweetness of the pie. Would you like a glass of water before you go?"

I sat back. "Yes, thank you." I'd thought she might have appreciated my concern, even if it were misplaced.

Nora took a pitcher and went out to the pump. Robbie made a small sound, and kicked, and the quilt covering him fell on the floor. I went over and shook it out and replaced it. As I tucked him in I noticed the gleam of something beneath the pallet. Perhaps Robbie had hidden one of his toys there, or a spoon had fallen underneath. I reached down.

What I touched I knew immediately to be the barrel of an Army Colt .44.

Such a gun could be a danger to a child! Nora was still outside; I checked quickly. The revolver was empty.

I could understand Nora's having a rifle; she lived far in the country, and might even hunt for food occasionally. But a revolver?

Jake had been killed with a Colt .44. His gun had not been found.

Nora and Aunt Cornelia had told me that after Jake left the Neilson house the day he was murdered Nora had been resting with Robbie, while Cornelia and Lidia were downstairs, preparing Emily in case she and her child would have to travel.

My hand shook as I replaced the gun where I'd found it.

"Robbie kicked off his quilt, so I covered him," I said as Nora returned and poured fresh, cold water into two glasses.

"Thank you. I'm sorry to have sounded ungrateful before, but you mustn't concern yourself with our family. You've been more than kind to both of us already. And remember, you're going to have to come back soon to help Robbie pull his wagon! His wall is very important to him." She smiled, and we both took long drinks. "Robbie is very fond of you."

"I'll be back," I said. "I promised Robbie. But now it's late, and I must get back to my aunt's house. It's been a long week for all of us."

I walked back along the rutted drive, holding my lantern in front of me, but hardly seeing the road.

Aunt Cornelia had never asked me to do anything but defend Lidia Neilson.

It would be a long night.

Chapter 39

Merely being in possession of a Colt .44 didn't make Nora Burns guilty of murder. I paced the floor that night in my small bedroom. I had no doubt Lidia Neilson was innocent. But had I managed to have one woman freed, and found evidence that would convict a second? And the second a woman I'd grown to love?

Two days ago saying "Nora" and "murder" in the same sentence would have been a contradiction within itself. It had to be. Nora had been in my thoughts since I'd met her. She was the beautiful, strong, and brave woman who'd struggled to raise her brother — her son, I corrected myself — without help from anyone. The woman who'd risked her own freedom to help other women find theirs. She'd been a victim, and she'd risen above her own pain to help others to escape abuse.

Nora, a murderer? But she'd killed her father. She'd told me herself. I now had no need to investigate the bones found in the north field.

Surely her father deserved to die. I had no doubt of that. But could she have killed again?

When he was killed Jake had knowledge that could have returned Emily North and her infant daughter to her abusive husband and might well have imprisoned Lidia, Nora, and Aunt Cornelia. Most likely the court would have consigned Robbie to the orphanage. The Bradford Asylum already had a high wall around it. Robbie's stones would mean nothing there.

What Jake knew could have ruined many lives.

Aunt Cornelia and Nora had convinced me the work they were doing was right. Both men and women had the right to expect marriage and family to provide caring support and structure. Consenting to marriage did not mean consenting to servitude, and certainly not to abuse.

I starred out my bedroom window into the dark. There were many Army Colt .44s in the world. Perhaps Nora's had been her father's. Or perhaps someone else had given it to her for protection. That was possible.

But not probable. I'd been an officer. I knew that particular Colt revolver had not been manufactured until 1860, and almost all of them had been sold to the Army of the Potomac.

Sheriff Newell had found no witnesses to Jake's shooting. No one had seen Nora, or anyone else, in the area between the Neilson's home and Proctor's Tavern. Now that Lidia had been cleared the sheriff would have no reason to question Nora further. Certainly no reason to search her house. No one would know about the revolver.

But I did.

Should I confront her with what I'd found? Ask her what happened?

I shook my head in frustration. Did I really want her to tell me what she'd done? Or, perhaps worse, have her lie to me?

I could go to the sheriff myself. But if I told anyone what I'd found, it would destroy Nora's life, and Robbie's, and quite possibly the lives of other women. How far away were the women who'd been helped to leave this area of New York State? Knowing part of their trail, how many might be found and brought back?

That would be legal.

But it couldn't be right.

By all accounts Jake had hurt Lidia repeatedly over the years of their marriage.

Jasper Field said he had seriously injured another soldier. If Field was not guilty of Jake's death, then he wouldn't be convicted. Would he?

I opened the drawer where I kept my supply of morphine, and starred at it, longing to end my agony in sleep. But the questions I was asking wouldn't be answered by a drug, or by postponing a decision. I had to decide myself.

Did I really want to know what Nora had done?

By morning I had my answer. Soldiers on the same side of a battle line sometimes injure each other, in confusion or error. The law was another battle line.

By morning I'd made my decision. I was going to align myself with Aunt Cornelia, Lidia Neilson, and with the woman I loved. I was not going to hurt someone on my side of the line.

At breakfast I told Aunt Cornelia I was going to return to New York City to see my parents, but that I would return, to set up a law practice in upstate New York. And to be with Nora and Robbie, if they would have me.

Chapter 40

Father shifted himself in his large chair. It had taken almost a full day for him to hear my story, but he'd listened. I'd told him everything. Everything except Nora's deepest secret. That remained safe in my heart and always would.

"So. You've decided to ignore your earlier training and settle in rural New York, taking on clients who may not be able to afford your services, for the sake of a girl? Son, you are contemplating the ruin of your life." Father shook his head as he looked at me, sadly. "Your mother and I had such high hopes for you."

"What I am contemplating is not my ruin. It's my rebirth, Father. I've found a use for my training and my talents, if they can be called that. I will not be living as you and Mother have, but I'll have a good life in upstate New York. Aunt Cornelia and Uncle Henry were happy there."

"This girl you're interested in. She's not only poor, but Irish and Catholic. How can someone from a background so different from yours make you the kind of wife you need?"

"I don't even know if she'll have me, Father. But if she will, then I'll be a lucky man, and the details will work themselves out. You would like her; she is good and honest and believes in justice and right. Just as you do."

"But the law .."

"Is not always right. Sometimes there's a higher law. Father, I've made up my mind to settle upstate and begin a local law practice there. I've already spoken with Aunt Cornelia. She's offered to help me, both by introducing me to people I should know, and by allowing me to continue living with her until my practice supports me to some degree."

"Then it sounds settled. What are you asking of me?"

"Your understanding. Your love. And your presence at my wedding, should Nora Burns consent to be my wife."

Chapter 41

By the time I'd taken the New York Central to Albany and then changed for New York City, talked with Father and Mother and a few friends in the city, arranged for my law books to be shipped to Hestia, and purchased a wooden train set for Robbie at Rowland Macy's store on Fourteenth Street, I'd been gone for a little over a full week.

Although Mother was clearly disappointed in my choices for the future, the night before I left she took me aside and handed me a gold and pearl ring that had been her mother's. "For your future wife," she told me, giving me a hug. "She's a very lucky woman, and I look forward to meeting the next Mrs. Stone."

The ring was wrapped in a piece of velvet in my waistcoat pocket on the trip north and west, which seemed to take three times as long as had the trip to New York City.

"Then your parents are supporting your decision," Aunt Cornelia asked as soon as we were settled in her carriage and on our way home from the Utica station.

"They remain hesitant, but they've accepted it," I told her. "I couldn't hope for more. They'd counted on my remaining in New York. Father wanted me to partner with him in his law practice, and Mother has been looking forward to my establishing a family nearby, no doubt with a half dozen grandchildren for her to pamper."

"They're welcome to visit. I haven't seen my sister in many years, and would look forward to her company."

"I told them that." Upstate had changed in the week I'd been gone. Tall elm trees and rounder maples were both sporting new green leaves, plowed fields stood ready to plant, and higher grasses and red and blue wildflowers crowded the roadside as soon as we had left the city of Utica. "How is Nora?"

"She's well. I told her you'd gone to New York City to see your family and settle some matters there, but you expected to return this week." Aunt Cornelia patted my hand. "Robbie's anxious for you to see the progress he's made on his wall."

"I've brought him a railroad set. I hope he likes it."

"He has few toys; I'm sure he will," said Aunt Cornelia. "I know you're anxious to see Nora. But she's still young, Aaron, and has been on her own a long time. She may take some time to respond in the way you would like her to."

"I'm willing to wait, Aunt Cornelia."

"She's lived a very different life from the ones of the women you knew in the city. Margaret - the woman you were engaged to - was prepared for a marriage that meant her own household and servants, a wardrobe supplemented by trips to Paris to buy dresses from Worth and Bobergh, and a husband who'd accompany her to the theatre and opera. Nora has no dresses but those she's made herself, no food but that she's grown or purchased with earnings from her sewing, and no experience with parties or theatres."

"I look forward to introducing her to some of those pleasures. But we will be living here, not in New York City. I would strive so she would not have to continue the heavy labor she has had to do, but we will not be making trips to Paris in the near future, Aunt Cornelia. Or possibly ever."

"She's cared for Robbie, and has made her own decisions, without anyone else to account to."

"And if she agrees to marry me, then I hope she'll continue to be the independent woman I've fallen in love with. Although I do hope she will allow me some input to her decision making." I smiled at Aunt Cornelia. "Trust me. I'll not rush Nora into making changes in her life she's not comfortable with. I'm looking forward to offering her the opportunity to improve her life in some ways, and to share it with me. In return, she'll bless my future."

After a brief meal I could wait no longer. I put the railroad set in a wagon borrowed from Owen, and set out to visit Nora.

She and Robbie were working in their garden, as they had been often when I'd visited. I stood in the rough drive leading up to their home and watched them. Robbie was kneeling on the ground, planting something on the far side of the garden. Nora was cutting rhubarb with a knife, putting the long red and green stalks in a basket on the ground. Sparrows flew overhead, and a pair of barn swallows swooped down close to the ground and then up again. I wondered if their nest was in one of the out buildings here. Barn swallows nesting meant good luck.

I stood for a moment, watching the two people I hoped would be my future. Then I raised my hand in greeting and called out to them. "Hello there! I'm home."

#

Notes from Lea Wait:

JUSTICE & MERCY is a work of fiction. The idea of repurposing the Underground Railroad to support women's rights is mine alone; so far as I know, it was never done. And Hestia is a fictional town. although other locations along the Erie Canal in New York State are real, and a number of Civil Rights, Women's Rights, and religious organizations began in central New York State.

A special thank you to my sister, Nancy Cantwell, who encouraged me (repeatedly!) to get this book out into the world.

And thank you to you, my readers, whose enthusiasm and encouragement keeps me writing, even on dark days. If you haven't already, please friend my Lea Wait/Cornelia Kidd page on Facebook so we can stay in touch, check my website (www.leawait.com) for a printable list of my books and links to free prequels of many, and write to me at leawait@roadrunner.com with your email address if you'd like to hear when my next book is published.

In the meantime, if you enjoyed JUSTICE & MERCY, please share it by telling your friends, or by writing a review on an on-line site or on your Facebook page.

Thank you all!

Lea Wait

Books by Lea Wait

Mysteries:

    1-Shadows at the Fair

    2-Shadows on the Coast of Maine

    3–Shadows on the Ivy

    4–Shadows at the Spring Show

    5–Shadows of a Maine Summer

    6–Shadows on a Cape Cod Wedding

    7–Shadows on a Maine Christmas

    8- Shadows on a Morning in Maine

    1-Twisted Threads

    2-Thread of Evidence

    3-Thread and Gone

    4- Dangling by a Thread

    5- Tightening the Threads

    6- Thread the Halls

    7- Thread Herrings

    8- Thread on Arrival

Death and a Pot of Chowder (by Cornelia Kidd)

Pizza To Die For

Historical Novels for Ages 8 and Up

 Stopping to Home

 Seaward Born

 Wintering Well

 Finest Kind

 Uncertain Glory

 Contrary Winds

 For Freedom Alone

Nonfiction

 Living and Writing on the Coast of Maine

Made in the USA
Lexington, KY
25 March 2019